**Mistletoe hur...
Directly...**

"Kiss her, Brennan!" someone in the crowd called.

Mary Paige shook her head and waved off the comment.

"Yeah, kiss her!" More voices, more laughter.

In a panic she glanced over to where Brennan stood. He laughed and waved off the remarks.

"Kiss her!" More people. Clapping started. All were merry. All were bright. All were insane.

She raised her hands to her cheeks. They were afire with embarrassment. For heaven's sake, couldn't they see she was not the type of girl who got kissed by the Brennan Henrys of the world? She wasn't elegant, beautiful or—

"Oh," she said as Brennan loomed above her.

Her gaze found his and there was amusement in the gray depths…and maybe something more. Satisfaction?

Maybe. But she didn't have time to think any more about it.

Because at that moment Brennan kissed her.

Dear Reader,

I'm delighted to announce exciting news: beginning in January 2013, Harlequin Superromance books will be longer! That means more romance with more of the characters you love and expect from Harlequin Superromance.

We'll also be unveiling a brand-new look for our covers. These fresh, beautiful covers will showcase the six wonderful contemporary stories we publish each month. Turn to the back of this book for a sneak peek.

So don't miss out on your favorite series—Harlequin Superromance. Look for longer stories and exciting new covers starting December 18, 2012, wherever you buy books.

In the meantime, check out this month's reads:

#1818 THE SPIRIT OF CHRISTMAS
Liz Talley

#1819 THE TIME OF HER LIFE
Jeanie London

#1820 THE LONG WAY HOME
Cathryn Parry

#1821 CROSSING NEVADA
Jeannie Watt

#1822 WISH UPON A CHRISTMAS STAR
Darlene Gardner

#1823 ESPRESSO IN THE MORNING
Dorie Graham

Happy reading!

Wanda Ottewell,

Senior Editor, Harlequin Superromance

The Spirit of Christmas

LIZ TALLEY

HARLEQUIN®
entertain, enrich, inspire™

Recycling programs
for this product may
not exist in your area.

ISBN-13: 978-0-373-71818-4

THE SPIRIT OF CHRISTMAS

Copyright © 2012 by Amy R. Talley

This edition published by arrangement with Harlequin Books S.A.

For questions and comments about the quality of this book, please contact us at CustomerService@Harlequin.com.

www.Harlequin.com

Printed in U.S.A.

ABOUT THE AUTHOR

From devouring the Harlequin Superromance novels on the shelf of her aunt's used bookstore to swiping her grandmother's medical romances, Liz Talley has always loved a good romance. So it was no surprise to anyone when she started writing a book one day while her infant napped. She soon found writing more exciting than scrubbing hardened cereal off the love seat. Underneath Liz's baby-food-stained clothes, a dream stirred. She followed that dream, and after a foray into historical romance and a Golden Heart final, she started her first contemporary romance on the same day she met her editor. Coincidence? She prefers to call it fate.

Currently Liz lives in north Louisiana with her high-school sweetheart, two beautiful children and a passel of animals. Liz loves watching her boys play baseball, shopping for bargains and going out for lunch. When not writing contemporary romances for the Harlequin Superromance line, she can be found doing laundry, feeding kids or playing on Facebook.

Books by Liz Talley

HARLEQUIN SUPERROMANCE

*The Boys of Bayou Bridge

Other titles by this author available in ebook format.

For Ursuline Academy, New Orleans, for teaching me the importance of *Serviam*—I will serve. I will always cherish my time walking those historic halls, teaching girls who could be angels one minute, devils the next and knitting together a foundation of education and service with the best faculty ever.

I may be gone, but my thoughts often drift back to the land of Merry Macs, Skips and Sioux.
Go, Lions!

And for the readers who reliably buy my books and tell others how great they are—there is no greater compliment than a friend who is a devoted fan.
Thank you.

CHAPTER ONE

MARY PAIGE GENTRY stepped into an icy puddle of water as she exited the taxi with not only one high-heeled shoe, but both of them.

"Darn, darn, darn!" she said, trying to turn back to the driver without stepping into the cold water again. The cabbie raised bushy eyebrows and she tossed him a glare. "I assume you didn't see that puddle when you pulled up?"

He shrugged.

"Yeah, right," Mary Paige muttered, blowing out a breath that ruffled her bangs. "Just wait for me, okay?"

She didn't hang around for his response because, after the day she'd had, something had to go in her favor. She slammed the door and leaped to the curb, managing to clear the puddle she'd previously waded through. Having the cab wait for her would cost a small fortune, but she was way late to her uncle's infamous Christmas kickoff bash, thanks to her boss, Ivan the Terrible.

The frigid water seeped into the toes of her shoes as she walked toward the iron-barred glass door of the convenience store anchoring a corner in Fat City. Stupid, stupid! If she hadn't let vanity rule, she'd be plodding around in her cute fleur-de-lis rubber boots with warm tootsies. But because the strappy high-heel, pseudo–Mary Janes had called her name that morning, she would risk frostbite for the remainder of the evening.

Flashing neon signs hung garishly on the front of the store, bright cousins to the various cigarette ads, and from somewhere to her left, music bled onto the street. The door to the convenience store swooshed open, and she moved aside to avoid a woman who burst out, clutching a paper bag containing a fifth of something potent. Her elbow caught Mary Paige's arm, but the woman didn't even acknowledge the offense. She merely growled something about skinny blonde bitches and waddled down the block.

"Really?" Mary Paige called after her, even as part of her relished the backhanded compliment since she'd spent the past two months doing Zumba and eating foam chips in an effort to fit into a size eight again. As she reached for the closing door handle, she heard a low moan to her right. Her hand paused in midair, hovering above the cold metal.

Pulling her jacket closer to her chin and nuzzling into the cashmere scarf her ex-boyfriend had given her last Christmas, Mary Paige peered into the darkness beyond the blinking lights lining the eaves. At first, she saw nothing in the shadows, but then spied movement.

She stepped toward the noise, her feet squishing in her wet shoes, her teeth starting to chatter. The light plink of sleet on her shoulders made her wonder if she was somewhere other than New Orleans. They rarely saw anything frozen—except daiquiris—so it had been quite the sensation when they'd gotten a blast of winter the day after Thanksgiving.

Newspapers stirred and she made out the form of an elderly man wrapped in a thin blanket, moving among discarded boxes and newspapers quickly becoming sodden with the sleet.

"Sir? You need some help?"

The man stopped his rustling and flipped her the finger.

"Guess that answers that question."

She turned around, ignoring the tug at her heart. Why didn't he go to a shelter, anyway? Too cold out for someone to be sitting around with nothing more than a thin blanket. She glanced to the corner and found the cab still waiting. Good. A man who listened. An early Christmas miracle.

She entered the warmth of the store, blew on her hands and scanned the cramped aisle. Nope, none of it would do. Bottled water, sanitary products and condoms. The necessities of life, sure, but nothing that would help her tonight.

The second aisle proved as fruitless. Nothing but potato chips, cartons of cookies and packages of those powdery little doughnuts. Mary Paige's stomach betrayed her with a growl as she eyed the pink snowballs. She shook her head and rounded the end cap, where she scanned the new offerings, methodically sweeping her gaze along the aisle, mentally discarding everything until… Bingo!

Hanging innocently at the end of the aisle was the most repugnant pair of Christmas socks she'd ever seen. They were bright green with sparkly silver-tinsel trees around the ankles, adorned with bright cherry-red pom-poms. The tops had garish silver lace that matched the flashy trees and small jingly bells. They were hideous and absolutely perfect for the white-elephant gift required for Uncle Fred's crazy pre-Christmas party. Mary Paige snatched them as if they were the Holy Grail. Finally, something had gone right.

She hurried toward the register, hating that she'd already taken too much time in this little stop, hating that the homeless curmudgeon outside the door weighed on her conscience. Yeah, he was a miserable old goat, but it *was* the beginning of the Christmas season, and it *was* colder than normal outside.

Perhaps she should get him a little something to warm him up?

A coffee bar sat to her right, featuring a self-service, instant cappuccino machine. Not the best, but certainly good enough. Mary Paige glanced at the register. Only one person in line. Surely five more minutes wouldn't hurt. She spun toward the bar, snatched a medium-size cup, centered it beneath the spout and pushed the button. It filled quickly. She plopped a lid on and grabbed two sugar packs along with a stir stick.

Darn. Two more people had joined the queue behind the woman paying.

She got in line, shifting back and forth on her frozen feet trying to restore the circulation and wondering why she even bothered with an old bum outside a convenience store in the middle of Metairie. He'd probably hurl the cup at her and ruin her only decent jacket. Par for the course considering the day she'd had. A run in her stockings, a nervous stomach that had sent her to the bathroom twice, a coffee stain on her pristine white blouse and a tongue-lashing from Ivan the Terrible when the towering pile of receipts on her desk didn't add up for their biggest client. She really wanted to go home and curl up in her ratty chenille robe with a glass of wine. Instead, fierce love for Uncle Fred sent her scurrying across the city in a cab she couldn't afford, wearing shoes now frozen stiff.

Mary Paige finally reached the register, where the cashier snatched the socks from her, scanned them and dropped them into a plastic sack.

"Ten thirty-seven," the cashier said, not even bothering to make eye contact with her.

Mary Paige rooted in her purse for her wallet. Ugh. She'd left it in her desk after doing some online Christmas shopping. But, luckily she always kept some cash in the side pocket along with her ATM card. Her fingers crisscrossed in a desperate search. No cash.

No way.

Thankfully a second swipe netted her the ATM card. She glanced at the cashier, who glared knowingly in return.

"Uh, do y'all have an ATM?"

The cashier pointed to a machine sitting below a glowing sign as a man behind her in line growled, "Jeez, get your cash before you get in line, lady."

Something inside Mary Paige snapped. "Listen, buddy. I have had a hell of a day and my ex-boyfriend stole all my cash. Give me an effing break here!"

The man stepped back, throwing up his hands before giving her a smart-ass gesture toward the ATM.

"Thanks."

She prayed as she entered her PIN that her account wasn't overdrawn. Things had been so hectic lately she couldn't remember the last time she balanced her bank statement. *Please, please let the stupid machine spit out the money.*

The machine whirred and coughed out the amount she'd requested—thirty bucks.

Whew. Hibernia Bank had just earned itself a place on her Christmas-card list.

Mary Paige popped back in line as the rude construction worker rolled his eyes and blew garlicky breath on her neck with theatrical exaggeration. Mary Paige shrugged at the cashier. "Happens to the best of us, right?"

The cashier held out a palm and gave no response,

making Mary Paige feel like even more of an idiot. She placed a ten-dollar bill in the outstretched hand of the cashier along with three dimes and a nickel, the sum of all the change she could scrape up from the bottom of her purse. The cashier cleared her throat and looked pointedly at the money.

"Oh, sorry." Mary Paige scooped two pennies from the take-a-penny, leave-a-penny container on the counter. "There you go."

She grabbed the coffee and the plastic bag, swerved around Big and Beefy, desperately wanting to give him the finger—much as the old bum had given her earlier—and stalked out the door.

"Ow." Hot coffee splashed on her fingers through the open drinking spout. "Double darn it."

She shook the liquid from her fingers and caught sight of the cab out of the corner of her eye. Thank God he'd waited, and thank God the ATM had delivered the money she needed to pay for the cab. Shoving the bag with the socks under her arm, she held up a finger indicating she would be a minute longer, then headed around the corner to the old man.

As she approached the alley, she was swamped by a feeling of déjà vu. How many other times had she done this kind of thing? Ten? Twenty? More? As much as she would like to be a hard-ass career gal, she knew her heart was of the Stay Puft variety. Not even rudeness would deter her from doing what was right.

"Yoo-hoo? Mister? I have a little something here to warm you." She stood in front of a Dumpster bookended by two large cardboard boxes. Flaps hung over, providing little shelter, and the man seemed to be curled into a pile of wet newspapers. A broken cyclone fence stretched behind him, leading the way to an abandoned bakery showcasing yawning windows. *Dismal* wasn't the word for the small corner of the world this man occupied in the frozen rain. "Sir?"

He said nothing.

"I've brought you some coffee."

The papers moved. "What the hell ya want?"

"Just thought you might like something to warm you."

"Coffee?" The papers shifted as the man unfurled like a gray troll from beneath a bridge, his grizzled face parting sodden sales flyers, pinning her with sleepy blue eyes. "Coffee, did you say?"

Mary Paige thrust the cup toward the man.

His eyes swept Mary Paige from head to foot, causing a flash of alarm within her, but then he looked away before extending a thin arm toward the steaming cup. As he leaned forward, the papers parted, revealing a body woefully unprepared for the frigid weather. His pants were thin and patched, his flannel shirt threadbare in a few spots, but most frightening of all were his bare feet.

Aw, heck, no. Not bare feet. Anything but bare feet.

The plastic bag holding the socks grew heavier.

Pretend like you didn't see his bare feet, Mary Paige. Just hand him the coffee and go.

But she knew she would not. Could not.

Triple darn.

No time to get another pair. Plus, the only other socks inside were a pair of plain blue ones. There had been only one pair of perfectly horrendous Christmas socks, and she knew they hadn't been intended for anyone at Uncle Fred's house. Not Aunt Betty with her giant mole, or Cousin Trav with his ugly comb-over, or Mr. Dan the eccentric butcher, who showed up to Uncle Fred's party every year uninvited. Nope, these Christmas socks were for the bum who had flipped her the finger.

She sighed and bent down, meeting his gnarled fingers with the cup. "You don't have any socks. It's awfully cold out here for bare feet."

The man took slurping sips of the scalding liquid as if it were nothing more than lukewarm tea. "Yes, socks t'would help, I imagine."

"Yes, well, I happen to have a pair right here. How about we put these on so you don't freeze your toes off? And then, I can take you to a shelter where you can get some hot food and a warm place to sleep."

The man peered at her over the rim, his disarming blue eyes measuring her. She ripped her gaze from his and dug the ugly socks from the plastic bag, eyeing his dirty but, oddly enough, well-manicured toes. She tore the tag from the socks and bent toward the man, uncertain as to whether she should actually lift his foot. "Should I help you put these on?"

The old man clasped her hands, stilling them as she picked at the sticker stubbornly gunking up a sparkly silver tree.

"You ever read *A Christmas Carol?*"

"I beg your pardon, sir?"

"You know...old Ebenezer Scrooge?"

"Oh, yeah, of course." She nodded and the blunt ends of her bob swung into her eyes. She tucked the wayward strands behind her chilled ears. "The socks. Let's get them on you."

"Yes," he said staring at the gaudy socks in her hand. "What I meant was the Spirit of Christmas."

"What?" Mary Paige said biting her lip and scrunching each sock so she could jab them onto his almost-blue feet. "You mean the ghosts, like the ghosts of Christmas past?"

"They were all part of the Spirit of Christmas, right?" His voice was low, intense and raspy...and also quite refined. Odd for a street person. She slid the first sock on his right foot.

"Mmm-hmm." She shifted her weight so she wouldn't fall on her butt onto the slick concrete. She wasn't the most graceful of gals.

"Well, you're the Spirit of Christmas," he said, jabbing a finger at her.

"Maybe so," she said, hoping to pacify the old man, as she put the other sock on his deathly cold foot. She prayed she had hand sanitizer in her purse. No telling where the man's feet had been even if he had trimmed his toenails.

"There. Nice and toasty. Let's get you out of this weather." She prepared to rise, but the man clasped her wrist. She pulled away but he held firm.

"I'm sorry I was rude to you earlier."

"That's okay. You're enduring a hard time right now," Mary Paige said, trying to wrench her arm from his grip, growing uncomfortable with his familiarity. "Living out on the streets makes a man defensive. I understand. If you will let go of me, I will see that the cab driver pulls around so we can find you a nearby shelter."

The man ignored her. "What's your name, my child?"

Mary Paige stared into his hypnotic blue eyes and responded without thinking. "Mary Paige."

"Well, Mary Paige, can I offer you a gift in return for the one you have given me?"

She shook her head. Jeez. There was no telling what the bum would give her. Visions of grimy bottle caps or shiny pieces of glass danced in her head. What valuable object would soon be hers? "You owe me nothing. Now let's get—"

Her words died as the man released her hand and fished around inside the pocket of his worn flannel shirt.

Dear Lord, please don't let it be his old socks. Or something dead.

She should get out of here. The old man could be nuts, rooting around for something more sinister than a piece of old junk. He could have a gun. Or a knife. Or…a piece of paper.

The man held a paper that had been folded several times and smiled at her, his teeth remarkably straight and white. A gold crown winked at her from the back of his mouth, sparkling as much as his blue eyes. "I needed to know your name, my child, so I know what to write on this."

He unfolded the paper and extended it to her. She took it as if she were in a trance before finally glancing down.

It was a check.

She blinked.

It was a check for two million dollars.

Signed by Malcolm Henry, Jr.

The Malcolm Henry, Jr., of Henry Department Stores.

She blinked. "I don't understand. Where did you get this?"

He grinned. "My child, *you* are the Spirit of Christmas."

A flash of light blinded her, forcing her to squinch her eyes together. When she opened them, she found another man emerging from behind the Dumpster. The light was so blinding and her feet were now so numbed by the cold, she stumbled back, tilted and fell, landing hard on the icy pavement.

She tried to get up, but her legs failed to comply, so she sat there feeling water seep through the seat of her newest skirt, no doubt ruining the charcoal tweed and her favorite silk panties.

The elderly man stood and shrugged into a long cash-

mere coat the cameraman handed him while shoving feet
still clad in the garish Christmas socks into a pair of lined
hunting boots stored within one of the cardboard boxes.
Then he extended one hand to her. She took it, bobbing
her glance nervously toward the man filming the odd-
est thing that had ever happened to her—and she'd had
plenty of oddness in her life…she'd once been bitten by
a llama, for heaven's sake. She still held the check, so she
shoved it toward the older man, who didn't look so much
like a bum anymore. His coat probably cost a week's sal-
ary. Maybe a month's.

He waved the check away. "No, no. That's all yours.
I feared we wouldn't find a kind soul at all. Been doing
this for four straight days."

She didn't say anything. Merely stood there. Shocked.

"By the way, I'd like to introduce myself. I'm Malcolm
Henry, and I must tell you I love these socks."

CHAPTER TWO

BRENNAN HENRY STUDIED the huge Christmas tree towering in front of the glass elevator of his office building. The thing was nearly thirty feet tall and took up so much space on the marble floor everyone had to walk several feet out of the natural path to the elevators. And the lights blinked in time with loud holiday music that spilled from overhead speakers.

Ridiculous.

He would have his secretary pen a strongly worded letter to the owner of the building—who happened to be his grandfather. Didn't matter. A letter would be official. After all, Brennan didn't mind people enjoying the upcoming holiday season, but not at the expense of others.

The elevator shot up to the top floor and swooshed open, revealing the tasteful lobby of MBH Industries, the company bearing his great-grandfather's initials. An attractive receptionist gave an automatic smile, which deepened when she saw him stride out. "Good morning, Mr. Henry."

Brennan gave her little more than his normal clipped smile. "Mr. Henry is my grandfather, Cheryl."

She laughed because it was a game they played every day. A small flirty little game he allowed himself, like an extra shot of cream in his coffee. He pushed on toward his office in a far corner, and entered his assistant's area.

"Good morning, Brennan," Sophie Caruso said, looking up from her keyboard and spinning toward the antique sideboard housing the coffee. The office smelled like cinnamon rolls fresh out of the oven and his stomach growled.

"Good morning, Sophie. You have those quarterly sales reports from Mark yet?"

She pressed the button on the one-cup coffee machine before sifting through the folders on the corner of her desk. "Right here. They were waiting for you this morning."

She pulled a folder covered with lime-green and red paisleys from the stack of plain manila and held it toward him.

He looked at it as though she'd handed him a writhing rattlesnake.

"What?" she asked. "He's trying to get into the spirit and swears paisleys are all the rage this year."

"This is a place of business," Brennan muttered, downing some coffee and heading toward his office, holding the ridiculous folder with the reports Mark had promised. Next time, Brennan would request his director of marketing send them as an email attachment. Mark was adamant about using a highlighter and doing things old-school. He swore it kept him from missing important trends, but if the man kept decorating his folders like a schoolgirl on crack, Brennan would insist on electronic versions.

He pushed the intercom button on his desk. "Hey, Mrs. Caruso, could you bring me a plain—"

The door opened and his assistant entered with a manila folder and his second cup of coffee.

"You're wonderful," he said, accepting the mug and placing it next to the nearly empty one, before sliding the stapled reports he'd already pulled from the colored folder into the much more businesslike one she handed him.

"I know," she said, turning toward the door. She spun around and snapped her fingers, the motion making her silver-strewn brown hair stand out like a flying saucer. "Your grandfather called and said he was bringing by the centerpiece for the new ad campaign. Said you needed to call Ellen and have her sit in on the meeting. Board-room B at ten."

She shut the door before he could mutter a really dirty word under his breath.

Oh, sure. He had nothing better to do than to be at the beck and call of his grandfather's shenanigans. What had happened to the hard-nosed captain of industry who had brought their company into the twenty-first century? Where had the iron-fisted, no-nonsense head of the most successful chain of small department stores in the South gone?

Because the man who'd flown a kite from the top of the building last week wasn't him. If the past few months were any indicator, Malcolm Henry, Jr.'s cheese had slid off his cracker.

Hell, the man sat up front with his driver holding a wiener dog he'd named Izzy in his lap. If that wasn't damning evidence, Brennan didn't know what was.

He couldn't wrap his mind around the change in the man who had skipped most of his grandson's birthday parties because there had been work to attend to. His grandfather had even arrived late at Brennan's graduation because of an emergency board-of-directors meeting about an acquisition of a small chain of stores on the East Coast. Malcolm Henry had been the sharpest businessman in the Crescent City…and now he called bingo at the local homeless shelter on Friday nights.

Brennan picked up the phone. "Get me Ellen. Please."

The VP of communications and community relations, who was also his second cousin, answered on the third ring. "Bivens."

"Ellen, tell me my grandfather isn't going through with this crazy promo idea."

"Your grandfather isn't going through with this crazy promo."

"You're lying."

"Of course I am. You told me to."

Okay, so he had.

"We can't throw money away like this. Giving a random stranger millions of dollars is irresponsible in this economy. We have investors who will flip when they find out MBH is handing out money capriciously."

"Wait a sec, it's not the company's money."

"You mean he's using *our* money for this?" Something hot slid into his gut. It wasn't as though his grandfather couldn't do what he wished with his own money. But over the past six months, the man had shelled out huge chunks of money to pet nonprofit agencies. Giving money away to a perfect stranger, declaring him or her the *Spirit of Christmas* and mapping out some crazy publicity stunt sounded dangerously negligent.

Worry started eating away at Brennan. What if the heart attack his grandfather had suffered six months ago had done other damage—like to Malcolm's head? Maybe a mild stroke that had gone misdiagnosed? His grandfather had always been extremely careful in spending money, both in business and his personal life.

Brennan wasn't ready to watch his grandfather turn senile, ineffective and dotty in his advanced age. He wasn't ready to let go of the one solid presence in his life.

"That's what he indicated," Ellen said, clearing her

throat uncomfortably. "I assumed you had spoken with him about this. We've been working on this for three months."

His grandfather had spoken to him. Brennan had just failed to "hear" the plan. "I have, but I was unaware of the particulars, and, honestly, I had hoped this crazy idea would fall by the wayside. After all, we have the Magic in the Lights gala coming up benefiting Malcolm's Kids. Grandfather has plenty of charitable causes to pursue, all of which demonstrate the Spirit of the Season."

"Actually, this idea of his is brilliant from a marketing perspective. All I have to do is splash this story on the front of the *Times-Picayune,* and we're golden. You can't buy this sort of goodwill."

Brennan frowned. "Story?"

"He didn't tell you how he found the person he wants to use as the center point?"

"No."

An awkward pause hung on the line, and he could tell Ellen didn't know if she should be the bearer of the news or not.

He saved her the trouble. "No problem. I'll get to the bottom of it when we meet in Boardroom B at ten. I'll see you then."

"Meeting? I can't attend—I have a report I have to submit to Don before the end of the day."

"Grandfather called it regarding this foolishness."

"Oh, well, then I guess I can't refuse Malcolm."

Of course you can't. He still writes the checks around here.

Brennan set the phone in the cradle and looked at his desk. He had too much to deal with to worry over his grandfather's stunt. He had a conference call at 9:00 a.m. about a new cosmetics line by some Hollywood starlet the company was considering for the stores, and he still needed to look at the reports Mark had sent so he could talk to the CFO, Don Angelle, about procuring extra commercial spots to be aired over Mardi Gras.

No time for crazy Spirit of Christmas ideas. Not when a healthy bottom line demanded more than mistletoe and Yule logs.

Bah, humbug.

He snorted at that thought. Man, he really was like Scrooge. Next thing, he'd be shuffling only one small lump of coal onto the fire to save a measly buck.

And with his grandfather pissing away all their money, he might be forced to play the Dickens character.

MARY PAIGE TAPPED HER FOOT in time with the Christmas music spilling out of the speakers, mouthing words about sleigh rides and walking in winter wonderlands. A huge Christmas tree sat on a platform in front of the lobby fountain, blinking in time with the music. She loved it and wished she knew how to sync music with her own small tree that she'd put up last weekend.

The doors slid open and she stepped inside the glass elevator with a well-dressed woman and pressed the button that would take her to the twentieth floor. As the doors closed, her stomach flipped over.

Maybe she should have told Mr. Henry she wasn't interested. No one in her right mind would give up two million dollars, but Mr. Henry wanted her to basically take a break from her job to be his poster girl for bringing the true meaning of Christmas to the Crescent City. Her boss, Ivan, hadn't been happy about her taking the morning off, and she still had half a study book to get through in preparation for her certified public accountant exam, which loomed in a couple of months. It felt like she'd be sacrificing all she'd been working so hard for.

Still, it was two million dollars.

And she was in her right mind. Mostly.

Late last night she'd considered all the things she could do with the money—pay off student loans, buy a car that didn't have rust spots around the wheel well and make donations to all her favorite charities. And she could help her mom pay off the loans taken to modify their old farmhouse to accommodate her brother's wheelchair. Yeah, two million could do a lot of good in her life…and in the lives of others.

So she should probably sign the agreement, cash the check and count herself a lucky duck…even if it meant tugging on a Santa hat and making merry with the entire city of New Orleans for the holiday season.

Besides, if during the meeting with Mr. Henry the whole crazy proposal felt like too much for her to handle, she'd refuse. She wasn't locked in to anything and had done nothing more with the check than hide it in the bottom of the ballerina jewelry box her granny Wyatt had giving her for her twelfth birthday.

"Are you with MBH?" the woman standing next to her asked with a polite smile.

"Uh, no," Mary Paige said, smoothing her skirt over her thighs, hoping the bottom of her Spanx wasn't showing. The skirt had fit her four years ago, and even though she'd lost weight, it was still a little too tight. She hadn't had time to go by the cleaners to pick up her more professional clothes, so she'd held her breath that morning and zipped. It worked but she had to keep tugging the hem into place because it inched up as she walked.

The other woman was dressed in a fine wool suit that fit her to perfection. A patterned raspberry-colored scarf was knotted at her neck, and her dark, heeled boots were absolutely gorgeous. She looked like an ad out of *Vanity Fair*.

"I'm just going to a meeting." Mary Paige swallowed her nervousness and pasted on a smile. She was glad she'd used the flatiron on her hair this morning. At the very least her short blond pageboy cut flattered her elfish chin and helped her feel more together than she was.

The woman tossed her wavy brown mane over her shoulders and nodded at Mary Paige as she stepped out into the lobby of MBH Industries.

A pretty receptionist looked up as the brunette walked by her desk. "Oh, Ms. Thornhill, Mr. Henry has a meeting soon."

"Really?" the brunette said, not bothering to even slow her steps. Instead, she pushed through the frosted glass doors to the inner sanctum, letting them swing shut after her.

The receptionist frowned and muttered something under her breath before donning a bright smile. "Welcome to MBH. Can I assist you?"

"Uh, hi. I'm Mary Paige Gentry, and I have an appointment with Mr. Malcolm Henry?"

Darn it. Why had she phrased it like a question? Like she was uncertain?

"Oh, of course," the receptionist, whose nameplate read Cheryl Reeves, said with a genuine smile. "Have a seat and I'll let Mr. Henry know you've arrived."

Mary Paige pointed her sensible heels toward the seating area housing several glossy magazines and a beautiful orchid on a glass table and sat on the leather Barcelona chair.

Just as she perched on the edge of the chair—tugging

the tight skirt over the edge of her Spanx—the frosted glass doors swung open.

But Mr. Malcolm Henry didn't emerge.

Instead it was a Roman god wearing an expensive-looking suit and a scowl. He zeroed in on Cheryl as Ms. Thornhill lollygagged behind him with annoyance evident in her brown eyes. "Cheryl, will you see that Creighton gets a cup of tea while she waits for me."

It wasn't a question.

"Of course, Mr. Henry," Cheryl said, rising from behind her desk. "I—" She snapped her mouth closed when Creighton shot her a warning.

"Don't bother with tea, Brennan," Creighton said, laying a hand on his forearm as if she could soothe the fiercest of beasts. "I have other things to attend to this morning. I thought you might be free for a little chat this morning. Nothing important."

Innocuous words, but not the way she said them. Creighton—the well-dressed, gorgeous brunette—had purred them, with a sort of raspy innuendo that made poor Cheryl pinken like a…a…shrimp.

"Good," he said, looking at the brunette as if he didn't appreciate the implication of what a *little chat* was.

"Fine," Creighton said, heading for the elevators with staccato click-clacks of her heeled boots.

Mary Paige shifted on the slick leather as the woman walked by, then slid right off the chair onto the floor in a graceless heap.

All three people in the lobby turned and looked at her.

"Oh, are you all right?" Cheryl squeaked, hurrying toward her.

The man named Henry—but not Malcolm Henry—got there first.

Mary Paige looked at him standing over her. His brow

was furrowed and he reminded her of how her younger brother had once looked at a baby bird that had fallen from the pecan tree in front of their house—confused, alarmed and sympathetic. She knew she was the color of her sweater—a vibrant fuchsia—and could do nothing other than laugh. Falling twice in twenty-four hours? Had to be a record.

Her laughter seemed to really confuse him.

He glanced at Cheryl, who pressed her lips together as if she were afraid she'd join in the giggling, and asked, "Who is this?"

Mary Paige swallowed her laughter and struggled to fold her legs under her, praying the man wouldn't spot her modern version of a girdle. Her heels failed to make traction so she looked even more awkward and her skirt rode even farther up her thighs.

Damn it.

His gaze zeroed in on the stretchy nude fabric, cutting into her white legs—yeah, her summer tan was long gone—and she saw the question in his gray eyes. He didn't say anything as he made eye contact with her and extended a hand. She grabbed hold and let him haul her to her feet.

Again he asked, "Who are you?"

Creighton wore a bemused smile as she pointed to Mary Paige and said, "I think that's your ten o'clock."

Mary Paige pulled her hand away and jerked the skirt down where it should be—just above the knee. The elevator opened and Creighton gave them all a little finger wiggle and a cat-full-of-cream smile as she glided inside. The doors slid closed as Mary Paige, Cheryl and the grumpy sex god watched.

Mary Paige smoothed her hands against the shiny fabric of the chair and tried to smile, hopefully distracting him from the fact she'd wallowed like a sow on the floor of the lobby. "Um, slick chair, huh?"

The man bent and scooped up her checkbook, tube of lip gloss and cell-phone charger that had spilled from her purse when she'd taken her epic tumble. He passed them to her. "Are you sure you're okay?"

She wasn't sure if it was legitimate concern or more of a legal thing. "Yeah, my dignity's a little bruised, but otherwise, I can walk."

His stormy eyes perused her and it made her feel squirmy, not necessarily in a pervy way, but more in a crackly way. The man may have been fierce-looking, but he *was* abnormally handsome. If not a little scary. It wasn't his size because he was a little over six feet, but it was the way his confidence oozed. No, not *oozed. Conquered.* The man conquered a room, demanding attention by his sheer presence.

She stuck out a clammy hand. "Hi, I'm Mary Paige Gentry. I'm to meet with Mr. Malcolm Henry, Jr."

The man took her hand. "So you *are* our ten o'clock?"

She shrugged. How was she supposed to know who *his* ten-o'clock appointment was?

His touch was warm and dry, which was good considering her hand had started sweating. Coming here wearing a too-tight skirt for a meeting about two million dollars then sprawling onto the floor and showing her "light" support girdle didn't inspire serenity in a gal. She waited for an introduction.

A little tremor went through him—subtle but noticeable—before he dropped her hand. "I'm Brennan Henry, Malcolm's grandson. I'm also the VP of acquisitions, and I'll be sitting in on this meeting. If you'll follow me, I'll see if I can find where my grandfather is hiding, and we can get down to brass tacks regarding this…venture."

She nodded. He didn't sound very pleased about this… *venture,* but she wasn't so sure about it, either. When Mr. Henry had helped her from the icy pavement—thus establishing a habit of Henry men hauling up clumsy blondes who fell on their asses—he'd explained his idea for bringing the true meaning of the holiday season to the city. And it had sounded sweet but implausible.

After all, how could she be the Spirit of Christmas?

She was an accountant…not even a certified one at that. She had nothing special that would mark her as the epitome of, well, anything. She had blond hair that she highlighted herself every two months to save a buck, she shopped at bargain stores and grew her own herbs under a growing light. And not *those* kind of herbs. Basil, thyme and rosemary. She skipped to the end of books to find out if there was a happily ever after before she read them and her bottom was a little too big for her frame. She was plain ol' Mary Paige from Crosshatch, Louisiana. Well, not even Crosshatch, considering she'd grown up on an organic farm five miles from the town-limit sign.

So how was she supposed to inspire the citizens of the city to be kinder, gentler and more loving as they enjoyed the holiday season?

Uh, yeah. Sounded like a really weird idea, but for two million dollars—money that could help more people than herself—Mary Paige supposed she could at the very least hear the man out.

Brennan held open the door from which he'd emerged minutes ago.

Well, at least he was a gentleman.

She slid by, praying she'd remembered to put on deodorant that morning. She really couldn't recall, and she could feel the anxiety seeping from her pores. Like literally.

"This way," he said, his voice all rich and yummy, like a vanilla cupcake—a particular favorite of hers and one of the reasons her bottom was a little jigglier than it should be. He might be aloof but his voice had a warm timbre, the kind made for reading bedtime stories. Yes, naughty bedtime stories.

She dashed the thought of Brennan in her bedroom from her mind and followed him to a room labeled Board-room B, where Mr. Malcolm Henry, Jr. stood holding something aloft. Below him sat an adorable red dachs-hund, balancing on his back legs with front paws waving in begging fashion. Mr. Henry tossed the dog something, which it caught neatly, then turned to them with a spar-kle in his bright blue eyes. "Miss Gentry, my own sweet Spirit of Christmas. You came."

The older man looked much different than he had last night. The dapper navy suit with a whimsical red bow tie complemented his tanned skin, and the cordovan loafers had to be Italian—only because that's what they always were on the wealthy men in the books she'd snuck from her mother's bedside table.

"Good morning, Mr. Henry," she said, moving close to the little dog looking up at the older man with expec-tant, beaded black eyes. "What a precious pup."

She bent and held out a hand and the dog trotted to her, sniffed her hand and allowed her to pet him.

"Her name is Izzy," Mr. Henry said, bending down and bestowing a kiss on the animal's head. "She's a good girl, aren't you?"

A full minute was spent in admiration of Izzy, who rolled over and gave them her belly to scratch.

"I love dogs," Mary Paige said, dutifully scratching Izzy's satiny chest. "I had a golden retriever growing up.

Toby was the best dog ever. He's buried under our pink dogwood because he always loved that tree best."

"Ahem." The sound came from above them.

Mary Paige stopped prattling and glanced at Brennan Henry.

He appeared disgusted. "Do you two mind?"

"Sorry," she said, standing and tugging her skirt. Again. "Never could resist a sweet face."

Brennan pulled a chair out from the table for her as his grandfather headed around to the armchair at one end. The dog loyally trotted after him, curling at his feet with an adorable doggy sigh.

"Brennan isn't fond of dogs," Mr. Henry said with a secret smile.

"Well, you wouldn't be, either, if you'd been humiliated at your tenth birthday party by a clown's dog."

Mr. Henry laughed. "That dog went to town on your leg, didn't he?"

Brennan glowered. "I don't think we need to bring that up. This is a meeting, right?"

Mary Paige sat—glad the chair had armrests to cling to—and hid a smile as she pulled hand sanitizer out of her purse and squirted some in her palm. She rubbed them together as Mr. Henry retold the story of his meeting Mary Paige, to which his grandson said a grand sum of…nothing.

As he'd finished talking about the check, the boardroom door opened and an older woman wearing an ivory suit entered. She carried several folders and a travel mug. "Apologies for being late. Don's barking up my tree on these reports."

The woman set her things opposite Mary Paige and held out a hand. "Hi, I'm Ellen Bivens, vice president of communications and community relations."

Mary Paige shook her hand and introduced herself, glad to have another woman to break up the testosterone oozing from one end of the boardroom table. Ellen looked to be around fifty years in age with a long face and quick smile. Mary Paige liked her on sight.

Mr. Henry cracked his knuckles. "Okay, time to talk turkey. This young woman is exactly the kind of person we wanted for this campaign. We're pulling out the stops for this—TV, radio and print. Hell, we're even using that social media everyone's talking about. It's time to bring goodness back to Christmas. Rip down the sparkly tinsel and self-serving commercialism. I want the world to know that Henry's embraces the spirit of service as part of the season."

Ellen nodded, flipping through a folder. "This campaign is brilliant. With so many other companies embracing 'me,' it's a good strategy to focus on this season being a time of sharing with others, reveling in the spirit of community, a time—"

"For making lots of money," Brennan added.

Mary Paige glared at the sexy grandson with his fingers tented in front of him.

What an ass.

"Excuse me," Mary Paige said, scooting her chair back. "If this is only about making money, I'll have to decline."

Brennan cocked his head. "Decline?"

Mr. Henry waved a hand. "Rest assured, dear girl. This is not about the bottom line, but the greater good. It's about what you showed an old bum who had a need. It's about the milk of human kindness."

"But the bottom line *is* important," his grandson persisted.

Mary Paige directed her attention to the ass. "I'm not

interested in tricking people so you can make a buck. It's deceitful to pretend the holiday is about showing love to your fellow man when you have a different motivation behind it. I can't imagine something so…"

His eyes clouded.

"Well, let's just say, I'll not be part of it." She turned her attention to Mr. Henry as she rose. Something about Brennan made her uncomfortable. Not just his concern for the almighty buck, but his distaste for his grandfather's plan. She could feel cynicism sheet off him in waves.

And maybe part of her discomfort was she was attracted to the man…a man who was about as far away from her usual type as she could get. Scary. "Thank you for the offer, Mr. Henry, but I'm not interested in being the Spirit of Christmas for Henry Department Stores."

Brennan stood politely, ever the Southern gentleman, a mixture of triumph and relief on his face. "So you'll be returning the check, then?"

CHAPTER THREE

BRENNAN WATCHED THE blonde with interest. What would she say at the thought of handing that two-million-dollar check back to his grandfather? Sure, she could buy a man a cup of coffee, but anyone could have done that…even an ax murderer. Here was the litmus test of her character.

Mary Paige shot him a look that curled something in his gut, and he felt the way he had when he'd disappointed someone he cared about. Except he didn't care about this woman. So why did she make him feel like scum? His job was to take care of his grandfather and this company, and that included safeguarding the bottom line. Lord, she made it sound like it was wrong to pursue profit.

"Of course I'll give the money back," she said, picking up her purse. "I certainly wouldn't keep it if I couldn't uphold my end of the deal."

"No, please wait, Miss Gentry," his grandfather said, standing and waving a gentling hand in her direction. "I think you've gotten off on the wrong foot with my grandson. Brennan doesn't mean to come across so harshly. He's looking out—"

"For this company." Brennan gave his grandfather a nod that said he could fight his own battles. "I'm sorry if that offends you, but we're a business and thus responsible to our shareholders and employees to, you know, make a *profit*—nasty word, though it is."

She hesitated and he wondered if this was what she'd

been after in the first place. Was she faking do-gooder or was she sincere? He couldn't tell. He'd never been great at reading women. His grandfather alone had raised him and there hadn't been a steady female influence in his life, so he didn't always trust the fairer sex. The women he was accustomed to were soothed by pretty words and shiny baubles…and would never give back two million dollars without a fight.

"Please, sit. Let's try this again." It was his one acquiescence to his grandfather. He didn't like the idea of this whole Spirit of Christmas thing, but after hearing Ellen's take, the idea had rolled around in his head, carving a comfortable nook in his thoughts of the image the company should present and, yes, the profit generated from the way they positioned themselves.

Ellen smiled. "You're obviously a good soul, Mary Paige, so I know corporate considerations can be, well, conflicting in their intent."

Mary Paige nodded. "I'm an accountant, Ellen. I understand the concept."

An accountant? His mind flashed to her tangle of arms and legs in the lobby…and that interesting piece of Lycra. Something about her wasn't businesslike and he couldn't see her chained behind a desk tapping on an enormous calculator.

"Oh, really?" Ellen said, eyeing Mary Paige. "Very interesting."

Mary Paige shifted her gaze from Ellen to the dog. "Listen, I see what you're trying to do, Mr. Henry, and it's admirable. It's actually a really sweet idea, but I'm not sure I'm comfortable in the limelight."

His grandfather smiled. "Don't worry, dear. Brennan will be right beside you every step of the way. We're not throwing you out front to tap-dance. We want the face of MBH beside you, showing all of the country we here in New Orleans believe in good works and good cheer."

The hell Brennan would be right beside her. He wasn't sure what the old man had up his sleeve, but if he thought Brennan would gallop all over this city with a silly grin on his face escorting the clumsy accountant as she put on a dog and pony show spreading Christmas cheer, he was certifiable.

In fact, maybe Brennan needed to pursue that possibility. Testing the old man to certify he was missing a few spokes on his wheel.

"Him?" Mary Paige pointed to Brennan.

"Once upon a time Brennan loved Christmas and his goal in life wasn't to frighten small children."

Ellen snorted.

"I'm not interested in promo stunts," Brennan said. "You like that sort of thing, Grandfather, so you do it."

"If you want to be the next CEO," his grandfather said, "the public needs to see you as the face of the company. Not me. Besides, I have a full calendar."

"And I don't? I'm trying to run this company, and I don't think the board of directors would appreciate the future CEO gallivanting around trimming trees and singing carols. I need to maintain a stable public image. This is ridiculous."

And it was. He was not babysitting his grandfather's project. If the old man wanted a Spirit of Christmas campaign, fine, but it had nothing to do with Brennan. Besides, it was illogical to spring it on him five weeks before Christmas. It felt a day late, a dollar short and very, very nutty.

"I don't see how standing next to Scrooge here and faking merry is going to help you spread Christmas cheer." The light from the window caught Mary Paige's hair, creating a golden curtain around her pleasant face. He really liked the wholesome thing she had going on. She didn't wear a lot of makeup or any heavy perfumes. When she'd passed him earlier, she'd smelled light and clean, like fresh laundry and sunshine. Like some crap on a commercial...but, he'd liked it.

And she'd just called him *Scrooge*.

"It will do more than you know, Mary Paige. Ol' Scrooge here—" his grandfather gestured toward Brennan "—needs to be a poster boy for Henry's in this city. I've seen him put on a smile when it behooves, and it need behoove him now if he wishes to move on to the large chair in the biggest office. The success of this company is not in the bottom line, but in the values we embrace and show to the world. I'll let it be known here and now that we have genuine concern for our fellow man. If that is the focus, it trickles down into every square inch of every store across the country."

Brennan had to mull that one over. Maybe his grandfather had a point. Sometimes it was hard for Brennan to see the forest for the bottom line. His goal was profit, but that alone would not sustain the company.

"I want you to understand, Miss Gentry, that this Spirit of Christmas campaign is not about making more money, but rather bringing something back I've been missing for so many years in my own life. It has been too long since I've felt the wonder of kindness and the generosity of my fellow man. I know change starts with me. I am looking at the man in the mirror each morning and expecting something more."

Brennan glanced at Mary Paige and he could see the cogwheels rotating through the windows of those chocolate-brown eyes.

"How can I help?" she asked. "By showing up at events

wearing my best smile? How is that going to make anyone feel any more charitable toward a fellow human being?"

"I have a hunch about you, my dear." The confidence in Malcolm's expression seemed to say he knew something no one else in the room did. "A very strong hunch about what you can accomplish in even the hardest of hearts." He then looked at Brennan with a sort of gleam in his eye.

Oh, hell, no. If his grandfather had some sort of notion about Mary Paige performing a bypass on the hardened parts of his ticker, he was sadly mistaken. Brennan wasn't damaged or bitter. He was merely a realist. And he absolutely did not need another woman in his life—not when he couldn't seem to shed Creighton at the moment. She'd become like a latex coating on his fingers… preventing him from feeling anything. He really wished he'd left her alone. Wished she'd get the message he'd tried to send her many times over the past few weeks.

So even if he felt a weird interest in the accountant, he wasn't letting his grandfather cook up some crazy matchmaking scheme with a stranger he'd picked up at a gas station.

But this blonde wasn't dumb. She narrowed her eyes at the old man then shifted her gaze to him.

"This *is* about Christmas, right? I mean, you're not trying to give me a babysitting job with McScrooge here, are you? I'm no miracle worker, Mr. Henry."

"Babysitting?" Brennan echoed, trying not to frown and scare poor misguided Little Bo Peep. "I'm not the one who fell on my ass in the lobby then crawled across a boardroom to fawn over some cur."

Izzy lifted her head and gave him a doggy glare as if she knew he'd slighted her.

Brennan tapped the arm of his chair. "Someone might

need babysitting, but it's not the guy wearing the striped tie and sitting in this chair."

Mary Paige blinked at him, making him feel a little childish for being so defensive. What was wrong with him? He never got emotional during business meetings. Of course, this was one of the strangest meetings, but nevertheless, he had to get hold of the situation. No way would he try to convince her to do this. If she refused, it would likely be game over for his grandfather's little idea. One less headache for Brennan.

"Before we send out a press release or make any further plans, why not do a test run?" his grandfather said, settling back into his chair and folding his hands across his still-flat stomach.

"Like what?" Mary Paige looked as if she might bolt for the door at any second.

Her reaction to him struck Brennan as odd. Most women found him charming. Okay, not charming, but intriguing. After all, he wasn't half-bad to look at, had money in the bank and treated them like ladies. What was this chick's problem? Hadn't he helped her from her fall, picked up her lipstick and held the door for her? He hadn't been an ogre. But she'd been treating him like he had horns. It was almost as if she didn't want to participate in the gig because she'd have to spend time with him.

So he was a bit grumpy this morning. And not totally on board with the whole Spirit of Christmas idea. Was that good reason to act like he was the Antichrist?

Or maybe just anti-Christmas?

Perhaps that was it. The woman was a bona fide Christmas jingle-bell ringer. Probably decorated her whole house with flashing lights and little red-nosed reindeer statues.

"Why not take Miss Gentry down for a cup of that new

eggnog coffee they're brewing at CC's? Show her your sweet side, grandson o' mine," Malcolm said.

It wasn't a suggestion…it was an order—iron buffered with gentility. His grandfather may have been slurping down the Froot Loops lately, but he was still his grandfather, the man who'd nearly single-handedly built Henry's into a reputable, reliable chain of department stores with net worth that kept Wall Street's eye on them. So if Malcolm Henry said "Jump," folks asked, "How high?" But Brennan wasn't *folks*. He was the heir to the throne with the key almost in his pocket. Wasn't it time he stopped dancing to his grandfather's tune? "I'm sure Miss Gentry has other business—"

"Yes, I do," she agreed quickly.

Her eagerness to avoid him stopped him. The woman didn't even want to go to coffee with him? Good Lord, when was the last time a woman had turned him down? Hardly ever. From the time he'd been knee-high, everyone had jumped to do his bidding, to be his friend, to have some of the limelight given to the Henry name shine on them. But this little accountant didn't want a thing to do with him…and that made her more interesting than her willingness to hand back the check.

"Maybe we should get better acquainted." He stood and politely pulled her chair back as she rose.

Her hair swished in front of his nose, releasing a light scent of innocence and simplicity that tumbled him briefly into childhood. He breathed deeply, then exhaled into the silky strands. And he felt her tense in awareness.

Something flared between them, causing an almost uncontrollable urge for naughtiness to overtake him. The wisp of an idea curled into his brain, featuring Mary Paige in silk stockings and a red-and-white Santa-styled push-up bra. Her ass would be spectacular in a garter and thong. And her smile. So warm and promising.

Ellen's phone went off, drawing everyone's attention to the BlackBerry jittering on the table. He popped the picture of Mary Paige playing the sexy ingenue from his mind with his handy dandy pin of reality. For heaven's sake, the woman was wearing some girdle thing that was about as sexy as corn bread.

Mary Paige stepped back, almost brushing against him. "I'm sorry. I'm not playing games with you, Mr. Henry. I'm merely convinced I'm not the right girl to be your holiday spirit. I've a lot on my plate, and while the money would be nice, I think it best if I bow out."

"Coward," Brennan murmured in her ear before he could catch himself. He had no clue why he'd issued the challenge. What did he care if she stomped out of the office, handed over the check and the whole stupid holiday stunt crashed and burned? He didn't. But something inside him had balked at watching Miss Mary Sunshine slip through his fingers.

He felt her response—the slight outrage, the nervousness at his presence invading her space and a little bit of the right kind of interest—just before she moved away.

"Okay, maybe just coffee," she said.

"Splendid," his grandfather crowed, leaning forward to toss a file onto the table. "Ellen and I have some work to do while you two talk about a partnership that will make this the best season for Henry Department Stores in its history...a season of kindness."

Brennan ignored his grandfather's donning of Christmas-colored glasses and gestured toward the door, allowing Mary Paige to slide through before following. He couldn't stop himself from watching her really nice backside.

She spun around as the boardroom door closed and

caught him looking. Her face went pink again and she pointed a finger at him. "If you think I'm sleeping with you, you're nuts. This is a business meeting."

His reconnaissance skills with regard to the opposite sex weren't usually this rusty. While many in New Orleans thought him a playboy, he truly didn't sleep around that much. He was no walking hormone even as visions of Mary Paige in sexy Santa lingerie had him tilting that way. "Since when is going for coffee code for sex? Jump to conclusions much?"

"So what were you looking at?"

"Whatever you're wearing that keeps showing under your skirt. Is that a pair of Spanx?"

Her eyes widened right before a vivid red swept up her neck. She jerked at the skirt riding high on her thighs. "Oh, my God. I can't believe…"

She turned and stalked ahead of him, holding her purse as if it were the last parachute on a plane.

He followed not because he had to, but because something inside him wanted to follow her.

Which didn't make a damn lick of sense.

CHAPTER FOUR

MALCOLM HENRY, JR. sat in his big office chair and smiled.

He couldn't have scripted a better meeting between his grandson and that adorable girl. Brennan had taken notice earlier than Malcolm had expected and it tickled him to no end. He was tired of watching a parade of beautiful empty girls wind through his grandson's life, and he wondered if this Mary Paige could work magic in the life of the person he held dearest.

Not that it had been his original intention—he wasn't a matchmaker and would never meddle in his grandson's love life. But when life handed you peaches, you made pie. And as he'd watched the pretty Mary Paige climb into his Bentley with such apprehension, he wondered if fate had pulled a fast one and delivered the very person who might help *Brennan* find the true meaning of Christmas.

Hell, the true meaning of life.

A real peach.

Malcolm sneezed and it scared the dog curled in his lap.

"Sorry, girl," he said, scratching under Izzy's chin. She closed her alert eyes and if a dog could sigh, well, then Izzy sighed. "Such a wonderful creature, aren't you?"

She didn't bother to open her eyes. That meant she agreed.

A knock at his office door had him spinning from the view of Poydras Street to face his assistant, Anton

"Gator" Perot, who'd been his bodyguard, driver and right-hand man for the past twenty years. Malcolm trusted Gator like he trusted no other. Raised on the bayou backwaters by a grandmother from the Houma tribe, Gator had pulled himself up from near poverty by sheer cunning, guts and smarts. He'd landed in Malcolm's doorway after refusing to take a job with the Garciano family—a true show of character that paid off when Al Garciano was tossed in the slammer for racketeering.

"I have the pictures from last night on this disk," Gator said, setting a plastic case on Malcolm's desk. "Want me to give them to Ellen or send them to the *Picayune?*"

Malcolm sighed. "Not yet. I'm still waiting to see if Miss Gentry will sign on."

His assistant raised his eyebrows as he eased into one of the red leather chairs across from Malcolm. "She did look at the check, didn't she? Two million's hard to say no to. Don't think I've met a broad who would turn down shoe money like that."

"This one's a bit different."

"Do-gooders usually are."

"Is that what you think she is? A do-gooder?"

Gator shrugged. "Never would have pinned you for one, either, but turns out you shoulda named that mutt Max."

"Max? Izzy's a girl."

"You know from that cartoon about the Grinch. Remember his dog's named Max."

The Grinch, huh? Well, Malcolm supposed it could be said his old shriveled heart had grown three sizes. Or, more accurately, it had repaired itself with a new mission in life.

Six months, three weeks and four days ago, Malcolm had stepped out of the Bentley, heading into the board-of-directors meeting, when a crippling pain struck him. He'd literally dropped to his knees, putting out a hand to a passerby who sidestepped him in panic. Gator had already pulled away from the curb, and there was no one there to help him. He collapsed on the dirty Poydras sidewalk, unable to talk or even breathe.

Someone had called 911 and a doctor dining in a hotel restaurant had seen him from across the street, left his eggs Benedict and administered first aid. By the time Malcolm had reached the hospital, he'd coded twice. The E.R. doctor was on record as stating there wasn't a prayer's chance in hell Malcolm would make it.

After a drawn-out surgery where he was nearly declared dead, Malcolm had awoken alone in ICU…and had remained there by himself for four days. When he'd been moved to a private room, he went a whole week seeing no one but his physical therapist, the doctors, nurses and Gator. Brennan had come by once to get him to sign power-of-attorney papers so he could run the company while Malcolm recovered.

Malcolm had received tons of flowers, plants and baskets of cookies, but no visitors.

And that had done something to him.

The reality of being Malcolm Henry, Jr., CEO of MBH, had slammed into him with the same crippling velocity of a massive heart attack. He was a shadow of a man who no one knew and, worse, no one really cared about.

And the realization had hurt.

And it had sobered.

And it had changed him.

As he worked to heal himself physically—changing his eating habits, work habits and exercise habits—he'd looked really hard at his life and what it represented and found it sadly lacking in the fundamentals of happiness.

He had no family who cared for him, save Brennan, who was headed down the same dead-end street Malcolm had already trod, and Ellen, who was focused on healing from a bitter divorce. His only other kin, his nephew Asher, lived in Europe and seldom visited. Malcolm had no true peace. No true purpose other than making money. No warmth of human kindness to buffet him when a cold wind blew. His life was a yawning pit of darkness with no light beckoning.

Malcolm needed a role model, someone to show him what true joy was. So he went to the bookstore and bought biographies on people who'd embodied it—Mother Teresa, Ghandi and the Apostle Paul. He read about their lives of service, about their lack of self-importance, about their sheer passion for living.

And his heart had grown three sizes.

"Maybe I should have named her Max," he said, rubbing her head and earning an adoring swipe of her tongue on his wrist. "I sent Brennan with Miss Gentry for a coffee. Right now, they don't see eye to eye on this endeavor."

Gator raised his eyebrows, making his thin, nearly feral face more attractive. He looked fierce but was putty in the hands of old ladies, small children and cats. Who woulda thunk?

"Brennan is a tough cookie, boss. He might eat Miss Gentry for lunch and pick his teeth with her pinky finger."

Malcolm smiled.

"What?" Gator grinned, a sort of dawning in his eyes. "You're not playing matchmaker, are you? She's not his type. He likes women who scratch."

"I have a sneaking suspicion Miss Mary Paige isn't as docile as she appears. She reminds me of a girl I once knew. And this isn't about matchmaking. It's more like waking Brennan from his money-drunk stupor."

Before it could take root, he struck the thought of Grace from his mind because it still smarted to think about his first love. She'd broken his heart and danced away with some schmuck from River Ridge after Malcolm had offered to set her up as his mistress. Who could blame her for wanting a full and respectable life, for refusing a man who would marry the "right" kind of girl while keeping the "wrong" one on speed dial? Malcolm had been too afraid of his father to choose Grace over adding to the family fortune as expected, so he'd lost her. And Malcolm hated losing.

"Well, let's hope they find some way to make this happen. Don't think you have time to play Hobo Hal again, and truthfully, I don't wanna sit in that Dumpster again. Got a sensitive nose, and I still can't get rid of the scent of rotten milk and molding bread."

"Pansy-ass," Malcolm drawled, spinning toward the window and the busy city cranking like gears on a clock spread before him.

"Managing mama hen," Gator said.

Malcolm had to think about that. "Oh, I don't have to do any managing of those two. I'm banking on something wonderful happening this Christmas."

Gator harrumphed.

"Besides Brennan knows the score. He wants to be CEO. I want Mary Paige as my Spirit of Christmas. He better make it happen."

"And you always get what you want."

Malcolm smiled. "Usually."

MARY PAIGE SCOOTED to one side of the elevator and pretended that she hadn't made a fool of herself.

Of course, he had been looking at her stupid Spanx and not her butt. It was very evident the man wasn't interested in someone like her. She'd seen his preferred type of woman earlier and Mary Paige was as far from put-together sophistication as a gal could get.

Not that she didn't try.

She wanted to be a confident, well-dressed career girl. To have a duplex uptown, shop in decent stores and get her hair cut in salons that offered tea while she waited.

But she hadn't gotten there yet. And she may never arrive at that particular destination if she let herself get sidetracked.

"I'm assuming you like coffee since my grandfather has sent us out on a playdate for the stuff?" Brennan asked, shrugging into his overcoat as the elevator descended. An older woman with puffy graying hair had handed it to him as they'd approached the lobby of MBH, making Mary Paige wonder how the woman had known he needed the coat. Psychic assistant?

"Uh, sure. Though I usually go for tea."

"They have tea."

And that was their brilliant conversation in the elevator.

They walked out of the building, greeted by a cold wind whipping around the corner. Mary Paige shivered and wished she hadn't left her sweater behind that morning. Brennan quickly took off his coat and handed it to her.

"No, I'm fine. It's a short walk."

He jabbed it toward her again. "I insist."

She tried not to sigh her frustration. He was already acting as though he had to babysit her. She didn't need his damn coat because it wasn't like they were in Minnesota. It was only forty-three degrees—she wouldn't freeze walking three doors down. But she took the dark cashmere coat and draped it over her shoulders.

It was warm and smelled like expensive men's cologne and for a brief moment, she felt safer.

Which was idiotic.

"Thank you. You're quite the gentleman."

He looked at her and stuck his hands into his pants pockets. "I try."

Monday morning in New Orleans swirled around them with businessmen hurrying toward offices, tourists sleepily contemplating maps and street signs and the French Quarter homeless folks lolling in doorways, siphoning heat from open souvenir shops.

CC's smelled like her mama's kitchen, resplendent with the scents of comforting coffee and pound cake baking. Tinkling jazz was overshadowed by the hum of conversation and the hiss of the espresso machine.

She approached the counter and perused the menu board. She didn't usually go to coffeehouses for tea because the prices added up fast. She was an at-home Celestial Seasonings kind of girl. "I'll have a cup of green tea. That's it."

She pulled her wallet from her purse.

"I've got it," Brennan said.

"No, you do not," she said, shoving a five-dollar bill at the girl behind the register, who took it with an unsure look.

Brennan shrugged, ordered a plain black coffee then reclined in a chair at one of the wooden tables, crossing his legs and looking very intense even in a relaxed posture.

Mary Paige took the cup steaming with fragrance and sat opposite him. "So?"

He gave a smile that didn't reach his eyes. Kind of an annoyed smile. A make-the-best-of-this smile. "My grandfather has an iron will, if you haven't noticed."

"I noticed," she said, pulling the tea bag from the water and setting it on a pile of napkins. She added one sugar packet then took a sip. It warmed her instantly. "Oh, here's your coat. Thank you for letting me borrow it."

He waved a hand. "Keep it until we get back."

She nodded, mostly because it seemed stupid to argue over a coat when they had more important things to iron out. "About this whole Spirit deal, I get the feeling you're not on board with it, and I'm unsure exactly what it is I'm taking on and how I can do anything near what your grandfather wants."

Brennan nodded, pausing a moment as if he were gathering the right words to say. She studied him in the yellowish light of the café…at the slight shadow of his beard, the intelligent gray eyes and the thick shock of brown hair, glinting with reddish highlights. He had nice broad shoulders and strong, blunt fingers, and though he wore a well-tailored suit, she could tell he'd look spectacular in athletic shorts and a T-shirt.

Something more than tea warmed her insides.

Okay, horny girl. Stop fantasizing about Scrooge as a man and see him for what he is—a not-so-nice person.

But could she really say that?

No.

She didn't know the man, and judged him based only on his reaction to the crazy scheme his grandfather had dreamed up and his intent to make a buck from the campaign. That didn't mean Brennan threw kittens in the lake or elbowed old ladies.

"I agree with you. This whole thing is absurd, but my grandfather's nutty Spirit of Christmas idea isn't a bad one. It could be brilliant for our company, bring in a load of customers buying into the whole true-meaning crap. It's just bothersome to have to spend the time making it happen."

Okay, he was a bit of an ass.

"Bothersome?" she asked.

"Well, don't tell me you want to skip all over the city doing Lord only knows what for the entire season? With me?"

He looked hard at her and something crackled between them.

What if?

That question floated out there between them.

Mary Paige snatched it back. "So this is a no-go?"

"I didn't say that."

What had he said, then?

Mary Paige cleared her throat. "Listen, I have plans for my life. Plans that don't include a crazy billionaire and five weeks of standing beside you pretending I want to be there."

He frowned and looked sort of offended.

"But I like your grandfather. And I like what he's trying to do. Christmas often feels so commercialized people lose sight of what is truly important."

"Which is?"

"Family, friends, love."

"Bah, humbug," he said with a smile.

She arched an eyebrow she knew needed waxing. Why hadn't she gone by the mall and attended to her wayward eyebrows? Because she hadn't known she'd be sitting across from a hot executive having tea.

"I'm trying to bring some humor into this," he said.

She rolled her eyes.

"Not working?"

She took another sip of tea. "You're behaving much better."

"Oh, goody."

"If we do this, we need to set ground rules."

"I know. You aren't sleeping with me."

She felt the blush sweep her face and wished she had more control of her body. "I'm sorry about that. I didn't mean to—"

"So you *will* sleep with me?" His gray eyes sparked and for the first time she saw that Brennan's charm might be way more deadly than expected. The man was downright gorgeous when he offered a genuine smile.

"Uh, that's not what I meant. I meant I didn't mean to imply that you were looking at my…uh…my butt in that way."

"What if I were? You have a nice-looking ass."

She snapped her mouth closed because it had fallen open again like the country bumpkin she was.

His eyes crinkled and she realized he enjoyed flirting with her. What's worse, she enjoyed it, too. "Stop playing with me, Brennan."

"Oh, I haven't even begun playing with you yet, Mary Paige," he drawled, his voice dropping an octave, making liquid heat flood her lower body.

Damn him. This man wasn't anything she should be meddling with.

"Okay, are we doing this or not, Brennan?"

"Doing what?"

"This Spirit of Christmas thing your grandfather wants."

"Oh, that."

She didn't bother with asking him what else he'd been

talking about because she knew. And she wouldn't give him the satisfaction he wanted. "Yes, that. The only thing on the menu."

His short laugh stroked the imp inside her who really, really liked playing the sexy word games with him. "Actually, I usually prefer things not on the menu, but we'll see about that, won't we?"

"No." She sipped her tea and stared out at people hurrying by the window. She wasn't allowing herself to go off the menu…she was barely convinced by what was on the menu. Spending time with Brennan felt dangerous, and that appealed to her. Which was peculiar. She didn't even like him all that much. "In all seriousness, should we do this thing your grandfather has in mind?"

"No," he said, leaning back in the chair, taking a draw of the dark roast he'd purchased. "But my grandfather usually gets his way. He's like that."

"I'm thinking you're both accustomed to getting your way," she muttered.

His smile was almost predatory.

Yeah, dangerous.

"At first I thought the idea ludicrous, but the more I think about it the more I like differentiating our stores from the pack. It's a good message for the holidays. A do-unto-others sort of vibe that seems right in this economy."

"You're back to thinking of it as a profit generator."

He cocked his head. "I'm always thinking of the bottom line, Mary Paige. Always. I can't apologize for doing my job. I want to be up front and honest here about the reason I'm considering throwing my hat into this promotion blitz—it's good for the company. And that's it."

She nodded, not happy that his only motivation for standing beside her as she became the Spirit of Christmas for Henry Department Stores was money, but appreciating his honesty. It was disappointing a person would be self-serving in the opportunity to help others and revel in the joy of the season. Very sad.

"Okay, I'll sign on as long as you promise to be a good boy."

He shrugged. "Who, me?"

She nodded, a bit amazed she was giving directives to a Henry. It was probably the most power she'd held in her hand ever…which felt heady. "Yes, you. I can't have someone standing beside me scaring the homeless with a frowny face as I serve them Christmas ham."

"We're serving ham to the homeless?"

"I don't know, but whatever Ellen and Mr. Henry have planned for us may put you outside your comfort zone. I'll be your Spirit of Christmas as long as you summon a little enthusiasm."

"I can fake merry."

"That's really pathetic, but I'll take that as a yes."

He extended his hand across the table and she stared at it for a brief second.

Did she really want to commit to spending the next few weeks with this man?

Her brother's sloppy grin popped into her head, followed closely by her mother's expression when faced with the mound of bills on the counter.

And then her own towering student loans.

And the animal shelter three streets away from her rented duplex in desperate need of funding.

Yeah, she could suffer through Scrooge for the next month. It wouldn't be bad. He'd be her shadow. Nothing more. And at the end of it all, she'd take that check and create good with it.

She took his hand, which was warm from the coffee, and tried to ignore how nice it felt as his fingers curled over hers. No stupid tingles or dumb electricity. Just a nice toasty shake that made her feel only slightly fluttery. "Deal."

He pulled his hand away and stood. "I need to get back. I have a luncheon meeting in thirty minutes, and I'm sure Grandfather will want to go over particulars with you. I'll let him know we're in on this Spirit of Christmas."

She rose, dropped her half-filled cup in the trash can and followed him out the door—which he held for her, of course. As they walked to his office building, she mulled over her decision to do this thing. Was she borrowing trouble? Probably. She didn't want to acknowledge it, but an attraction to Brennan lurked at the edge of her consciousness. That's why agreeing to Malcolm Henry, Jr.'s plan felt dangerous. Because of Brennan and the way she kept looking at his stormy gray eyes, his drool-worthy shoulders and the nice butt that peeked through the back slit of his suit jacket.

But she's wouldn't be one of his playthings. Oh, she knew his reputation—New Orleans's own playboy, favorite of the jet-setters and a cousin to those alpha heroes in her mother's British romance books.

Of course he wasn't some emotionally stunted Greek tycoon. He was an emotionally stunted New Orleans tycoon.

Surely there was a difference.

And she wasn't his secretary…or mistress…or nurse.

Mary Paige was her mother's daughter, Caleb's sister, future CPA and card-carrying member of the SPCA and about as far from Brennan Henry's type as a gal could get.

And that was her only reassurance.

They walked into the lobby of the building and she

watched Brennan cringe at the large tree near the fountain. The music spilling out was jolly and reminded them of how cold it was outside.

Brennan gave another disgusted glance at the tree flashing in tune and turned to her. "When you get the schedule for whatever they're planning, will you insure Grandfather forwards it to me so I can sync my calendar? He's forgetful in his old age."

"Sure," she said, shrugging out of his coat, inhaling the scent of his cologne as she surrendered the warmth. "Anything else, master?"

She was being a smart-ass, but didn't care. She wasn't his assistant and didn't have to pass along messages for him. Okay, it wasn't hard to utter a simple sentence, but still, his presumptuousness irked her.

His eyes glinted approval at her sarcasm, which had a peculiar effect on her stomach. He pointed to the tree. "Yeah, tell him to take down that blinking monstrosity. It's offensive."

Mary Paige studied the good-looking miser who seemed to have tumbled from Dickens's book into the here and now. "Tell him yourself."

CHAPTER FIVE

MARY PAIGE OPENED the door to her duplex in midtown and smelled something burning. Simon must have made himself dinner because her place always smelled like this when Simon cooked. She also knew the dirty dishes would be in the sink and he'd be gone. Wonderful house-guest, he ain't.

"Simon?"

His head poked out of the kitchen. "Oh, you're home early."

A giggle from the kitchen proved she'd been off base about what Simon had been doing in the kitchen.

"I took the day off," Mary Paige said, zipping her purse and setting it on the table in the narrow foyer and trying to gauge whether she should leave or blaze into the kitchen and kick her goat of an ex-boyfriend out of her life for good.

"Uh, Mary Paige, I kinda have a friend here," Simon said, jerking his head toward the depths of her tiny kitchen.

"I heard, but I need a drink," she said, heading toward the fridge where, hopefully, she'd still find her dime-store bottle of Zinfandel.

"Stop," Simon said, flinging out a hand. "We're not exactly decent."

Mary Paige almost skidded into the sofa table she

stopped so fast. Oh, heck to the no. He better not be naked with some floozy in her kitchen.

Disgusting.

"Simon, please tell me you're not—"

"We're doing some experimental art. That's all," he said with the shrug of a thin naked shoulder.

"*Fun* experimental art," someone of the female persuasion called out with a slight giggle.

"Okay, fine. I'll go to my room for a moment while you two get decent and clear out of my place. Both of you. Clear out." Mary Paige hurried toward her room because though she'd seen Simon without clothes, she never planned on doing so again. Letting him crash here had been a favor…one that had long ago proven a huge mistake.

Because she couldn't get him off her couch or—obviously—out of her kitchen.

But she'd reached the end of her charity.

"Okay, we're good," Simon called after Mary Paige studied the wonder of her new cherry sleigh bed covered by a cream batiste spread. She'd looked hard at it, making sure Simon and whoever was posing for his *experimental art*—aka sex in the kitchen—hadn't tried to use her new bed.

She stalked out to find Simon slouching on her couch wearing a pair of sweatpants and tank top. His bare feet were propped on her new *Glamour* magazine, and the bimbo—Mary Paige recognized her as the girl who sold her fancy cookies at a bakery down the street—perched on the corner of the couch. Her hair fell around her shoulders in a sort of dirty-looking dreadlock do that wasn't flattering and hadn't been in style for ten years.

"What's up, M.P.?" Simon said, folding his arms behind his head and giving her a quasi-smile.

"What is *up* is your time," Mary Paige said, nudging his bare feet off her table with her knee. "You said you only needed to crash here for a few days, and it's turned into almost a month. This little escapade was the last straw. You need to pack your stuff and leave."

"Come on, M.P. As soon as Rick gives me that commission, I'll get a place."

"No. My couch hasn't been my own for too long and I miss it. Go stay with her." Mary Paige pointed to the cookie girl, who made a funny face.

"He can't stay with me. I live with my boyfriend."

Right. Of course she did.

"Babe, if you'd let me sleep with you, I wouldn't be out here on this couch." Simon spread his hands and tried to give her his little-lost-boy smile, the one she'd fallen for over a year ago—before she knew that her highly artistic, creative boyfriend was a slug in disguise. He'd milked her checking account while bleeding her heart dry. And she found out she wasn't so into a carefree, bohemian lifestyle when he asked if she was up for a three-way.

She'd ended the relationship last spring and hadn't seen him until almost a month ago when he'd shown up at her front door with a hangdog expression and a pretty good reason why he'd cheated on her before—he had a large sexual appetite she couldn't handle, which meant he'd actually been doing her a favor, right? Mary Paige had been caught so off guard by his tale of woe regarding some scheme a gallery owner had pulled on him, she'd agreed to let him sleep on her couch for a few days.

Yeah, she was a dumb-ass that way.

Not only that, but she owned all those Dead Sea salt scrubs and lotions sold in kiosks in the mall.

Giant sucker.

But not today.

"Get out of my apartment and take the cookie girl with you. Now." Mary Paige stomped her foot. Twice.

"Babe, just a few more days. I swear. Rick's a man of his word and he'll get me my money."

"And I'm a woman of mine. I told you that you could stay here for a few days…a month ago. Now it's time to find some other sucker to mooch off. And you better leave the forty bucks you took out of my purse on the table before you leave. Oh, and the extra key."

Simon straightened. "I didn't take your forty bucks. I borrowed it."

"Well, I want my *borrowed* money back or I'll walk my butt down to the police station on the corner and file charges."

He threw his hands up. "Whatever. I'll write you a check."

Not even worth the paper it was written on, no doubt. But it was better than nothing. "Fine."

"Don't know why you're busting my ass for forty bucks when you got a two-million-dollar check squirreled away." He gave her a little-boy smile aimed at making her feel crummy for holding out on him. "Naughty little M.P."

His guilt trip didn't work.

"You went through my jewelry box?" Mary Paige curled her hands and parked them on her hips so she wouldn't wrap them around Simon's scrawny neck. What had she ever seen in him? Okay, he was cute in a starving artist, funky, unconventional way, but that was where the charm ended.

Cookie Dreadlocks's eyes widened. "She's got a check for a cool two mil?"

"Looks real," Simon said, stretching before glancing

at the girl he'd more than likely bopped on Mary Paige's grandmother's vintage table. "Is it real?"

Mary Paige glared at him. "Of course not. Why would I have a check for that much lying around for you to find? It was a joke gift from my uncle's party."

The doorbell dinged like the bell in a boxing match.

Sweet relief.

"I'll get it," Cookie Dreadlocks chirped as she skipped to the door.

"This isn't your—" The door swung open to reveal Brennan Henry standing on Mary Paige's stoop.

"Yo, lookie," Cookie Dreadlocks said, glancing over her shoulder at Mary Paige. "You got money in your doorway."

Brennan slid off his sunglasses and glanced at the brass numbers affixed to the weathered exterior boards.

"Fake check, huh? Yeah, I know who that is." Simon pointed toward Brennan. "Saw him at a show once."

Mary Paige had no clue what to do when a hot, rich guy showed up on her stoop in the middle of kicking Sir Simon the Leech and his consort from her life, so she took a good thirty seconds to think about it.

Why now? Why here? Why her?

No answers.

"Oh, wow, is that your ride on the curb, dude?" Cookie Dreadlocks asked.

"Um, yeah," Brennan said.

"Goddamn, that's a good lookin' car." Simon checked out the ride through the slotted blinds.

Mary Paige finally snapped out of it when she saw Simon sliding toward the door with an opportunistic gleam in his green eyes. She pushed skinny Simon against the couch and stepped in front of Cookie Dreadlocks then she squeezed out the door, shutting it behind her.

"Mr. Henry," she said, glad she hadn't already changed into her usual end-of-the-day sweats and fluffy socks. "What are you doing here?"

He stepped back, nearly falling off the postage-stamp-size stoop. "Uh, I had to come this way for an appointment and thought I'd bring over the contract and schedule Grandfather and Ellen put together. Got my hands on it right before I left the office and thought you might want to look at it before you sign since there are some negotiable areas with regard to appearances."

Mary Paige caught a flutter at the window and knew Simon was spying on them. She almost shushed Brennan. "Oh, okay."

Brennan turned as the curtain was drawn back. "Who's that?"

"Who's who?"

"That guy staring out at us. Is he your boyfriend?"

"No," she said, holding firm to the doorknob and pretending that Simon and the weird girl didn't exist.

Simon knocked on the window and waved.

So much for pretending Simon the Mooch away. She tried to smile.

"Well, he's waving at us. And he's in your place. This *is* your house, right?"

"I'm actually leasing it, but, yes, I live here," she said, turning toward her ex-boyfriend. She shot poison arrows out of her eyes at him. Not for real, of course. But if she'd had the ability, she might have used it.

She hadn't wanted Simon to know anything about the Henry Department Store thing.

Yet.

Of course, Simon would find out when he saw her in the media, but she really wanted to get him out of her life—and off her couch—before he learned she'd become the centerpiece of a multimillion-dollar campaign. Who wanted the headache of Simon and his puppy-dog eyes and sad-sack stories of someone ripping him off facing her every time she turned around? Oh, and his palm out, too.

"So?"

She glanced at Brennan, who seemed out of place against the sagging rail of her porch steps and the scraggly grass creeping over the cracked sidewalk. Mr. Ledbetter, the guy who owned the duplex, had had surgery and hadn't been able to do any repairs, much less weed eating. The whole neighborhood still showed the effects of Katrina like a dry-rotted badge. So Brennan standing akimbo in his charcoal cashmere coat, dark pants and shiny shoes looked like a prince who'd stumbled upon a broken-down duplex in a questionable area of midtown to save the poor, clueless wench.

Well, she wasn't a wench or clueless.

But still he looked awfully yummy for a gripe-ass.

"He's leaving. Now," she said loud enough for Simon to hear. The curtains swished closed and she sighed. "He's been staying with me for a few weeks. Uh, just as a friend, but he's worn out his welcome today. Kind of an inopportune time, you know?"

Brennan's eyes widened and he shoved his sunglasses into the coat pocket. "You were kicking him out?"

"Not that it's really any of your business, but, yes, he's leaving," she said again loudly, to emphasize the point.

One of his dark eyebrows lifted and a smile played at his lips. "You're fired up, aren't you?"

"That amuses you?" she asked, pushing her hair behind her ear and trying for some inner control. She needed to get Brennan off her stoop and Cookie Dreadlocks and Simon out of her house, and then eat a Lean

Cuisine dinner. In exactly that order. "Now, if you'll hand me the contract and schedule?"

Brennan didn't budge. Just stared hard at the window where the curtains had started fluttering again. "You need some help convincing him?"

"No, I'm pretty sure he's going. For good."

"I'm not convinced."

"You don't have to be. I don't need your help."

"I'm sure you do." He beckoned at the window with one finger.

The doorknob wiggled in her hand. She clamped down on it, but even though she weighed the same as Simon, he had that whole manly arm-strength going for him. Brennan caught her before she stumbled into Simon.

"What's up?" Simon said, scratching his head and looking very much at home. He'd tossed away his standard slouch for some puffed-up chest posturing.

"You giving Mary Paige a hard time?" Brennan folded his arms across his chest, which seemed to poke holes in Simon's defensive pose. Mary Paige could almost hear the strains of the theme song from *High Noon* in the late-afternoon chill.

"Why would I give her a hard time?" Simon shrugged.

"She said you're leaving. You've worn out your welcome with her."

Simon shrugged again. "Mary Paige got a little ruffled, but that's Mary Paige for you. A sweetheart of a girl. She didn't mean—"

"The hell I didn't." She poked Simon in the chest. "I want you and Cookie out."

"My name is Chloe," the girl chirped, peeking over Simon's shoulder. "I really don't like being called 'Cookie' just because I sell cookies. I sell donuts, too. And lemon squares. And I'm studying to be a social worker."

Mary Paige felt a flash of guilt. Hadn't been fair of her to lump Chloe into the same pile as Simon—the girl had ambition. "Sorry, Chloe, but I really do wish you and your new boyfriend would vacate my apartment. I'm tired and want a bath."

"No prob," Chloe said, sliding by them all and trotting down the steps, backpack swinging behind her. "Later, Simon, who is *not* my boyfriend."

"Later," Simon said, failing to move from the threshold.

"Now it's your turn," Brennan said in a growly voice, eyeballing Simon like something he'd found on the bottom of his shoe.

Simon gave Brennan his own version of a withering look. "Who are you to tell me anything? Don't remember your name on the lease of this apartment."

"Come on, Simon, it really is time to move on. After the whole deal with the money and then this episode today in the kitchen, I think we're really done here," Mary Paige said, in the same voice she used when she had to milk Betty Ann, her mother's Jersey cow. Betty Ann was a cow version of bitch supreme and kicked hard.

"Are you doing this guy, M.P.? Is that what this is? 'Cause now it makes sense why you wouldn't let me connect the dots." Simon drew a line from one of his nipples to the other.

Brennan moved as quick as a cat—a pissed-off jungle cat—and twisted a fist in Simon's T-shirt. "She said *get out.*"

His words were low and lethal. Mary Paige could almost imagine her grumpy Scrooge as a supersecret spy… or simply a guy who had a personal trainer. Fear flashed in Simon's eyes before he threw up his hands. "'Kay, dude. Lay off the testosterone next time."

Brennan released Simon, who immediately slunk inside her apartment, tossing Brennan his own fierce look. She clasped her hands behind her back, unsure whether she should thank Brennan or fuss at him for manhandling Simon. "Uh, thanks for being so insistent."

Brennan ran his hands down his coat and tilted his head toward her. "Are you going to ask me in?"

She thought about that. "Do you want to come in?"

"Don't mind if I do," he said stepping into her world like a man who owned every room he entered—as a Henry, that probably happened often. The Henry family owned plenty of yard all over the Crescent City.

She followed him and shut the door only because it was still abnormally cold and the sun had gone to bed early. Otherwise, she might have left it open so as not to shut herself inside with two men who made her nervous. Simon shoved clothes into an old duffel while muttering under his breath. Brennan monitored him like a prison warden. As if he expected Simon to pull something funny. Which was weird considering Brennan had no idea what belonged to her or what belonged to Simon. It was moot, but she figured Simon didn't know that.

"I'll grab your stuff from the bathroom," Mary Paige said, trying to escape the drama by giving her hands something to do.

"Already got it," Simon said, tossing deodorant and body spray into the bag with the velocity of a major-league pitcher. He zipped the bag with angry flourish. Mary Paige handed him the bag that held his camera and various photography supplies, and he jerked it from her hand.

"Well, guess I'll see you later, Simon," Mary Paige said, feeling a little ping of regret at the circumstances of his leaving. No. She shouldn't feel that way. That's what got her in this mess in the first place. She had to stop picking up strays and getting walked on by everyone in her world...especially guys like Simon.

"Yeah, whatever," he grumbled as he dashed a go-to-hell look at Brennan and headed for the door. The slam literally shook the house and a picture Caleb had painted for her fell off the wall.

"Well, that was fun," Brennan said, picking the bright attempt at postmodernism from the old mismatched chair into which it had thankfully fallen.

He studied the childish rendering that she was proud of, given how difficult art was for Caleb with his cerebral palsy, before setting it against the end table.

"So why are you really here?" Mary Paige said.

WHY WAS HE HERE?

Brennan really didn't have a good answer. He'd used the contract as an excuse to see her again, and he had no clue why he even *wanted* to see her again. Hell, Creighton was probably at his place now reclining against his headboard wearing a racy thong and sipping a martini... which wasn't comforting in the least since he didn't want her there.

But really, why was he here with Merry Sunshine?

He hadn't the foggiest.

Maybe it was the idea of Creighton that had him detouring toward the shabby neighborhood harboring weird people like the two who'd just left, along with several stray dogs. He'd nearly hit one out front, and he hadn't missed the food bowls hidden under the scraggly azaleas. He'd be willing to bet Mary Paige fed the strays. Very irresponsible.

Creighton and her dog-eared copy of *Bride* magazine fled to the back of his mind as he contemplated the woman in front of him. Mary Paige looked at him expectantly before picking up a small fob and pressing it.

The Christmas tree in the corner came to life in brilliant color.

He *knew* it. She was a Christmas nutso.

"I came to give you the contracts," he said.

"Why not send them with a courier? Or fax them to my office? Or send them via email?"

He didn't have a good response. "I told you. I had a meeting this way and thought I'd save time."

"You mean spy on me," she said, dropping the remote on the table and kicking off her shoes. Her skirt still inched up her thighs but he didn't see the girdle thing peeking out. For some reason he wanted to see it. Maybe he had a girdle fetish he didn't know about. Or maybe he hadn't had enough water today. Didn't dehydration make a guy do dumb stuff like drive across town to see a clumsy blonde with a too-big bottom?

Or maybe it was something more than that? Not something he wanted to contemplate.

"I'm not spying on you. That's ridiculous." He shifted his weight and averted his gaze. Mostly because she was right. He'd been curious. "Though I have to say seeing you in your world makes things clearer."

Her brow creased and her pretty eyes narrowed. "'Clearer'?"

"Suffice it to say, I understand you better."

"'Suffice'?"

"Am I not being articulate enough for you?"

"You haven't convinced me you aren't here to snoop around. So did you see what you needed?" She swept her hand around dramatically. "It's not much but it's clean… or it will be as soon as I clear out all traces of Simon."

"It wasn't a bad idea for me to stop by. I helped you with Simon, didn't I?"

"Yeah, but I wouldn't nominate myself for Prince Charming just yet, if I were you. I've seen you in your world, too, you know." She walked toward the kitchen. "Would you like a cup of tea or a glass of wine?"

Drinking wine with her sounded intriguing, but he shouldn't. This wasn't a social visit. "Wine would be good."

"All I have is pink Zinfandel," she called from the kitchen.

Ugh. "That will be fine."

She returned moments later with a plastic wineglass full of pink liquid and gestured to her couch. "All I have are plastic—the cat kept knocking the glass ones off the table and breaking them. I got tired of picking slivers out of my toes."

A vision of Mary Paige's naked toes flashed in his mind. Good God, he really was in trouble. "Cat?"

"Well, there are a lot in this neighborhood that run wild. I'm not irresponsible and I've called animal control many times, but it's a losing battle for them. I kept one little cat. She's blind, thus the broken dishes."

"Where is she?" He sat but not before checking for cat hair. He didn't much care for dogs, cats or any other absurd pets like ferrets, parrots or gerbils.

"Under my bed, most likely. She hates Simon."

"Good judge of character."

Mary Paige smiled and something inside him warmed. Her face had a sort of glow…or maybe it was that absurd tinsel Christmas tree beyond her shoulder. "My relationship with Simon was as much my fault as his. I enable people because I'm too soft. My greatest weakness."

"A weakness that brought you fortune."

"Fortune isn't everything." Her eyes appeared as deep as any lake he'd ever dived into during all those years of summer camp. She believed what she said.

Huh.

Maybe that was the reason for his fascination with her—she didn't seem to care about money, unfathomable as it seemed. Anyone else faced with a dangling carrot of two million dollars would tap-dance, stand on his head or eat worms, but this woman didn't give a rat's ass. Money truly meant little to her.

Maybe she was soft…in the head.

But he knew that wasn't true. Oh, she was soft all right—from the lovely curve of her ass to the goose-down heart beneath that ill-fitting, bright pink sweater. And that had to be the other part of his attraction to her—the softness that was so opposite of most of the women in his life, with their sharp cheekbones and even sharper tongues. "Not your fault for being decent, but I wouldn't have let him in the door in the first place."

"You wouldn't have, would you?"

He took a sip of wine and tried not to grimace at the sweetness. "Nope."

"So did you do enough reconnaissance? Satisfied I won't wreck your company's image with a heroin problem or bipolar personality?"

"No, you're surprisingly consistent."

He took a big gulp of the wine, grimaced because he couldn't help himself this time, and stood. "I should be going. Here's the contract and schedule. We're moving fast out of the gate with the lighting of the Henry's Christmas tree downtown on Wednesday evening. We'll meet at the Fern and St. Charles stop to take the streetcar there. Work for you?"

"That soon?"

"My grandfather will work you like a mule."

"He wants his money's worth." She gave another pretty smile. "I've yet to talk to Ivan the Terrible, but I'll break the news tomorrow."

"Ivan the Terrible?"

"My boss." She followed him toward the door. "He reminds me of you—all business, no charm."

He turned around, and she stopped, her nose a few inches from his chin. "No charm?"

Her mouth curved and her eyes glimmered like a jolly elf's. "Kidding."

"Yeah," he said, almost reaching out to tuck her hair behind her ears. His compulsions around Mary Paige were *so* abnormal. He shoved his hands into his pockets. "Ivan's an accountant. They don't need charm."

She made a face and it struck him that Mary Paige had totally chosen the wrong profession. Hard-nosed business gal trying to inflate net profits was a far cry from the girl wearing the cheap clothes and nursing a blind cat…and charming him without lifting a pinky.

"Well, I'll check that off my list." She sidestepped a couple inches as if suddenly aware she stood dangerously close to a man who had an unexplained urge to kiss her.

"See you on Wednesday," he said, opening the door.

"Yeah," she said with a little wave.

Brennan exited into the New Orleans evening pleased he could walk away from the strange pull that had cropped up between him and this woman who'd fallen into his life. Literally. He was, after all, a man who could control his passions.

Exactly the kind of man MBH Industries needed as the next CEO. A man who wouldn't be moved by his heart.

And who cared about the bottom line.

CHAPTER SIX

MALCOLM HENRY, JR. watched as the young man wearing the platform shoes got jiggy with it. Or at least that's what the boy kept telling all the people around him.

"I'm getting jiggy with it," he shouted, throwing a fist pump as he thrust his hips toward every other person dancing around him. Everyone laughed. Not at him. But with him. It was refreshingly different from the last few parties Malcolm had attended—exuberant, joyful and actually fun.

"We're going to have to keep our eye on David. He's pumped and primed," Judy Poche remarked as she scooped ice from the chest at their feet and set cups on the table.

"He's filled with the Spirit of the Season," Malcolm said over the beat of the bass from the speakers sitting beside the stage. The room swirled with strobe lights and was draped with red and green crepe paper.

"Or too many soft drinks." Judy smiled and cast her eyes over the young adults twisting, shaking and generally cutting a good, old-fashioned rug on the gym floor of the Catholic ministries center. Mixed in with the handicapable and mentally challenged adults from Holy Trinity were the student-council members from Ursuline Academy, who were teaching some of the group-home members a new dance move. All looked to be having a grand time.

"Back in my day, we waltzed," Malcolm said, filling a cup for a sweaty kid whose sweet grin and shy ducking of head was in direct opposition to the polka dots and plaid pants he wore.

Judy sighed. "Oh, those were the days. I can't even understand what this music says much less attempt to dance to it."

"You probably don't want to know the lyrics." Malcolm swiped a damp cloth over the plastic table. "But I love watching them have fun. Blesses me."

"Me, too. You've gotten quite involved with this group. They really seem to respond well to you considering you've been volunteering for only a few months."

Malcolm had started volunteering with many organizations, no longer content to merely hand over a check. He'd wanted to contribute more. Many of the charity directors had been surprised by his desire to interact with those on the receiving end of his donations, but he'd learned one important thing when he woke up alone in that hospital room with scarcely a soul to care whether he lived or died—he'd learned his was a life not well-lived. And he'd wanted to correct that…which was why he now poured soft drinks at the Holy Trinity Center's annual Christmas dance. He refused to spend one more night smoking smelly cigars, reading prospectuses and swilling scotch hundreds of feet above the dirty, teeming masses safe in his moneyed world. Not when he could make a difference. "I truly love being a volunteer, Judy. Thank you for letting me be a part of this."

Judy had been the director of the center for over twenty-five years and Malcolm had encountered no better human being than the sweet soul standing next to him. She barely came to his chin, but was a dynamo of energy with soft chestnut hair that brushed her shoulders, a face well-lined with character and elegant arms that matched her trim form. She'd been a member of the Dominican order when she was younger, and he had no clue why she'd left, and didn't know her well enough to ask. What he did know was that each evening or afternoon he shared with her made him feel like a better man.

It kept him volunteering at her center each week.

A slow song started and the room dimmed a few notches. Several other volunteers appeared, shooing both he and Judy aside so they could mingle with the kids.

Malcolm smiled at several of the boys he often played basketball with. None of them were very good, which made him perfect to teach them the game. He'd always stunk at sports, other than running. He'd been a fine cross-country runner and had been on the Tulane track team back so many years ago it didn't bear thinking about.

"You gonna dance, Mr. H.?" one of the boys asked mischievously, eyeing a cluster of girls nearby.

"You want to dance with me, Carter?"

"No way. I'm a boy." Carter laughed, rolling his eyes comically. "You're supposed to dance with a girl. Like my mother. But she's not here."

One of the girls, Bea, smiled shyly at him, obviously overhearing Carter's remark about dancing. She laughed because Carter laughed, but didn't take her eyes off of the boy. In a true show of male obliviousness, Carter ignored her.

"Shall we?" Malcolm said, holding out his arm to Bea.

She looked confused. "What?"

"Shall we dance, Bea?"

She looked at Carter before nodding like a friendly puppy and taking Malcolm's arm. He led her onto the floor, complimenting her dress, which had a glittery overlay. Bea wore a floppy red bow pinned against her straight red hair. Malcolm showed her how to hold her arms and then swept her around as best he could. A few Ursuline girls danced with some of the other residents, but most looked to have taken a break.

Bea danced enthusiastically for several minutes then broke away suddenly, abandoning him in the middle of the song. For a moment, Malcolm stood there stupidly.

Until Judy saved him.

"She does that sometimes," Judy said, placing her hand on his shoulder and swaying to the rhythm of the song. "Too much contact can overwhelm Bea and she just, poof, disappears."

"Remind me to thank the girl later," he said, curling Judy into his embrace and waltzing toward the perimeter.

"Why?" she asked, peering up at him with warm brown eyes that reminded him of the walnut cabinets that had lined his *grand-mère*'s kitchen. Judy looked so different in his arms. Better than he'd ever expected.

"A thank-you for leaving me out here by myself. Otherwise, I wouldn't have been rescued by my lady on a white steed."

Judy glanced down at her shoes. "They're actually black. And they're pumps."

"You are a delightful woman," Malcolm said, wishing the song would never end. Maybe after the dance, he could ask Judy out for a cup of coffee.

Suddenly he was as nervous as a boy holding a boutonniere and meeting his date's father for the first time. He wanted Judy to like him, to see beyond his millions in the bank, to see a man worthy of her attention.

Even though he knew he couldn't hold a candle to her.

"And you are an old fool if you think so."

Malcolm smiled. "Never enjoyed being called an old fool more."

Judy laughed and looked pleased at his flirting.

Life felt extraordinarily good at that moment.

Like anything was possible.

THIS WASN'T GOING to work.

Mary Paige shoved a pile of folders onto her desk and looked under the credenza for her other shoe. Where had it gone? She'd kicked it off earlier, which meant it had to be in the office somewhere.

She found it under some papers she'd thrown toward the wire trash basket just as Ivan the Terrible roared into her office.

"Where's the Hogue file with all the 1099s? You had it last."

Mary Paige slipped the red stiletto onto her foot. "I put it on your desk an hour ago."

Growl. Roar. Snuffle. He disappeared.

She pulled a brush from the drawer and gave her bob the twice-over, making sure it curved against her jaw, then she touched up her makeup—what little she wore—before shrugging into the red swing coat her mother had given her last Christmas.

"Where are you going?" the beast called through his open office door.

"I told you this morning. I have to leave early for the tree lighting."

"You can't leave now. We have to have the McKays ready by tomorrow morning. You still have to call Randy and get the disclosures."

She closed her eyes and performed her serenity prayer. "Mr. Gosslee, we went over my upcoming schedule this morning. I have to leave right now if I'm going to make it to St. Charles in time. Traffic's about to kick up on the bridge. I'll come in early tomorrow and make sure we have everything in order for the McKays."

"This is unacceptable."

Another silent plea to her Maker. Another sigh. "Shall I tender my resignation?"

His hoary head appeared in her doorway. "Is that the sort of employee you are? One who wants to quit when the going gets tough?"

"No."

His black eyes narrowed. "Have it ready in the morning."

She saluted, ducked under his arm and tucked the tag back into his sweater. The man was forever untucked and wrinkled, but he was a hell of an accountant. "See you tomorrow, Ivan."

"That's Mr. Gosslee to you," he grumbled.

"I love you, too, Ivan."

She shut the door of the faded shotgun house in Gretna that served as their office as she heard him say, "Cheeky."

Ah, free until tomorrow morning. And a date to boot. Okay, not a date really, but something inside her tingled at the thought of seeing Brennan again.

Which was not good.

The man was so far off her map she'd have to enter another realm to locate him. Brennan Henry was too rich for her blood. Too everything for her, including grumpy, materialistic and sardonic. Not qualities she'd *ever* look for in a man.

Still, those tingles wouldn't go away.

The drive to the east bank of New Orleans was painfully slow because of an accident in one of the lanes near the Superdome. By the time she hit Carrolton, a crawl would have been fast compared to the current flow of traffic. She pulled into a safe parking lot and tugged off her heels, glad she kept an extra pair of running shoes in the gym bag in the backseat. She didn't want to arrive in her sneakers, but there was no way she could cross the mile and a half to Audubon Park in her heels.

She gathered her purse, keys and the contracts then locked her car. By the time she reached the park, it was too late to go back to her car for the red high heels she'd forgotten on the passenger seat. Darn it.

When her nerves jangled, she forgot stuff. Now she'd look like a moron at the lighting. She felt the prick of tears, tasted the embarrassment that would come.

Crap. Why had she agreed to this? She was not the kind who could function in front of large crowds. Riding a tractor in a parade and clogging at the Watermelon Festival in her hometown was as close as she'd ever been to the public spotlight.

Too late now.

She choked down the panic and scanned the fading sky for the decorated streetcar they would use to carry Old St. Nick into the city. Finally, she saw it sitting jolly and bedecked at the very place Brennan said he would meet her. She headed toward the throng of people clad in business suits and elf costumes, and spied Mr. Henry, Brennan and the man who'd leaped out to take her photograph that night in the alley. These men were not in elf suits. If they had been, it would have been more than surreal…and amusing.

"She said she'd be here, but I'm having my doubts," Brennan said to his grandfather as she approached.

"She'll come," Mr. Henry said, straightening his bow tie.

"Her middle name is probably wishy-washy," Brennan said.

"Actually, it's Paige," she said, smiling at the gentlemen assembled.

Brennan didn't even bother looking embarrassed at being caught talking ill about her behind her back. He raised a smug eyebrow. "And she arrives."

"As I knew she would," Mr. Henry said, holding out a hand to her. "An honorable woman is above even rubies."

Brennan snorted. She shot him a withering look. "But only to her husband."

"Touché," Mr. Henry said, taking her hand. "You remember Gator, don't you?"

"Of course," she said, nodding toward the crafty-looking assistant—or whatever he was for Mr. Henry.

After a few moments of introducing her to the elves and the older gentleman who'd played the role of the Henry Department Store Santa for the past fifteen years, Mr. Henry stepped away to take a phone call. Gator trailed after him, leaving her with Brennan.

For a moment, they were as silent as the live oaks surrounding them.

"Any further problems with Simon?" Brennan asked, shoving his hands into his pockets and glancing around at the busyness of the scene. The streetcar driver gave orders to a couple who were festooning the car in Christmas lights. Brennan seemed even more aloof than on Monday, as if he'd had a stern talk with himself about being a proper businessman who did not partake in festivities.

"Nope. Guess he found a better situation."

"Good."

"Yes, it's good to have my couch back…and my TV."

He nodded. Then silence sat on them. A strange awkward silence, sort of like being in a room where a comedian bombs or a doctor gives bad news. She didn't know why it felt that way. Maybe Brennan's dread of the task at hand. Maybe the fact she still felt out of breath and uncomfortable around him. Maybe it was the weather. Or the way the last rays of light fell as the sun sank over the Mississippi River in the distance.

Mr. Henry approached, interrupting…well, nothing. "Time to roll—it's nearly six and it will take a good thirty minutes to get downtown. I will be waiting for you on the dais along with the mayor. Mary Paige, you and Brennan will bring the ceremonial torch—the flambeau—to the stand and place it beside the unlit tree."

"There will be a stand," Brennan clarified.

"Yes, then you will be seated while the St. Bartholomew's choir sings several Christmas carols. There will be a welcome from the mayor, a reading by the archbishop and then finally I will announce Mary Paige as the face of Christmas for Henry Department Stores. Then both of you will together light the tree at seven-thirty."

"Why both of us?" she asked.

"Well, usually I do it," Malcolm replied. "But Brennan is the future of MBH. It's time he assumed some company responsibilities. And you are an important part of our season, aren't you?"

Mary Paige looked at Brennan, who wore a semigrimace at the directive. "I spend every day at the office, so I'm certain I've already assumed some company responsibilities, ones more important than lighting a Christmas tree."

"Oh, but you're wrong. This is a family and a New Orleans tradition. If you want—"

"I get it. Tradition, frivolity and lots of blinking lights. Ho, ho, ho," he said, taking a few short steps to where Gator stood eyeing an elf. Something about the way his grandfather dangled his future as the possible CEO seemed to bother Brennan. Or maybe it was the entire holiday.

Mr. Henry looked at her. "Are you ready, my dear?"

"I suppose. Oh, and here is the signed contract. There was only one day I must bow out—the Gosslee-and-Associates Christmas mixer is on the same night as the St. Thomas's Bingo Bash. Otherwise, I should be able to attend all of the events."

"Wonderful," Mr. Henry said, tucking the folded contract into his breast pocket and whistling. Izzy, wearing an elf hat and a doggy smile, leaped out of the streetcar and sat at attention. Mr. Henry tossed the dog a kibble treat then attached a leash to her collar. "Izzy will ride with you. Thought the children might think she was cute."

He handed Brennan the leash and, without further word, Mr. Henry walked toward the Lincoln Town Car Gator had idling in a no-parking zone.

Brennan's expression at being saddled with the tiny elf was classic horror.

She almost laughed.

But she didn't, mostly because she was afraid her laughter would send Brennan stomping off, leaving her to face the streetcar, Santa and the city business district armed only with a wiener dog.

Mary Paige took the leash. "I'll take her."

"I can't believe he shoved his dog off on me. And not only that, but he gave me this atrocious elf hat to wear." Brennan held up a green felt hat with little jingle bells dripping from the ends.

One of the other elves heard Brennan's comment and handed Mary Paige her own jingling elf hat. "For you, too. All of Santa's elves must be properly attired."

Mary Paige plopped the hat on her head, arranging her

hair so it didn't stick out crazily, then stepped onto the trolley, waiting for Izzy to navigate the steps.

She wasn't going to wait for the big grumpy elf.

Why hadn't she laughed at him and sent him running? What was the attraction of riding a streetcar with a man who hated dogs, hated Christmas and thought she was wishy-washy?

Nothing.

Okay, she knew she lied to herself because she was interested in Brennan Henry.

Too interested.

She sat on a wooden bench three rows back, making room for Izzy to stand at the window if she desired. Instead, Izzy curled into a little dachshund ball in Mary Paige's lap. The hat tilted crookedly onto the dog's neck, but Mary Paige didn't try to fix it. Izzy closed her eyes and sighed.

The bench creaked as Brennan sat beside her, and Mary Paige tried not to feel pleasure at the brush of his sleeve against her arm, or the warm male scent that emanated from him. She tried to look nonchalant. Like she had no interest in a sexy soon-to-be CEO with an attitude problem.

"You're going to let that dog sit in your lap? Won't it get hair on your coat?" He still hadn't put on his elf hat.

"I own a lint brush. Plus, Izzy is tired."

"I'm tired, too. Can I curl up in your lap?"

"Will you be a good boy?"

His smile was pure wolf...and made those tingles start again.

"You don't want to know the answer to that, Mary Paige." His stormy gray eyes dipped to her neckline... like the wolf he was. It made her heart speed up.

Damn it.

"Probably don't." Mary Paige waved as the Town Car drove away. Then the streetcar jerked and started forward with a zipping sound. "Better put on your hat. Time to make merry."

Brennan looked at the offending object in his hand and sighed. "Fine."

He shoved it on his head but it was too small and didn't fit properly. Brennan looked like a cartoon character—sort of like SpongeBob when he put on his ball cap.

"Here, let me fix it for you," she said, tugging the locks of hair into a more appealing look. She felt something inside her stir at the feel of his hair beneath her fingertips, at the raspiness of the stubble on his upper jaw.

Lord have mercy, the man smelled good.

And his skin was soft for a guy. Maybe he moisturized. Or maybe she hadn't been with a guy in a long time and had started making Brennan into some kind of fantasy man.

She pulled one last piece toward his ear and then examined him critically. "That will do."

Then she made the mistake of looking into his eyes.

What she saw there had her swallowing hard.

Unabashed desire shone from those depths and something ignited between them. She felt it. He felt it. Hell, Izzy probably felt it.

The dog had to have because she unfurled and crawled into Brennan's lap.

Eye contact was broken when Brennan looked at the dog, who'd settled with another doggy sigh. "I can't believe I'm going down St. Charles wearing this stupid hat while holding this fleabag. Disgrace, I tell you."

"Hope your grandfather took her for a constitutional."

"What?" Brennan wore the same expression as when his grandfather had handed the dog off to him.

This time Mary Paige laughed. "I'm joking. She shouldn't christen you."

"She better not," he grumbled, looking more like a disenfranchised court jester than a jolly elf.

One of the other elves handed Brennan a bag of candy and a bag of Christmas-colored plastic beads. "This is for the folks who will be lined up to watch Santa's arrival."

Brennan opened the bags and set them between the two of them, not even disturbing the dog curled in his lap. Pretty telling that he was considerate of the pup. Maybe Brennan wasn't such a Scrooge after all. Could be he was totally redeemable.

"Okay, let's start throwing this crap. Sooner we get this done the faster I can take this absurd hat off and give this beast to my grandfather."

Or maybe not.

"Cheer up," she said, "it's Christmas."

Brennan hurled a strand of beads out the window toward a group of revelers. "Bah—"

"Humbug," she finished for him.

CHAPTER SEVEN

BRENNAN OBLIGED THE waving throngs gathered along the route of the streetcar by throwing the baubles and pasting a smile on his face.

What he really wanted to do was drop the bags to the floor, shove Izzy away, pull Mary Paige onto his lap and kiss the living daylights out of her.

What was coming over him? Was he getting seasonal fever? She was as much as his type as hair ribbons or pink cupcakes. Brennan ate kittens like her for breakfast.

"Oh, look at that darling little girl," she said, waving like a lunatic and making him want to both roll his eyes and kiss her. "Isn't she cute?"

He looked at the kid in question, noting her perfect little blond curls and furred parka. His imagination took off—he envisioned Mary Paige with a blond toddler on her hip and a goofy smile on her face. She looked so happy. Natural. Just right.

"Brennan?" She elbowed him.

"Huh?"

"You okay?"

He nodded but realized she couldn't see him because her focus was on the crowds lining the street. It was mini–Mardi Gras out there. "Yeah, sure. Just a long day."

"Have you always done this?"

"What? Ridden on the streetcar for the lighting?"

She nodded, still smiling and waving like the spirit

his grandfather had envisioned. And the onlookers waved back like trained seals, their smiles equally happy.

What was he missing that he couldn't abandon himself and be like those people? Wouldn't life be easier if he could yank some joy from it? But he didn't know how. He was who he was.

"Yeah, like, did you do this with your family when you were young? Your grandfather said this has been a tradition for over thirty years, so I'm assuming it was something you did as a child."

His mind went back to the boy who sat upon his mother's lap, laughing and tossing trinkets all along St. Charles Avenue. That boy had loved riding the streetcar with Santa Claus, sneaking glances at the jolly fat man, worried that perhaps pulling his sister's hair had earned him a lump of coal. He could remember the smell of his mother's perfume—something French and expensive— and his father's booming laugh as he directed Brennan's sister, Brielle, to clear the window with her throws. Brielle had giggled and teased Brennan the way older sisters did. It had been wonderful to be a six-year-old Brennan, a boy loved, worshipped, safe in a world that never should have shattered.

"I rode when I was small."

Mary Paige must have heard something in his voice because she turned toward him. "So you stopped when you grew up?"

"Something like that." He didn't want to talk about his childhood. About Brielle. About love and loss and things coming unraveled.

About the real reason Christmas made him nuts.

"Must be good memories," she said, patting him on his thigh, waking Izzy from where she dozed. Izzy looked up with sleepy eyes and a yawn.

"Let her sit in your lap so the kids can see her," he said, shuffling over the dog to Mary Paige. He didn't want to think about what the heat of Mary Paige's hand had conjured within him. Not only a physical want, but also a spiritual desire he couldn't name. Izzy seemed reluctant to move, and for one brief second he thought about letting her stay. Something about a dog curled in his lap seemed…satisfying. He probably needed a drink or something.

"Come here, girl," Mary Paige said, fixing the silly elf hat atop the dog's head and holding her up to the window. The people immediately responded with bigger smiles and laughs. Izzy was, indeed, a hit.

It made Mary Paige laugh.

Which made his heart do weird loopy things.

Shit.

He needed to get off this well-used streetcar with its childhood memories, with the warm laughter and Christmas carols.

But still the car rocked down the historic street spreading Christmas cheer like a rash. It had its mission of bringing Christmas joy, Brennan's desires be damned.

"Did your parents ride with you?"

Mary Paige's question was like an arrow to his chest. His parents. He tried not to think of them. Of the days they'd spent together, happy and oblivious to what would befall them. Lucinda Magee Henry and Malcolm Henry, III, New Orleans's golden couple. Everyone had called his father Trent and he'd been the life of the party. King of Brennan's world. Prince to the Henry fortune. And for a few years, Duke of the Diamond, pitching his way through the minors before returning to New Orleans as a cherished son, sitting beside football great Archie Manning's boys and the Connicks on committees, feted, honored, loved. His mother had lovingly looked on. Until that day.

The day Brielle died.

"Yes, actually they did participate." He hoped his voice conveyed the fact he didn't want to talk about it.

"Oh, I'm sorry. I shouldn't be so nosy." She gave an apologetic smile and shrug. "I'm from a small town."

As if that explained it. Perhaps it did. They tended to know everyone's business in small towns, didn't they?

"My parents are deceased. Plane wreck over twenty-five years ago, so it's been a while since anyone asked me about them." Twenty-five years, eleven months, ten days to be exact.

Brennan locked down the memories and emotions, and instead pulled more candy and beads from the bag and handed them to her.

Okay, closed discussion.

"I'm sorry." Her words were simple yet seemed heart-felt.

They neared Lee Circle and would soon reach the downtown core. Everyone came out to celebrate the lighting of the huge tree that sat where Poydras and Canal Streets joined, and where the anchor store of Henry Department Stores sat. New Orleans loved a party. Anything to tear them away from the mundane and give them reason to forget their cares.

It was the theme of Mardi Gras, after all.

"Ho, ho, ho!" Santa called from his perch at the front of the streetcar. The Christmas music seemed to grow louder and even Izzy tossed out a bark…mostly when she saw other dogs on leashes.

The cacophony was enough to make Brennan hop from the moving streetcar.

But he didn't.

Because he'd given his grandfather his word. And he really wanted to be CEO. Lately, his grandfather's requirements for the job seemed to include service and goodwill, as if those qualities were markers for a good leader. So Brennan would wear the damn elf hat and look like a fool in front of the entire city.

Finally, they stopped before the dais, where local dignitaries and his grandfather sat. The crowd let loose a cheer as Santa stood at the open doors of the streetcar.

"Ho, ho, ho!" the elderly man bellowed, spreading his arms wide.

Two elves slipped beneath the arms of Santa and rolled out a red carpet that extended all the way to the platform. It looked impressive and Brennan wondered what minion of MBH Industries had traipsed out to the tracks and measured the distance between it and the platform.

Large speakers crackled with a tinny version of "Santa Claus Is Coming to Town" as the man himself laid his black boot on the red carpet.

"Come on, Izzy. Time to go see your daddy," Mary Paige said in that falsetto voice people used when they talked to pets. It should have annoyed the hell out of Brennan, but it didn't. Somehow his brain had interpreted it as kind of cute.

"Let's get this over with." He sighed and stood.

"Like taking a spoonful of cough syrup," she said. "We'll survive."

"With each other's help?"

"Of course, I'm the Spirit of Christmas."

He snorted, but he followed her off the streetcar and into the chaos.

MARY PAIGE PLASTERED A SMILE on her face as she stepped from the car with Izzy. The idea of climbing up onto that huge platform with the mayor, a few city council members, the archbishop and a crazy billionaire turned the butterflies in her stomach into fat, strong crows slamming their wings against her rib cage.

I will not throw up.

I will not pass out.

I will not embarrass myself by freaking out.

The affirmations didn't do much to help her as she walked toward the smiling politicians. She was too preoccupied, feeling both ashamed at wearing her white Reeboks and relieved that she didn't have to navigate the steps in those cheerful red heels.

Didn't really matter that she wore tennis shoes, did it?

Of course it did.

She looked like a bumpkin.

That Creighton chick who'd probably done the horizontal mambo with Brennan wouldn't have been caught dead in Reeboks.

"Oh, that's the cutest dog!" Someone crowed as Izzy trotted like a queen at Mary Paige's side. At least the dog distracted people from her fashion crimes—elf hat, swing coat and tennis shoes.

Izzy and Brennan made her look good.

That was, if Brennan followed.

Oh, and the flambeau!

She turned to see Brennan balancing the traditional torch carried to light the uptown Mardi Gras parades in both hands. He nodded and smiled at the crowds, who good-naturedly tossed coins in his path the way they did during Mardi Gras. A few elves followed behind collecting the coins, which would be donated to charities like Malcolm's Kids.

She waited for Brennan and could nearly feel people's curiosity. They had to be wondering who the chick with the weenie dog was. Why was she part of the festivity? And why was she wearing gym shoes with her flared gray skirt?

"I forgot about the torch," she whispered when Brennan got close enough. "And I forgot about my shoes."

He grinned at her footwear. "I think they make you interesting."

"You're lying."

"Of course I am, but it makes you feel better, doesn't it?"

"Kinda," she muttered.

They reached the steps and climbed onto the platform. *Whew.*

Mr. Henry stood and gestured that she take the seat next to him as Brennan placed the torch in the holder sitting next to the giant tree rumored to have been purchased from the same farm where the presidential tree was harvested. Brennan sat next to her, giving her a comforting pat for good measure. Izzy hopped into Mr. Henry's lap.

Then the mayor rose.

As far as ceremonies went, it was typical. Blah, blah, blah from mayor, beautiful holiday songs from choir, blah, blah, blah and a prayer from archbishop. Then finally Malcolm Henry, Jr. approached the lectern. He welcomed the throngs with genuine kindness and then turned to her. "Mary Paige, will you please stand, my dear?"

With trembling knees, she rose, pressing her lips together before offering a tremulous smile.

"I would like to introduce you all to a remarkable young woman, a woman who embodies everything I respect in a human being, a woman who is Henry Department Stores' Spirit of Christmas."

There was a expectant hum among the crowd.

"You may ask how she embodies this spirit we wanted to focus on this year, so I will tell you—by exhibiting pure kindness to the 'least of these.'" He proceeded to share the tale of their meeting, of icy sleet, warm coffee and really ugly Christmas socks.

"And here are the very socks that sweet young lady placed on my frozen feet." Mr. Henry lifted his leg and tugged up his trousers to show everyone the hideous silver-balled socks.

There was laughter and a spattering of applause.

Mr. Henry smiled and dropped his leg. "Do you know what that cup of coffee and pair of socks meant to an old frozen bum?"

He gave a dramatic pause.

"It meant life."

Mary Paige wiggled as a poignant silence descended upon the spectators. Mr. Henry was making her sound like some kind of saint. She wasn't. She was just a normal human being doing what normal human beings did.

"So this Christmas, MBH Industries wants to do something a little different. We want Christmas to not only be a time to make merry and get shiny-wrapped presents. We want it to be a time to show love to your fellow man in small, yet significant ways. It's your turn to be an angel, just like Mary Paige. It's your turn to offer kindness and hope to strangers all over our city."

He gave a big grin. "That generosity earned Mary Paige Gentry a check for two million dollars."

A collective gasp went up in the crowd, followed by the buzz of chatter.

He really had their attention now.

"All over the city, I have elves watching, waiting to catch people showing others they care."

The buzz got louder.

"Your kindness may get you one hundred dollars, a Henry's gift card or tickets to a movie. It may get you a pair of diamond earrings or a free dinner at Commander's Palace. Or it may net you a new friend, a sense of goodwill and a few points with the Big Man upstairs."

Excitement stirred. Mary Paige hadn't realized the extent of the campaign.

"This is no gimmick, folks. This is a sincere attempt to show everyone what I have learned over the past six months. People deserve compassion and dignity. Everyone, even a homeless man, deserves kindness, deserves something to warm him on a cold, heartless night. This year Henry's wants to celebrate the true Spirit of Christmas. The eternal gift bestowed by our heavenly Father. The gift of love."

The applause was deafening, and many of the people were looking at her.

She felt the heat at her cheeks and smiled.

"I give you Mary Paige Gentry and the future of MBH Industries, my grandson, Brennan Henry. Together they will light the tree…and perhaps something more within you all."

More applause.

Brennan took her elbow and moved her toward the torch.

"Steady hand. I don't really want to go to the emergency room," he whispered. He waved and looked quite merry for a Scrooge. She moved with him because he had a good grip on her elbow.

As Brennan lifted the torch, the choir softly sang "O Christmas Tree." He extended the handle of the torch toward her and she grasped it, her hand landing on top of his. Together they moved the flambeau toward the box that would trip a switch to light the huge Christmas tree.

Mary Paige had lived in New Orleans for a few years and had never been to this ceremony, so she wasn't quite sure how it worked. Strings of LED lights covered the branches and she knew the flickering flames on the end of the torch had nothing to do with the actual lighting— it was only symbolic.

As the torch touched the switch the flames went out and the tree came alive with thousands of twinkling white lights.

Applause broke out as the choir launched into "The Most Wonderful Time of the Year" and elves frolicked on the stage, juggling red and green balls, doing cartwheels and pirouettes as Santa waved to children. The mayor shook Mr. Henry's hand, as did the other dignitaries.

She stood there stupidly, still holding the torch as Brennan smiled and waved like a true son of the city.

The crowd joined in the singing and Mary Paige felt awash in the holiday spirit.

What a wonderful event.

Her reservations about participating in the whole affair melted as Brennan started to sing. She managed to belt out a few choruses herself. Brennan tugged the flambeau from her fingers to place it in the metal stand.

The last strands of music faded as she noticed the crowd's attention turn to her.

Why?

She felt movement behind her and turned around. A silly elf held a long stick extended above her head. Mistletoe hung from a string. Directly over her.

"Kiss her, Brennan!" someone called.

Mary Paige shook her head and waved the comment off.

"Yeah, kiss her!" More voices, more laughter.

She glanced at Brennan in a panic. He laughed and waved off the remarks.

"Kiss her!" People began chanting the directive. Clapping started. All were merry. All were bright.

All were *insane*.

Her cheeks were afire with embarrassment. Couldn't they see she was not the type of girl who got kissed by the Brennan Henrys of the world? She was nothing elegant, beautiful or—

She felt his arms wind around her waist, cradle her, tilt her back.

"Oh," she said as Brennan loomed above her.

Her gaze found his and there was amusement in the gray depths...and maybe something more. Satisfaction?

Maybe.

But she didn't have time to think anymore about it.

Because at that moment, Brennan kissed her. And it wasn't a peck. It was full-blown, wide-open and absolutely wonderful.

She grabbed hold of him so she wouldn't fall and kissed him back.

The crowd went nuts.

Her heart exploded.

And in that moment, everything changed.

CHAPTER EIGHT

"WHOA, WAIT A SEC," Mitzi Cascio, her neighbor and friend, called from across the street as Mary Paige climbed the steps to her duplex, her mind still wrapping itself around the fact she'd kissed Brennan Henry.

Or rather, he'd kissed her.

Either way, her world had tilted and spun a little faster.

"Mary," Mitzi called with another frantic wave of her hand.

With a longing glance at her front door—she really wanted to put on comfy clothes and process all that had occurred—Mary Paige turned and smiled.

"Oh, my God, why didn't you tell me? This is huge. Huge!" Mitzi squealed, shuffling forward wearing a ragged-looking sweatshirt and big pink piggy slippers. Her grin was bigger than the St. Bernard at her knee. "Heel, Elvis."

The dog sat with a groan and Mitzi pulled Mary Paige into a hug. "You're rich, bitch!"

Mary Paige broke the hug with a laugh. "Hey, Mitzi. Elvis."

Elvis chuffed a hello since he was a sensitive dog and liked to greet and be greeted. Mary Paige had never known such a canine gentleman.

"You didn't tell me. How could you not tell me? This is crazy big, M.P. Crazy big." Mitzi's words got louder and louder.

"You're talking about this whole Henry Department Stores thing, right?"

"No, I'm talking about the Christmas tree in your window," her friend said, taking her elbow. "Come over and tell me about this money, this man and your new gig as a Spirit. Ma made red sauce and meatballs."

"Ah, you know I love your mama's cooking, but I'm so tired. I want to get into my pajamas and watch TV. Plus, I need to feed the cat. How about tomorrow?"

"You know Ma makes the best red sauce this side of the river. I told her I'd invite you, but I forgot. Then I saw you on TV and remembered, so…"

How could she refuse and not be consumed by guilt the whole night?

"Sure," Mary Paige said, giving Elvis a pat and allowing Mitzi to link an arm through hers and maneuver her toward the big blue house across the street. So she was a marshmallow and couldn't say no to her friend. At least she'd get a meal out of it, and Mitzi's mother rocked anything she put on a stove.

Mitzi was nearly forty but dressed like she was ten, choosing Hello Kitty and Strawberry Shortcake vintage T-shirts to wear to the music store she ran with her uncle Rup. She also wore bold wigs. Today she wore platinum curls that brushed her shoulders.

"You like?" Mitzi twirled a curl at her ear.

"Very Hollywood starlet," Mary Paige said, already feeling happier. Mitzi was that kind of person. She insisted on equal parts sarcasm and sunshine no matter what the heavens spat her way.

"That's what I was going for. I'll be glad when my own hair grows in."

"But then you won't be able to assume different personas. I loved the black bob you had last week." Mary

Paige climbed the fifteen steep stairs that led to the wide porch, with its spidering paint and cheerful poinsettias sitting outside the oval-paned door. "Very Veronica Lake to counteract the Jane Mansfield look."

Mitzi had been undergoing chemotherapy since September. In August she'd found a lump in her breast, had a double mastectomy and was on her last round of chemo. It had been a long painful journey, but Mitzi had made the best of it—which was a constant inspiration for Mary Paige. She felt blessed to live this close—it was like a slice of home in the midst of midtown New Orleans.

"Ma," Mitzi hollered as she opened the door, letting Elvis bound in first. "Mary Paige's here."

"Okay," Cecily called from the kitchen. The Cascio house was an elevated shotgun house like most of the ones in this neighborhood, a few blocks off North Carrolton Avenue. The front parlor/dining room melted into the living room, which led to the kitchen and finally to the three bedrooms, fulfilling the suggestion that one could fire a gun from the front door of the house and hit someone coming in the back door. Straight shot.

She came out of the kitchen drying her hands on a dish towel. Her smile matched her daughter's earlier one. But that was all that matched. Mama Cascio was as wide as she was tall, with dark hair knotted at her nape…just like a grandma on a commercial for Italian sauces. "Welcome, Mary. Hope you're hungry, darlin'."

Mary Paige barely had time to nod before Mama Cascio enveloped her in a bear hug, laying a fat kiss on her cheek.

"It smells like heaven in here, Mama Cascio."

"Yeah, it does," she nodded. "Been cooking my sauce all afternoon. That's the secret—you can't rush a good red sauce."

Mary Paige nodded as though she knew what Mama Cascio talked about. The closest Mary Paige came to making a homemade sauce was melting butter.

"So big news, huh? Simon got the boot, Brennan Henry's giving you tongue action and you're two million smackers richer. Like a dream, huh?" Mitzi sank onto the sofa, curling her legs beneath her. One pink pig dropped to the floor while the other hovered over Elvis's head.

A timer dinged and Mama Cascio clapped her hands. "That's the bread. You girls talk." Then she toddled into the space she loved, muttering about Parmesan cheese.

Mary Paige sat in the armchair that had a piece of plastic covering the area where a person's head rested. "I'm not seeing Brennan Henry."

"Looked like a really friendly kiss on TV," Mitzi said, stroking the big dog's head absentmindedly.

"Publicity stunt." Mary Paige resisted the urge to raise her hand to her lips. It had been a hell of a kiss. One she'd felt all the way down to her white Reeboks.

"Sign me up for those kinds of publicity stunts. He's smokin' hot *and* rich. It's like you won the lottery, Mar."

Mary Paige didn't want to talk about the money. For some reason it felt surreal, which is why the check still sat in her jewelry box. And she darn sure didn't want to talk about Brennan. "He's not my type."

"Baby, he's every girl's type."

On the surface.

"Actually, he's sort of sad. Hates Christmas. Hates people. Loves money."

"Well, there's that," Mitzi said.

"Besides, I don't want to feel like every man I meet is a potential candidate for love of my life. My main goal for this next year is passing the CPA exam. And all this publicity stuff for the Face of Christmas is—"

"Spirit," Mitzi said.

"Huh?"

"I thought it was the Spirit of Christmas. That's what they said on WNOE. I remember because it made me think of ghosts and things that go bump in the night."

"Yeah, Spirit. Anyway, I don't have time for a man, good-looking, rich or otherwise."

"That's a bad attitude for a twentysomething single gal. I get the whole career thing, but why wouldn't you be open to tall, dark and wealthy if the opportunity showed up? Think I'd pass that up? Even if I have cancer and could be dead in a few months?"

"Don't you dare say that, Mitzi Cascio." Mary Paige stiffened, her inane problems fading at her friend's words. Cancer did that. Made a gal feel silly for fretting over men, work and having to attend functions. Mitzi had been positive about her diagnosis and recovery, but still tossed out morbid zingers Mary Paige struggled with. "You're getting well. I refuse to believe any differently."

Mitzi smiled. "Me, too, but I'm just saying. Brennan Henry might be exactly what you need—a sexy rebound. God, he has to be good in bed."

"Yeah, being rich and handsome makes you a good lover. Probably the opposite. He probably lies back with his hands behind his head and lets the girl do all the work."

The image of her rising above a naked Brennan Henry while he looked on with gray eyes no longer hard as steel, but molten and stormy, while she moved her hands all over his taut abs made her mouth water.

Great. Now she was having fantasies about doing Brennan. And she didn't even know if he had taut abs or not.

"That would be a travesty." Mitzi's expression had

taken on a faraway look that told Mary Paige she might be having her own Brennan fantasies. "So tell me about this money. Two million? Really?"

"Yeah. Two million, but here's the thing. I don't know what to do with it. I haven't even told my mom about this whole campaign because I wasn't sure if I could go through with it."

"Why wouldn't you do it?"

"Because it's invasive and it puts me out in the spotlight. I'm not comfortable with that. Look at me." Mary Paige indicated her sweater, skirt and pristine white Reeboks. Realizing she still wore the stupid elf hat, she jerked it off her head and growled, "I'm no show pony."

"Mare," Mitzi corrected. "M.P., this is a once-in-a-lifetime opportunity. You can't pass it up."

"I haven't because it's not a totally bad idea. Maybe a few people will look at Christmas as an opportunity to show love to their fellow man. That's Mr. Henry's goal—to make people think about what is really important, who they should value."

Mitzi laughed. "I swear you're like an insurance commercial."

"So I wear rose-colored glasses. Not a crime to care."

"Nope. Not a crime at all."

"Let's eat," Mama Cascio cried, her New Orleans *yat* accent no doubt as thick as her marinara sauce. "And I heard you fussing at her, Mitz. Let Mary Paige decide things for herself."

"Mary Paige needs wild, hot sex and a man who lavishes stuff on her. After that prick Simon sucked her dry, she needs—"

"Spaghetti and Italian gravy," Mama Cascio said, shooting her daughter the Sicilian stink eye. "She said she's not interested in the Henry boy, so let it die already."

Mary Paige knew deep inside she was interested in Brennan, but where would that desire lead? Brennan Henry was a dead-end street for a girl like Mary Paige. It wasn't only that she wasn't his type, it was also the man's nature. If the gossips were to be believed, he was adverse to commitment. She'd spent the past year struggling with Simon the Leech, and she swore the next man she even thought about in a romantic capacity would have integrity, heart and generosity of spirit. From what she'd seen so far, Brennan Henry had none of those qualities.

More like selfish, damaged and intolerant.

"Come in the kitchen," Mama Cascio said. "We're family and we'll eat like family."

The woman's words washed over Mary Paige like warm bathwater. She appreciated Mitzi, and her mother saw her as family, even though they'd first met a little over two years ago. Going through cancer, bad boyfriends and the launch of Mama Cascio's catering business had knit them tightly together and had solidified in her heart that moving to New Orleans had been the right decision for her.

From that perspective, working to bring the Spirit of Christmas to her city seemed the right thing to do.

BRENNAN LOOKED AT his piquant sauce and grimaced. Clarice's Bistro had superb cuisine, but tonight nothing sat right on his stomach. Probably thanks to the fish he'd had for lunch.

Or the fact all of New Orleans had seen him kiss the crazy accountant wearing ridiculous tennis shoes.

And, Christ, it had been soul-stirring.

He shoved the still-steaming dish aside and contemplated the man who'd raised him. Malcolm was extraordinarily cheerful tonight, as was Ellen, who also seemed pleased with the tree-lighting festivities. After sending Mary Paige home in a private car, Malcolm had insisted on a celebratory dinner at his favorite uptown restaurant. Clarice's had occupied an unassuming wooden house on Prytania Street for the past forty years, and Malcolm had dined there at least twice a month since it had opened.

"I'd say tonight was a resounding success," his grandfather crowed, sipping a dry pinot and spearing another smoked oyster from the plate in the center of the table.

"Absolutely. And the mistletoe kiss was the icing. Nothing better than the public falling in love with a couple—gets people engaged. The heir to the Henry throne and his charming country mouse has *love story* written all over it," Ellen said, nodding like a good dog. Izzy waited in the car with Gator so Brennan assumed Ellen took the weenie dog's place. Though, he supposed it wasn't fair to his cousin to compare her to a canine. At the moment, Brennan wished she'd show some resolve, some sense, some damned fortitude against the assumption he and Mary Paige should act like a couple.

"I'm not pretending to be in love." Brennan folded his napkin and set it beside his plate.

"I would never ask you to fabricate something as important as love," Malcolm said.

"It's not that I don't like Mary Paige—she's a nice girl—but I draw a hard line at creating a false relationship."

"You don't have to kiss her again, just be considerate," Ellen said. "Pretend she's Great-Aunt Vergie."

"When last I saw Great-Aunt Vergie she didn't have a tooth in her mouth and she hit me with her walker."

"Well, don't do anything to make her hit you. Merely summon the charm from your arsenal," his grandfather said.

Ellen nodded again. "Yeah, just allow some speculation. The promise of romance builds interest and goodwill for our name. It builds—"

"Customers." Brennan didn't like the way his older cousin manipulated him with the promise of a healthier bottom line. Because even he wasn't so hardened that he'd fake affection for Mary Paige to manipulate the public into buying more sweaters. "So, Grandfather, you think I should dupe the public? What of your newfound integrity?"

His grandfather stared at him hard for a moment before shaking his head. "I'd consider that an insult from anyone other than you."

Brennan held his grandfather's gaze, refusing to flinch under the stare of the man who had taught him to guard his emotions. *Never let 'em see you sweat...or drink cheap whiskey.*

"I don't give a fig about what develops, or doesn't, between you and Miss Gentry. I do give a fig about you being courteous. You're a Henry. It's expected," Malcolm said, focusing his attention on his filet.

Ellen took a sip of her drink. "I still think allowing folks to think it's a romance is brilliant. What's the harm?"

Brennan didn't answer. If Ellen couldn't figure out the harm, he could see good reason her marriage hadn't lasted more than a few years. Dishonesty bred harm. Lots of harm. Even he knew that.

"I won't deny the idea of Brennan settling with a nice girl appeals to me," his grandfather said, regarding him again with intensity. It was as if his grandfather was testing him, which pissed him off.

"As I recall, you considered Creighton a nice girl from a good family with a U.S. senator in her back pocket. You introduced us and gave me use of your lodge in Park City, remember?" If his relatives were going to mess around in his personal life, Brennan thought it only fair they be reminded of their earlier interference. "So now, what? She's not pure enough for the Henry family? She has to go around buying bums coffee to make the grade?"

He didn't know why he felt so defensive. Not so long ago he would have agreed with Ellen's plan. And he'd certainly been of the opinion that Creighton wasn't well-suited to him. Could it be that one simple kiss had not been quite so simple? That little kiss had made him feel something more complicated than lust...something scarier than the company books dipping into the red.

Malcolm sighed. "As with much in my life, I regret encouraging that particular relationship. Creighton knows only one life, and she eats, breathes and sucks it down. She's not a bad girl, no, but she's not a good one for you, either. She wouldn't inspire you to want to be a better man."

His grandfather's judgment was harsh, but laced with truth. Creighton looked good on the arm, and she had excellent social standing right down to the crumbling mansion on St. Charles, Creole bloodlines and a sizable bank account. Still, their relationship had always been based on convenience rather than affection.

"Even so, Creighton deserves some consideration. We've been dating off and on for the past year. Not fair to splash a fake relationship all over the city for the express purpose to make this ridiculous campaign a success," said Brennan, knowing his words were hollow. He'd tried to break it off with Creighton several times and, had he wanted to pursue another woman, he would have had no qualms about doing so. "Besides, this campaign will succeed because you offer rewards for being decent to one's fellow man. People will be looking over their shoulders to see if they might get something for dropping a nickel in the Salvation Army's kettle."

"True," his grandfather said, stroking his gray goatee. "But if it results in someone being relieved of a burden, or five cents richer, because of what we're doing, then I can live with that. Generosity doesn't come cheaply."

Brennan lifted his coffee cup and waved a hand when Ernesto brought the dessert menu. This day had been long and exhausting, and the trip down memory lane triggered by Mary Paige's questions still echoed in his soul. He kept remembering his mother smiling at him, his father tossing him into the air and Brielle playing silly games involving cracks and breaking their mother's back—all fuzzy warm memories that left him a little lonelier than before.

Just ghosts knocking about inside his head.

"Strange. You never seemed serious about Creighton. More annoyed than anything." Ellen took the dessert menu and pointed to the Creole bread pudding she got every time she came to Clarice's. "And that kiss tonight looked friendly enough."

"I kissed Mary Paige because everyone chanted 'kiss her' and that was the only reason."

"Could have kissed her cheek," Ellen said, arching an eyebrow.

"Now that would have been anticlimactic, wouldn't it? It meant very little to me," he said, offering his empty cup to the waiter as he paused beside Brennan with a silver carafe in hand.

His grandfather's gaze never left him, and Brennan suspected the man saw through him. He knew Brennan had enjoyed every second of that kiss. Something about that knowledge squirmed inside him.

"What?" he asked his grandfather.

"Nothing," Malcolm said, nodding to Ernesto as he sat a fat piece of pecan pie in front of him.

"You think I'm lying?"

"Did I protest when you said it meant nothing?"

"But you think this girl is better than Creighton because she bought you a damned coffee and put a pair of ugly-ass socks on your bare feet."

"Defensive, aren't you?" Malcolm looked around at the half-filled restaurant with clear eyes that glinted with devilment. The small upscale restaurant had started emptying and the clatter of silver and tinkling of glasses had dulled to the occasional clink over the jazz played by Nico Batiste at the piano.

"Not defensive. Just clear in saying I will not fake romantic entanglement with Mary Paige. Good girls aren't my thing, old man."

Ellen snorted. "Yeah, you're apples and oranges. Oil and water. Cats and dogs. Brooms and—"

"Point made, Ellen, dear, though I can't fathom what brooms are opposite of." Malcolm set his fork down by his half-eaten pie.

Ever since the heart attack, his grandfather had followed strict dietary guidelines, but tonight he'd indulged in some of his favorite foods, although he ate only half in begrudging compliance with his doctors' decrees. More worrisome than that was the fact Brennan had caught him halving the blood thinners a few days ago. When Brennan confronted him, his grandfather had claimed the medicine made his stomach ache. These little tiptoes over the lines set by the doctors scared Brennan, but he didn't dare push too much and risk making his grandfather even more stubborn about eating what he wanted.

"Do whatever makes you feel comfortable, Bren,"

Ellen said. "Tomorrow you'll help the Greater New Orleans Food Bank prepare Christmas food baskets and take a tour of one of the shelters in St. Bernard parish. Decidedly unromantic."

Her comments led Brennan's thoughts back to the kiss, to the way Mary Paige felt in his arms. He would never admit it, but it was one of the better kisses of his life. Not frenzied like the ones he'd shared with Meredith Vittre the first time he'd gotten laid, nor was it slow and erotic like the ones exchanged when lying in twisted sheets with a woman. No, it was different. Kind of like the feeling of lying in the sun on an autumn day, lazy and completely relaxed, in tune with one another while also aware of your place in the spectrum of the universe. Sort of transcendent. That's what he'd felt when he kissed her. And he'd known Mary Paige would be a comfort to him.

He didn't know what to think about that.

And he wished he hadn't caved and kissed her.

But…he'd wanted to touch her so badly, to know how she felt in his arms, to eliminate the intrigue. It had backfired. He was intrigued more than ever.

"Change of subject. I'm asking someone special to the Christmas gala next weekend," his grandfather said, leaning back and giving his stomach a pat. The cable-knit sweater pouched slightly over the buckshot belt his grandfather bought at Perlis.

"Oh?" Ellen asked.

"Her name's Judy Poche and she's the director of Holy Trinity. A fascinating, remarkable individual," Malcolm said, his eyes lighting with something more than benign admiration. The man looked smitten, an expression Brennan had never seen on his face before.

"You're not taking Margaret?" Brennan asked. Margaret Pride was the high priestess of New Orleans society. Her displeasure with a person immediately resulted in invitations being rescinded, the name being left off guest lists and being branded a social pariah. She welded power like a chain saw, hacking off personal connections like withering limbs on a tree. She often attended events with Malcolm, mostly because she liked arriving with a billionaire.

"That asp? Heavens, no. I'm done with that set, haven't you noticed?"

Brennan had. And part of him was glad Malcolm no longer entertained the waspish elites of their city. The other part of him was scared to let go of the familiar. He scarcely knew this man sitting in front of him anymore.

"I look forward to meeting Judy," Brennan said, using his polite voice. "Ellen?"

"Originally, I'd thought to bring Asher, but his plans for Christmas are still up in the air, so I'm bringing Mark Naigle."

"Mark of the paisley folders?" Brennan asked.

"Well, he's trying so hard to be fashionable. We're just friends, of course."

"Of course," Malcolm said with a smile. "I like Mark. He's got energy and he's good at his job. You could do worse, my dear."

Ellen gave an embarrassed smile. "I know I haven't been the same since the divorce, Uncle Mal, but I'm pretty certain Mark is gay."

"Eh?" Malcolm said, raising an eyebrow. "Who would have guessed?"

"The lime-green and red paisley folders sealed the deal for me," Brennan said. "And what's this about Asher, Ellen? He may come home for Christmas?"

"He planned to come to New Orleans when I spoke

to him last month, but you know my baby brother—he goes where the wind blows."

Brennan nodded because Asher had the freedom to go where he wished thanks to a string of good investments he'd made after selling his stock in MBH. In addition, he was a silent partner in a luxury leather goods company, so had to spend little time at a desk. For so many reasons, Brennan had always admired Asher. "Perhaps the wind will blow him to us."

"I hope so. I miss him and wish he'd move back. Maybe when Elsa retires, she'll agree to spend at least part of the year here," Ellen said, waving at someone across the room before returning her gaze to Brennan. "So who will you bring?"

"No one." Brennan hadn't intended on escorting Creighton even before Mary Paige and her captivating girdle had tumbled into his life. Ever since her best friend in Charleston had married this past spring, Creighton had marriage on the mind. He suspected that she wouldn't see attending a society gala together as only a friendly gesture the way he would intend it…even if he'd broken things off with her.

Of course, so far Creighton had ignored all of his let's-be-just-friends, farewell speeches—she'd texted him three times during dinner.

"You're still number one on the top ten most-eligible-bachelors list in the *Crescent Quarterly.*" Ellen passed her credit card toward her uncle, who waved it off as he always did when they dined together. Brennan had to give Ellen props for still pulling it out, not making assumptions that Malcolm would pay.

"Such quality subject matter," he drawled, eternally perturbed his friend and *Crescent*'s editor Cason Scott placed him at number one each year. Cason liked to poke things with a toothpick wit.

"Cason sent the framed list again. Told me it was good for business." His grandfather smiled, scrawling his name on the bill. "Maybe I'll hang it in the lobby this year."

"I'll sue," Brennan growled.

"For what? Displaying your eligibility?" His grandfather rose, indicating dinner was complete. "Enjoy your afternoon out of the office tomorrow, Brennan, and give Mary Paige my thanks for all she's done."

Brennan nodded and watched his grandfather work the room as he left, shaking hands with several remaining diners, tossing out Merry Christmases to the waitstaff and generally playing lord of the manor.

"He still has it, you know," Ellen said, placing her napkin on the table and pulling her purse onto her shoulder.

"But he's not the same man. Not the man who taught me the company is above all else."

"Nope. He's better."

Brennan said nothing as his cousin took her leave. Before he left, he slid a hundred-dollar bill beneath the already generous tip his grandfather had left. Their server, Ernesto, had two kids in college and had lost his home during Katrina.

It was another unstated rule in the Henry household—take care of those who take care of you.

Simple as that.

CHAPTER NINE

"I NEED MORE peas." The homeless man jabbed a finger toward the section of his plate where Mary Paige had placed a scoop of sweet peas. Was she supposed to give more? The woman in charge of the soup kitchen had said "one small scoop" like it was a law, but she hadn't said if she could give an extra serving of "one small scoop."

"I don't think—"

"Here," Brennan said, dishing out red beans. "Have some red beans. Balances out the peas."

The homeless man looked like he might argue, but when he caught Brennan's fierce look, he snapped his mouth shut and moved down the line to where Gator slung mashed potatoes.

Mary Paige smiled at the next person in line—an older woman with a dirty shawl and a sweet smile. "Here you go."

"Thank you kindly," the woman said before shaking her head at Brennan's beans.

"No one likes these beans," Brennan said, his tone fittingly grumpy.

"I don't like beans much, either. My mom used to cook them all the time. You eat enough beans, you—"

"Get a lot of gas?"

She looked up then at him to make sure the ceiling wasn't falling. Brennan Henry cracking fart jokes? "I guess that, too, but I was going to say you develop a bias against them."

For a few moments, silence fell.

"So about that kiss last night." His voice was low and serious. No more fart jokes.

Mary Paige swallowed and bade the butterflies to still in her stomach. She'd gotten up this morning, fixed a cup of tea and found the headline of the *Times-Picayune* Living section to be, well, interesting. Playboy Gets into the Spirit blazed above a picture of her arching backward in Brennan's arms, the two of them lip-locked while wearing absurd elf hats. It had been alarming, exciting and mostly embarrassing.

Even worse, the reporter had insinuated the passion evidenced at the tree lighting was an indicator she and Brennan were falling into the spirit of love. She'd tried to call her mother to share all that had occurred last weekend before Freda saw the paper and flipped out for being out of the know, but she hadn't been home.

Was it only last weekend? Seemed forever ago she'd bought that coffee and pair of Christmas socks.

"Mary Paige?"

"Huh?" She jerked around and found Brennan staring at her.

"Give the gentleman his peas."

"Yeah, I like peas," the man standing in front of her said.

"Sorry," she said, giving him a big scoop. To heck with the small-scoop directives.

Mary Paige Gentry, pea-scooping rebel of 2012.

"So about that kiss," Brennan continued as though they hadn't been interrupted. "The papers are making us out to be a couple, spinning this as some kind of romantic story nonsense."

"Yeah, I read that. But we've already established this is business only." Her gaze met his. His gray eyes were unfathomable, but for a moment she thought she glimpsed fleeting regret. Which was odd. Because the idea of him and her together was ludicrous. Outlandish. *Not going to happen, pea-scooping rebel.*

"Of course," he said, nodding at the family of four who sloughed by, gazes averted, trying to blend in with the faded blue linoleum underfoot. "But if we protest, it will look worse. No benefit in correcting the misconception. If the general public wants to create smoke where there is no fire, they will. The upside is that innocent kiss has generated more interest in the Spirit of Christmas campaign. People are fascinated with you. The whole gauche, country-girl routine makes it even more delicious paired with—"

"The city's most eligible bachelor?" she said, lifting an unsculpted country-girl-comes-to-town eyebrow.

He rested the spoon in the vat of beans and stretched. "If that's what you want to call me."

"So you're seeing dollar signs?"

"I seriously don't understand your aversion to profit. You're an accountant, for Christ's sake. Y'all get boners when businesses are in the black."

"I don't think you have to bring the Lord into it." She set down her own spoon since the line had dwindled to a few people seeking extra banana pudding. No one had come back for peas. "Or boners, for that matter."

"What?"

"Besides, I don't have an aversion to profit. At all. But I do dislike plucking the heart strings of the general buyer for pure profit. I dislike lying to her by creating a heartwarming illusion that will lure her into spending more money."

"Good thing you didn't go into marketing." He sighed with disgust. "I'm not trying to trick anyone. I'm doing this for the company, for my grandfather and ultimately because it will get me what I desire. The more money we make, the more we can spare for places such as this since MBH Industries donates a huge percent of its profits to charities. That was in practice before my grandfather started having nut-ball ideas and giving all our family money away. We did what was required before you put ugly socks on him and he launched this half-cracked Christmas cheer plot."

"Required?" Mary Paige echoed, wondering if that was exactly how he felt. Required to be with her. Required to scoop beans. Required to write checks to those less fortunate.

He frowned. Or maybe it was a glower. She wasn't sure because she'd been good at math, not vocabulary.

"Can we talk outside?" She jerked her head toward the open door. She'd rather argue with him in private since several of the people at the folding tables stared at them. Fortunately, the cold front that had spat sleet at them had moved on to the east leaving them with typical December weather, which meant it was sixty-two degrees outside.

He inclined his head and followed her.

When they emerged into the ripe-smelling alley, she closed the door and spun on him. "What is your problem? Why do you hate Christmas so much? And why do you resent me?"

He blinked. "I don't resent you."

"You do. Your grandfather rewarded my kindness with your *family* money and that irks the hell out of you."

"Mary Paige, did you just use an obscenity?" He smirked at her like she amused him, and that made her even madder.

"You know, I wouldn't pretend to like you, much less love you if Mr. Henry gave me another million dollars. You're an ass. There. Another obscenity."

He smiled. Again. Like a Cheshire cat. "Technically, an ass is an animal and not an obscenity. Now, if you'd called me an asshole, that would be another matter."

"Asshole," she said, crossing her arms. She meant it, too. He was irritating and hopeless and—

Something flared between them that had nothing to do with the potshots they'd been taking at one another.

"So you really think I'm an asshole?" His expression seemed to contain a mix of emotions, maybe even hurt. That shocked her. Did Brennan Henry have feelings?

"Gotta call a spade a—"

His lips covered hers and she forgot calling anyone anything because he tasted delicious.

Following close on the heels of desire came anger. How dare he kiss her to shut her up? He wasn't in charge. Who put him in charge?

She struggled against the sweet taste of him, breaking their embrace. "Don't you dare kiss me. If anyone is doing the kissing, it will be me."

He drew back, his dark eyes intense, measuring her. Mary Paige reached up, cupped his head and jerked it toward her. Then she kissed him because she wasn't some helpless, clumsy accountant who waited on a man to do what she was perfectly capable of doing herself.

She felt his laughter against her lips, and the rare sound flooded her with satisfaction, fueling the urge to do more than kiss the sexy millionaire. She doubled her efforts to maintain control of the kiss, but, like before, she faltered before being completely sucked under by a current of desire she had no power against.

Brennan's arms wound around her, hauling her against

him, and a hot heaviness bloomed low in her belly. The kiss grew bolder and the need rising inside her expanded.

Brennan groaned and tightened his hold on her, sliding one hand to her waist, bringing her into tight contact with the hardness of his body. He felt so good, so warm and so manly—a feeling a woman couldn't get enough of. Her hands slid up his shirt front, past his jaw and into his thick dark hair, and met his mouth with an abandon she hadn't experienced in any of her dealings with the opposite sex.

Finally, he lifted his head and peered at her, his gray eyes dilated, his breathing ragged. "Damn, you really know what you're doing, don't you, Miss Merry Christmas."

"Uh, I shouldn't have—" Mary Paige shook her head, before releasing the death grip she had on his hair and stepping away. "I don't know why I did that. Sorry."

He didn't say anything, simply looked at her as though he couldn't figure out why he'd been kissing her in an alley that smelled like a fast-food Dumpster on a hot day. Well, if he wanted answers, he needed to look elsewhere because she had no good reasons for why she'd taken the wheel and pounced on him like a love-starved psycho chick.

"It was bound to happen." He thrust a hand through his hair, which made it stick up a bit, softening his hard corners.

"Why?"

"Because that kiss on the stage wasn't real—it was playacting to satisfy a bunch of people hopped up on spiritual eggnog. Only natural it stirred curiosity in us."

Sounded logical but something about his words pricked her pride because the kiss on the stage had felt real to her. In fact, it had totally tilted her on her elf hat and spun her for a loop. "Well, I don't make a habit of going around kissing people. I mean, I kiss guys, just not as many as you."

"I don't kiss guys."

"You know what I mean."

A shadow from the crumbling building adjacent to the shelter stretched into the alley.

"I know why *I* kissed you," he said finally, his low voice breaking the silence. "I wanted to see if it felt the same."

"Felt the same? How did it feel?" Was she some kind of strange experiment? Or was she actually a bad kisser?

"Just felt different when I kissed you last night."

"Different bad or different good?" she asked, her heart beating harder despite the fact she shouldn't give a flying tomato what McScrooge Moneybags thought. Maybe she was bad at it and no one had been honest enough to tell her until now. After all, Sam Schneider had been the one to teach her in high school, and he'd later fessed up he'd learned all he knew from Cinemax After Dark.

"Different different."

"Oh." What could a girl say to that? Um…nothing?

"We should get back," he said.

"You never answered my question about your deal with Christmas," she said, propping her hands on her hips. She wasn't going to be dismissed like an employee. She may have signed on with MBH Industries, but she wasn't under him.

A naughty vision flitted through her mind…this time with him above her, running his fingers across her not-so-tight abs. Okay, they were tighter than before thanks to Zumba, but still not as awesome as his probably were. She'd been imagining that rippling six-pack and she knew they had to be *ah-mazing*.

"Listen, no need to hash and rehash who we are. I'm a realist. A capitalist. And I don't like Christmas. You're a romantic, a Christmas nut and, I don't really know… a communist?"

"I'm not a communist…or a nut."

"Okay, but we're different, from different worlds, so let's respect that and we'll get along fine."

"Fine. I'll respect your right to be grumpy and inflexible."

He arched an eyebrow. "Are you trying to argue again?"

Was she? No. Though their earlier argument had ended nicely—a hot, steamy, forget-you're-probably-standing-in-urine-and-other-icky-stuff kiss. So maybe there was something to be said for trading barbs with Brennan if it ended in bliss.

"No, and you're right. We should respect our differences, but I asked why you don't like the holiday not to reiterate what we already know. Are you avoiding the question because you don't have a good answer?"

His eyes went blank—death-stare blank. "I have a good answer, but I fail to see why I'm required to share it with you."

"Because I asked."

"So…"

"So what? You didn't get a pony or an expensive gaming system when you awoke one Christmas morning? Or maybe Santa didn't eat your cookies because they weren't homemade?"

The death stare remained.

"Or maybe your high-school girlfriend kissed someone else beneath the mistletoe. Or did you get pink bunny pj's from your aunt Mabel. Or maybe—"

"My parents died in a plane wreck on the way to pick

me up from boarding school for the holiday break. I spent Christmas Eve on the headmaster's mother's couch in Connecticut."

She swallowed the rest of her comments. But it was hard to swallow the idea of parents dying around Christmas.

"Yeah, really nice opening gifts while funeral arrangements are being made by a grandfather you barely know because he virtually lived at his office. Makes for loads of Christmas cheer."

"Oh, Brennan," she breathed, wanting to stroke his arm, but knowing she had no right to offer such comfort. They weren't even friends.

Still, her fingers sought his. "I'm sorry. I didn't know."

He looked away but didn't pull his hand from hers. "How could you? You don't know me at all."

"No, but I shouldn't have been so obtuse. Very thoughtless of me."

He shook his head and allowed his fingers to curve around hers. "I'm certain those words are seldom used about you. It's fine."

The image of a dark-headed boy curled into a ball on an aged couch popped into her mind. It would be so easy to weep for that boy, to hold him while he cried against the brutality of the world.

But Brennan wasn't a little boy. He was a man who should understand the holiday had little to do with mechanical failure or icy conditions or whatever had brought the plane holding his parents plummeting to earth. Yet, she knew the human mind was a complexity never to be explained. Fear and anger could twist unrelated facts into something seeming quite sensible. "How old were you?"

"Nine, almost ten. I had been at Billings Academy for only four months—sent because my parents were in the process of separating. My sister's accidental drowning a year before put both of them in a tailspin of grief, anger and finger-pointing. The weekend before they flew to pick me up, they'd reconciled. My father said he couldn't spend Christmas hating my mother, blaming her for Brielle's death. I had thought it meant the end of Billings, thought I could smile again." Brennan's eyes were focused on a distant spot, his voice different from his usual timbre.

"When Headmaster Jennings's eyes met mine after I answered my dormitory door, I knew. Knew my visions of laughter under the Christmas tree wearing the matching pajamas my mother had ordered from L.L.Bean were shattered like...like—" he pushed a broken piece of glass with the toe of his loafer "—glass."

Mary Paige squeezed his hand but offered no words. What could a person say to something so devastating? What right did she have to berate the man for disliking a holiday that reminded him of his shattered family?

His head jerked up and he released her hand. "Hell, I don't know why I dragged up that tale of woe. I don't usually wallow in melancholia."

"I asked," she said, hoping her voice sounded steady. She wanted to hold him, to smooth away the grief etched on his face. To offer this hard man something she hadn't seen a lot from him—simple kindness.

"But not for that out-and-out pity party. I apologize."

"For what? For being human? For hurting? For wanting someone to understand why this time of year makes you sad?"

"I don't need your sympathy." All trace of emotion had left his face, leaving him closely resembling that cold businessman she'd first met. "Bad things happen to people all the time. I'm sure you could go inside and talk to those people and find thirty different hard-luck tales that would make mine look like a fairy tale."

She shook her head as he reached for the door handle, but he didn't see her. He was determined to dismiss his confession, to carry on as he'd always done. Maybe like a good little soldier or a stoic oak or some other metaphor for men when they swallowed grief and pretended not to feel. Her hand closed over his and he stilled.

When his gaze met hers she felt a shiver. "You feel exposed?"

"Don't play games with me."

"I'm not. Nothing wrong with being human, Brennan. Nothing wrong with vulnerability. Nothing wrong with giving me the small gift of understanding you better."

"I don't need to be fixed, Mary Paige."

"Who said I was trying to fix you? Who said I give a roaring flip about whether you sing carols or toast the Yule log? I'm not trying to rehabilitate you, only understand the disdain displayed by someone who doesn't believe in the magic of the season."

Again, he gave her a flat stare. "Shall we?"

"Shall we what?"

For a long moment he regarded her, as if measuring intent, cataloging possibility. One eyebrow crooked. "Serve the poor."

"We shall."

He pulled open the door, withdrawing his hand from beneath hers, shedding her easily as he pulled on the cloak of control he usually wore. The only difference was now Mary Paige had seen beneath the protective armor to the frightened boy who hid beneath, and for the first time since she'd met Brennan, a certainty about what he needed settled into her conscience. She'd lied when she said she didn't give a roaring flip about healing Brennan.

Because somewhere deep inside, Mary Paige knew this whole crazy campaign was more than what it seemed.

She had to be the Spirit of Christmas, not only for New Orleans, but also for the child who had cried silent tears on an unfamiliar couch. A boy who had grown to hate Christmas after being robbed of all it should have meant.

Her mission was clear. Show Brennan what service and love could do…not just for the people they served, but for the person scooping beans or writing checks.

"I'll serve the beans this time. You're too impatient and dribble juice everywhere. You got KP." She slid past him as he held open the door.

"What's that?" He followed her, executive mask firmly in place.

She gave him her flirtiest smile, raising her hands and wiggling her fingers. "Dishpan hands."

His expression might have been intimidating had it not been for the tiniest sparkle that lit his eyes.

Yeah, she could teach Brennan to embrace the spirit of giving.

Maybe.

CHAPTER TEN

BRENNAN LOOKED IN the mirror and adjusted his tuxedo tie for the third time. Damn thing wouldn't stay straight.

"You're looking awfully dapper," his grandfather said, entering the formal living room where Brennan stood sipping a cognac and contemplating his whirligig bow tie. Izzy trotted in behind Malcolm like his entourage. She hopped daintily onto her elaborate doggy bed, turned twice and curled into a ball.

"Thanks. Thought I'd confirm Mark's delusion that paisley is back, therefore the tie."

"No doubt you'll set styles this holiday," his grandfather said, a faint smile hovering at his lips. Brennan knew sarcasm when he heard it. In fact, Malcolm was the former King of Droll, but seemed to have abdicated in favor of sincerity.

Brennan offered a crystal cordial glass to his grandfather, whose breast pocket sported a bright red handkerchief that matched the blinking Rudolph nose he'd snapped onto his face. "No, thank you."

Brennan tried not to roll his eyes. He really did. But they seemed to have a mind of their own. "A blinking nose?"

"What? It doesn't scream 'fun'?"

"More like insanity."

Malcolm laughed. "Indeed, I fear I've finally gone

mad, but I'm loving every second of it. I've another blinking nose if you wish to board the crazy train."

"Save it for the accountant. She'll probably revere it
more than the Hope Diamond," Brennan said, sinking
onto the damask slipper chair flanking the marbled fire-
place. The room was New Orleans formal with a few
funky original paintings from noted abstract painters.
Malcolm had dated a noted, much sought-after interior
designer who'd used their St. Charles mansion as a showcase for all that was luxurious and expensive. Brennan
knew. He'd paid that bill and nearly choked at the cost
of the rug where his feet now sprawled.

"Mary Paige is a gem, is she not? I don't think I could
have picked a more perfect or deserving person to be
our centerpiece for this campaign. I'm extraordinarily
pleased."

Brennan grunted and tried not to think about Mary
Paige and her silky hair and soft lips. He didn't know why
she bedeviled him, drew him to her like a kid to fire-
works, but she did. And it bothered him that he couldn't
get her out of his mind. His mind should be filled with
sales figures and the new line of bathing suits they were
launching for plus-size women, not a nosy accountant
with a too-big smile and an ass that fit incredibly well
in his hands. But his mind, like his eyes, seemed to have
a will of its own randomly popping up images of Mary
Paige sprawled naked on his bed, maybe tied to the headboard with a string of Christmas lights. Now those were
lights worth enjoying, ensnaring that blonde elf so he
could enjoy the satin of her skin, capture her sighs with
his lips as he showed her how to get into the spirit of
things best not shared with anyone but him.

Yes, only for him.

"Brennan?"

His grandfather's voice ripped him from his naughty Christmas fantasy. "Yes?"

"I asked if you were riding with me to the benefit. Is that why you're here?"

"No, thought I'd take the Virage for a spin. Nice night for it." In most aspects Brennan was practical. He wore expensive clothes when necessary, but otherwise pulled on Levi's and Dockers. His one true vice, the one thing he indulged in, however, was fast cars. Beautiful, luxurious, expensive fast cars and the silver convertible Aston Martin Virage coupe he kept in the secure Henry estate garage was testimony to a wicked part of him.

The Virage was beauty in motion.

He'd once dated a woman who'd viewed shoes as art, and when he'd seen the closet she'd designed filled with display cases for shoes, he'd been disparaging that a person would build a museum for shoes. Then she'd held up the shoes, one by one, her voice full of admiration for the details, the supple leather, the towering, glittering works of art, and Brennan understood. Everyone had his or her peccadilloes, embarrassing collections or self-indulgent fripperies that on the surface seemed ridiculous, but beneath spoke to a basic human quality—people liked pretty things.

And his Virage was very, very pretty.

He wondered what vice Mary Paige indulged in. Perhaps beautiful, expensive French underwear? That would be a nice collection to see. Or maybe erotic literature? No. Mary Paige wouldn't dare.

"Brennan?"

"Yes?"

"Awfully distracted this evening, aren't you?" Malcolm said, smoothing a hand over his silver hair and tugging the lapels of his jacket into place, keeping one eye on the mirror like a sixteen-year-old on prom night. "I had hoped to introduce you to my date before the gala. Judy's nervous about attending, and I thought it might set her at ease to know at least one more person."

Judy What's-her-name was such an odd choice of dates for his grandfather. The thought of Malcolm dating a woman who'd once been a nun seemed like a joke. A nun and a billionaire walk into a bar…

It was nearly as bad as Brennan dating the accountant who wore cheap clothes and fed homeless animals.

"I'll be glad to stay and meet her." Even if he was ready to go. For some reason he felt antsy, a feeling that had settled over him since admitting to Mary Paige the real reason he wasn't filled with Christmas cheer.

"Good. I had hoped I might convince you to escort Miss Gentry to the gala. Has to be intimidating for her, too."

"I told you I'm not perpetuating the idea there is romance between us. She's not my type."

Malcolm frowned but said nothing.

Brennan tried to believe his own words even though his body had been singing a different tune, indulging in crazy fantasies about the simple, not-so-much-his-type woman for the past two nights. Crazy, hot fantasies.

He was horny.

No other explanation…at least not one he wanted to admit. He pushed himself off the chair and started to pace in an effort to release some of the antsy energy plaguing him.

"Just a minute, Brennan, if you will."

Brennan paused. "Yes?"

"Perhaps it's not the time or place for such a conversation, but I need to apologize to you and that bill is past due. It's hard to swallow my pride and admit to being something other than what I should be, but—"

"You don't have to apologize for anything." Brennan wished he'd left before his grandfather had come downstairs. He hated arriving at events early so had settled in for a drink, leaving himself open to a dose of his grandfather's sentimentality before meeting his date.

"No, I must say it, Brennan. You deserve as much."

"I don't deserve anything, and all this craziness you're going through, I don't understand it. You've changed so much I don't recognize you sometimes."

"Good. I don't want to be recognized as the man I once was. Was I all bad? No. But there was so much of me I didn't access. So much of me that lived without feeling. Places in my heart filled with…with rot. I've spent the past few months trying to cull the weeds and seed the flowers of something better."

Brennan didn't know what to say to his grandfather's proclamation. "Well, I never thought you anything but admirable."

"No, you didn't." Malcolm sighed, heavy and resigned. "In many people's eyes I was a success. Have you ever thought about what true success is?"

"I'm guessing it's not having money or influence."

Malcolm sank onto the couch, a smile twitching at his lips, the blinking nose absurd. "You've always been a bright boy, taking to business like a duck to a pond, navigating treacherous waters, ignoring what could distract and spreading your wings quite commendably."

Those words filled him with equal parts pleasure and pride. He had worked hard to get to where he was. Malcolm had laid down a decree long ago that no positions in the company would be given without merit. If Brennan did work worthy of the mail room, there he'd stay.

The position Brennan held had been earned through hard work, late nights and concrete results.

"But you have no comfort, my boy. You've no true friends, no feathers to support your head. I know, for I discovered much the same not so long ago. An epiphany washed over me, and I haven't the time this evening to share all I've learned, but I *will* say I'm sorry for being less of a man, for being unavailable to you when you needed me most, for leaving you in that godforsaken boarding school to grieve alone for all you'd lost. I was callous and shortsighted."

Like a bandage ripped from a wound, the pain of the memories waded through only yesterday with Mary Paige came roaring back. The smell of the couch he'd cried himself to sleep upon, the rawness of his nose from the sobs, the empty room lit only be a garish Victorian Christmas tree…and the days that followed. Black suit, lemon polish and red carpets of the funeral home. Waxy flowers, hushed whispers and empty platitudes to remember the man and woman who'd chaired the tennis social, donated generously to the campaign fund and mixed the best dirty martinis. Empty. Numb. Grief.

And here, over twenty-five years later, his grandfather wanted to apologize to the boy he'd left behind? Too little, too late. Brennan didn't want an apology and he damned sure didn't want to remember how shitty he'd felt. How absolutely alone he'd been.

"You know, I turned out okay," Brennan said, trying to keep emotion at bay. That agony had knitted together into a tough determination to succeed, to grab control and to never feel like that young, bewildered boy again.

And he hadn't.

Until yesterday.

"Yes, you're a good man even if you hide it beneath

that very businesslike, busy facade. Don't be afraid to find some softness, to reach for more pleasure than making profit, to take some time to remember what should be the most important parts of life—loving, laughing and sharing."

"For what reason?" So he could feel that same pain he'd felt as a child studying the way the funeral home lights fell on the patina of his mother's coffin? To again know he had no control over anything? He'd promised himself he'd never allow himself to feel that way again.

Malcolm looked down at the carpet. "Ah, vulnerability is a weakness for you, eh? I seek it now because it reminds me I'm human."

"I'm not making light of your apology or your advice. I just fail to see how I'm a bad person because I work hard, because I don't fly kites or play with dogs in the park or because I don't put up a Christmas tree or light a menorah."

"You're not Jewish."

"That's not the point. The point is the sound of 'Grandma Got Run Over by a Reindeer' gives me hives. What's wrong with cutting through the do-gooder crap and getting down to the meat of life—which is eat or be eaten?"

The doorbell rang, causing Malcolm to snap to attention and hop to his feet at a speed belying his seventy-two years. "I do believe that's Judy. Let's continue this talk another time."

So much for his deep philosophies. Brennan couldn't help but notice how quickly the arrival of his date distracted Malcolm. Or that the woman's name on his grandfather's lips was an endearment.

"You're not picking her up?" Brennan asked as Gator passed to answer the door.

"She wouldn't allow it. Said she lived only four blocks away and her two legs were perfectly capable of walking. I argued, but she's a stubborn sort."

Gator appeared, using a flourish never witnessed before as he waved Judy Poche into the enormous room.

"Oh," she said, her eyes taking in the over-the-top grandeur inspired by 19th-century plantation owners and 1970s drugged-out abstract artists. "Wow, this is… breathtaking."

"Come in, my dear," Malcolm crowed with more enthusiasm than a midway carnival hawker, the color in his face high, his blue eyes twinkling with a pleasure Brennan had never before seen. So strange.

She was small, brown-haired and very underdressed for a formal gala. Her coffee-colored hair lay straight and unadorned against the almost matronly black sweater set with little pebblelike pearl buttons. A long plain black skirt almost touched the tips of the black flats. A schoolmarm would have been pleased with Judy's outfit. New Orleans's society, however, would make her chum and feed her to the fashion sharks.

He saw this realization dawn in Judy's eyes as she took in the tuxedos and something inside him flickered at the embarrassment he saw in her eyes. Her discomfiture would do neither here, nor at the pavilion in City Park.

Malcolm took her hand. "You look lovely, my dear."

Judy's fingers fluttered to the simple strand of pearls at her throat. "I guess I didn't understand how formal the event is. I should have worn something finer, I think. And brought my blinking nose."

"You are lovely no matter what you wear," his grandfather said, bestowing a courtly kiss upon her hand. "And this is my grandson, Brennan."

Judy turned eyes the color of root beer on him and

smiled with sincerity. Oh, yes, he could see the softness in this woman, the very feathers for which his grandfather had been searching. His mind flashed to another woman with soft brown eyes and an unpretentious nature—a woman he had to stop picturing naked. "Pleasure to meet you, Miss Poche. My grandfather has told me how much he admires you."

"Well, your grandfather is as charming as you are, no doubt."

Brennan turned to his grandfather. "I'm off and shall see you both at City Park."

Judy nodded and took a few steps toward the Jackson Pollock hanging above the mantel, giving Brennan the opportunity he needed to whisper in his grandfather's ear.

"Take her to Gigi, or Margaret Pride will eat her alive and wash her down with champagne."

Malcolm straightened. "Yes, we should be leaving, too. I've a special little treat for you, Judy, and I won't hear of your refusing me."

"A treat?"

"I want to spoil you a bit, my dear. Say you will let me."

She shook her head. "I don't need spoiling."

"Adieu," Brennan said as he headed toward the garage, checking his pocket for both his keys and his money clip. Yes, Judy reminded him of Mary Paige and he rather liked that about the woman.

"This is going to be quite a chore," his grandfather called back, obviously exasperated with the angelic Judy and not bothering to temper it in front of the woman.

Brennan shook his head. Do-gooders and angels. He hoped the Christmas season would be over soon.

He also hoped his grandfather left him well enough alone. He didn't need lessons on living—particularly those that contradicted all he'd learned from the same man. And he didn't need to change all that he was just because certain people made him feel like—

Bah…he wasn't thinking about it.

MALCOLM WATCHED JUDY as she set her chin at a ridiculously high angle. Where was his sweet, reasonable Judy? "Come now, Judy, I want to treat you to something most women would love."

"I'm not most women. What I'm wearing suits me. I'm not flashy and don't wear jewels. In fact, I'm almost embarrassed to ride in a chauffeured car to a party. Feels wrong."

Gator drove the sedan through the ornate iron gates enclosing the Henry mansion and onto the street. Malcolm shifted next to Judy, wishing he'd been more specific about what was appropriate dress for the event. Of course, Judy was right. She looked lovely wearing light pink lipstick and tasteful clothing. But no one would be dressed so plainly and the thought of Barracuda Margaret making Judy feel less than what she was angered him. Character counted and a person shouldn't judge by outer trappings. Wasn't that what his point was about when he'd dressed as a homeless man? He should let Judy be and admire her for who she was, not what the glittering, phony society would think of her.

Still, something inside him wanted to lavish this woman with something as beautiful as she was. Silks to slide against the softness of her skin, amber jewels to match her eyes and beautiful heeled shoes to finish off those legs he'd once caught a glimpse of when he helped her hang the new shelves for the academic center at Holy Trinity.

"Please," he asked, pouring all the desire he had for her into that one word.

Judy tilted her head, an endearing habit, and those eyes narrowed. "Are you ashamed to be seen with me?"

"Not even if you wore a burlap sack and scuba flippers."

"Now that would be something."

"I'm not trying to change you, but when you care about someone, you enjoy doing nice things for them."

"Care about me?" Her throat worked as she swallowed hard.

He nodded, unable to look away. "Did you think I asked you to be my date tonight because—"

"You care for me?"

He took the hand lying upon her maidenly skirt and squeezed it. "Honestly, Judy, I want to do things to you that you've never even imagined possible."

"And you know my intimate thoughts, Malcolm Henry?" Low, intimate and somehow sexy, the words were surprising from a former nun.

His pulse skipped a beat then galloped off. "Oh, how I'd like to know them."

Judy's smile widened and her fingers traced the crisp hairs on the back of hands that had once looked much like his grandson's—strong, virile and capable—but had weathered into those of an old man. Yet, there were parts of him that, at that moment, didn't feel quite so old.

He crooked his finger so she leaned toward him as if she might hear a secret. His lips brushed the silkiness of her ear as he whispered, "Let me dress you tonight, Judy."

Allowing his lips to linger near her ear, he reached around to cup her nape. Her hair felt as soft as down and her breath came in short little puffs. Stretching slightly he pressed the button to raise the glass partition between the front and backseats.

"Oh," she breathed. She seemed not to know where to place her hands. They fluttered in her lap, telling Malcolm his sweet Judy didn't have much experience with a man, so he caught them with his one free hand, stilling them.

"Ah, my lovely Judy. How I've wanted to kiss you."

"You have?"

He softly kissed her ear and drew back so he could look at her. The sun had long set and the dark shadows settled around them, but the full moon hanging low in the sky and the passing streetlights illuminated her, softening the lines on her face, creating a glow in her eyes. "If you only knew, woman."

She leaned forward so her lips covered his. Wasn't the best kiss he'd ever been given, but it was the absolute sweetest. He smiled against her mouth, adjusted his hand to tilt her head so he could kiss her not so properly. No, not properly at all. *Indecently.*

Judy was game and opened to him, placing one hand on his neck in much the same manner his held hers.

Age-old desire swept over him, this time as ripe as cherries or some other similarly plump fruit. It stirred his blood and for a few seconds he wasn't nearly at the end of his life, but rather stepping into a beginning. He fell back through time, riding the elixir of passion, as if he were once again wearing dungarees and a white T-shirt, with a pack of Lucky Strikes in his pocket.

Judy trembled against him like a young girl in his '57 roadster. Then and there in his sedate sedan, Malcolm found something he thought he'd never find again—a welling of hope.

Gently he broke the kiss and she blinked at him, startled at the abrupt ending.

"Enough for now, sweet woman. We have shopping to do."

"You don't have to do this." Her lips glistened from a pretty dang spectacular kiss.

"I want to."

And Malcolm Henry, Jr. gets what he wants.

Of course, he didn't say those words out loud, but they were implied just the same.

"Okay," was all she said, keeping her hand wrapped in his.

The Henry flagship store materialized like a great ship against the glittering downtown skyline. Pride welled in him as he gazed upon that storefront that had changed over the years, but had never lost the moniker *Henry Department Store* scrawled in the deep turquoise his father had chosen from the discount sign shop in Metairie in 1937. The red color his father had wanted was too expensive and, thus, the almost Tiffany-blue logo was born.

"Doesn't it close at eight o'clock?" Judy asked, eyeing the doors where people bustled by heading home from jobs in the adjacent buildings.

"Not during the holiday crush," Malcolm said, watching the front of the store as Gator pulled into an empty parking spot at the curb. "Besides I have a key."

For the first time, a glimmer of anticipation flitted through her eyes. "So have you ever dressed a woman?"

Malcolm gave his sharkiest of grins. "Not quite. Usually the opposite."

"Promises, promises," Judy said as she opened the car door, not bothering to wait for Gator.

"Whatever you desire," Malcolm said to the place she'd vacated, unable to stop smiling like a blooming idiot.

CHAPTER ELEVEN

MARY PAIGE WAS late. Not wholly unexpected since Ivan had insisted she finish a huge account or find a new place of employment. His threat was, of course, empty because she didn't have to work for him any longer and he would never fire an employee who made him money and kept fresh coffee ready throughout the day. Besides, she wanted to work for Ivan, even if he was caustic and overly hairy. Ivan was a damn fine accountant and had taught her more than she'd ever learn working for some huge tax-return corporation.

As she was busy getting dressed, the phone rang, flashing her mother's number on the caller ID. Even though it would compound her lateness, Mary Paige knew she couldn't keep avoiding talking to Freda. They'd played phone tag long enough.

"Hello," she huffed into the phone, pulling off her shoes and wiggling her toes in the rug.

"About time you answered," her mother said in a voice that took Mary Paige back to Crosshatch, back to being the obedient daughter. "I thought I was going to have to send Lars down to find you."

"Sorry, Mama. I've been so busy—"

"Too busy to call your mama and tell her about two million dollars?"

"Yeah, that."

"Yeah, that," her mother said, irritation as thick as the

strawberry-blond hair she still wore past her shoulders. "When were you going to tell me about this whole deal? I had to read about it in the paper. My own daughter, and I get the news from the *Alexandria Journal*."

"I'm sorry, Mom. I didn't know how to tell you. What I mean is—"

"You're in over your head?"

Mary Paige rolled her eyes. "Well, if you'll stop finishing my sentences, I'll explain."

The silence on the line gave her permission.

"I guess you saw the whole story about how I came to be chosen as this Spirit of Christmas person, but that's not the problem so much. I like doing charity work."

"Of course. It's what we do as a family, so I couldn't see you having an issue with doing what is right." Her mother's voice had softened and Mary Paige knew the anger ebbed. Her mother always understood her, so she didn't know why she'd waited so long to call the one person who always had her back. Maybe because saying it to her mother meant everything, including that check still in her jewelry box, would be real.

"But I haven't cashed the check because it feels...I don't know...scary."

"It's a lot of money."

"Yeah, and if I put it in the bank, then it becomes mine with all the complications and problems. I'm not prepared to be a millionaire. I'm not prepared to change who I am."

"Why would it change you?"

"Money always changes people. Suddenly, that person's very popular, expected to pick up the check, wear clothes that don't come from discount stores and invest in an art show."

"Simon?"

"Yeah, he's left me three messages." Mary Paige

pulled out the sparkly bobby pins holding her hair back. "But I'm not loaning him a dime. He took enough from me."

"Good girl. I'm glad you're finished with him once and for all. I didn't agree with you loaning him your couch—I've known slime like him and they keep taking until there's nothing left. So good riddance." Her mom paused then and Mary Paige suspected she was in for an interrogation. "But this kiss? Who is this Henry guy?"

"That was nothing," Mary Paige lied.

"Your voice says otherwise," her mother said, using the decoding device all mothers seemed to possess. "You're a sweet girl, Mary Paige, and I've had qualms about your moving down to that city alone. You—"

"I'm sweet, but I'm your daughter."

And that was something. Freda Gentry was as strong as those redwood trees she'd once protested against being cut down. Resilient as the weeds she yanked out every day on her organic farm. And as stubborn as the waters of the Mississippi River flowing not far from that same farm. Sweet was one thing. Being her mother's daughter quite another.

"You are," her mother conceded. "Just be careful, my baby girl, playing with a man like that."

Mary Paige wasn't playing anything with Brennan. No way would she admit that her dreams had been filled with being with him. Naked, clothed and everything in between "with" him.

Which was nuts.

"I'm not playing with him. It was promo and we got a little carried away. No harm in that."

"But he's the kind of guy who'll eviscerate you with a smile. Like playing with a lion—he looks regal and you wanna touch him, but you'll draw back a bloody stump."

"Mama, it's basically a job. The papers can say what they want, people can speculate, but I know I don't belong with him and I won't squeeze into a dress that doesn't fit."

Her mother didn't say anything for a moment, and Mary Paige wasn't sure whether she believed her or not. But really, it didn't matter. Mary Paige loved her mother, but she'd never quite agreed with the way Freda treated men—keeping her distance, dating, but never making a commitment. So Mary Paige doubted her mother gave the best relationship advice.

"So, how's my brother?"

Freda took the bait and launched into a tirade about the local school system cutting the special education budget so severely, she was afraid Caleb would have to share a teaching aide with another student. While her mother berated the superintendent, the school board and the entire parish, Mary Paige grabbed the dress she *would* have to squeeze into from the closet.

She was a round peg and Brennan was a square hole. She knew that and knew better than to borrow trouble in an Armani suit. But that didn't mean she had to stand on the sidewalk and watch the parade.

The next several weeks were an opportunity to experience things she'd never have the chance to experience again—galas, benefits, charity work—all while being on the arm of New Orleans's most eligible bachelor. Was there anything wrong with getting the teeniest bit of pleasure from wearing fancy dresses and sipping champagne?

As long as she didn't let her head fly into the clouds and stay there.

But first she had to squeeze into her remade prom dress. She only hoped Mama Cascio had been able to let it out enough and cover up the ruffles ripped from the hem with the beaded trim Mary Paige had scored at

Hobby Lobby. Last thing she wanted was to have to wear those damn Spanx.

Maybe she should have put the check in the bank and bought herself something nice to wear to these shindigs. She was certain no other woman would be wearing her old prom dress.

But as ridiculous as it seemed, Mary Paige didn't know how to handle two million dollars when it was her own money. It was too daunting, too intimidating. So until she could wrap her mind around what that money would do to her life and how she should manage it, the check would stay where it was.

"Mama, maybe that charter-school idea has merit." For a few years Freda had been researching the process for running a school that would address Caleb's particular needs as well as assisting some of the other local families with the needs of their kids. She hadn't gotten as far as she'd like, in part because of the funding costs. "Let's talk more later. Right now I'm late for a gala."

"A gala?"

"Yeah." Mary Paige yanked her sweater over her head, then wiggled out of her pants. "I'm going to an adult prom in the dress I wore for high-school prom."

"Maybe you should have cashed that check."

"And miss wearing the dress you made from that bargain satin you found in a flea market? It still fits and it's still pretty."

"Dear God, you are my daughter."

THE GLITTERING TREES sprawled throughout City Park like magical creatures from a storybook, leading the way to an adventure filled with beautiful fairies, handsome princes and, no doubt, smoked salmon.

Mary Paige had no clue why people liked smoked

salmon. It was virtually raw fish, and she'd cleaned enough perch to lose any taste for raw fish.

But it didn't matter because she was lost. She'd driven all over City Park and still couldn't find the right parking lot. The Pavilion of the Two Sisters should be easy to find, but for some reason she'd ended up in the parking lot of Storyland, which was filled with whirling rides, a restored antique carousel and loads of laughing families wandering around under the thousands of glittering light strands—all part of Celebration in the Oaks. Maybe the reception hall was beyond the gated park. She could take the path through the trees and perhaps they would lead to exactly where she needed to go.

She climbed out and tugged the satin dress into place, happy she hadn't had to wear the Spanx after all. She sucked in her stomach and made sure the beaded trim around the top of the dress covered her boobs. The sapphire fabric fit her like a second skin, cinching in her waist and dropping to the tops of her one pair of designer shoes. The sheath was classic and needed no other adornment save the iridescent beads and high slit up the leg. It wasn't haute couture, but it did look good on her.

She grabbed her clutch, locked the car and started up the path toward…well, she didn't know.

"Mary Paige?"

Brennan's voice came from behind her. She turned to find him sitting in a no-doubt absurdly expensive car in the parking lot. The lights were on and the car idled.

"Oh, hello, Brennan."

"I drove past and saw you climb out. What are you doing here? You know we're at the Pavilion?"

He looked startlingly handsome. Not so much like a lion. More like a storybook prince ready to rescue her from perishing in the woods…or, in this case, the lit-up oaks. "I know but my direction doohickey on the phone kept taking me here, so I thought it was up ahead."

He shifted the car into gear and roared into a parking spot, putting up the top of the car and climbing out. A beep later and he strode toward her, looking elegant and sexy in a classic black tuxedo.

She didn't want it to, but her heart skipped a beat.

He stopped to take in the view. Not the park. But *her*. And she swore hot flames licked up her body as his gaze lazily perused her. "Stunning."

That simple word pooled pleasure in her belly, and she felt her cheeks ignite in a soft blush. "Thank you. You look very nice, as well. Like the paisley bow tie."

"Paisleys are making a comeback."

"Well, then," she said with a smile. "Should I go back to my car and follow you to the right place?"

"It's not far and we can walk as long as you're good in those heels." His gaze slid down her body again, landing on her toes. And again, she felt the heat of his perusal. Her body hummed and she reminded herself not to be seduced by Brennan Henry. Teeth and bloody stumps and—

He smiled—a secret little masculine smile that told her there was more on his mind than a stroll—and she forgot about warning herself. He glanced at the lights twinkling above them.

"I've decided to like Christmas lights," he said, a slight huskiness in his voice.

"Oh? Well, these are pretty."

Christmas music played softly in the background, almost drowned out by the shrieks of children on the carnival rides. The night was festive and magical already.

He took her elbow, and she curved her arm through his, pleased to have the solid warmth of a man next to her.

"Have you ever been to City Park Storyland or ridden the carousel before?"

She shook her head. "I've taken walks in the park and even went to a concert by some philharmonic but never visited this part before. Guess I have no reason to ride the carousel or tilt-a-whirl."

"Now, that doesn't sound like the Mary Paige I know. You seem the type of woman who'd do whatever she wished as long as it made her smile."

"You don't really know me, do you? I'm not all about pleasure, Brennan." God, the way she said it made it sound like it was about sex.

Bingo. His body tightened beneath her hand.

"What I mean is I pay attention to consequences, to the impact on others, to social responsibility. Ugh, this is not coming out right. What I mean is—"

"You wanna ride the tilt-a-whirl?"

"Wha—" She snapped her mouth closed and looked at the spinning cars. "You want to ride that? In these clothes?"

Brennan nodded, something she couldn't read hidden in the depths of those eyes that didn't seem so cold this evening. "I haven't done it since I was a small boy, and oddly enough, I don't think I can leave Storyland without riding it. You're exactly the person I want to do it with."

She didn't know whether to be insulted or flattered. "But we're dressed like…this." She indicated her gown.

"I like the irony. Storyland and the Carousel Gardens. You looking like Cinderella and a rollicking ride." He pointed in that direction. "Come on. Let's do it."

Mary Paige really didn't want to hike up her dress and climb on a carnival ride, but something inside her nudged her to fulfill this man's request. Perhaps riding the tilt-a-whirl proved Brennan was fallible, silly…human. "Yeah, let's go ride the tilt-a-whirl in heels and a bow tie."

He grinned and she caught sight of the boy he must have been at one time. Something about his expression motivated her to do whatever the man wanted her to do. Tilt-a-whirl? Sex? Rob a bank? Whatever. Sign her up. "I'll get the tickets. You get in line."

"This is going to make us late," she called to his retreating back. He didn't turn around because obviously he was a man on a mission. She looked around, feeling like she'd been plunked down in Oz. She lifted the hem of her gown. Nope. No ruby slippers.

So she got in line behind two preteen girls who kept looking at her with curious stares.

Well, yeah. She'd stare at a woman in a full-length gown standing in a line for a carnival ride, too. In fact, lots of people stopped, stared and then whispered. One man laughed.

She felt Brennan before he spoke—maybe because he smelled of expensive leather or something rich-guy-like. Then he touched her and she felt her pulse speed out of control.

"I got the tickets. You ready to ride?"

Was she? Ready to ride? Because suddenly it felt more than a carnival ride. Maybe she was in line for something more with Brennan. And like the anticipation of an imminent thrill ride, her stomach flipped, her breathing quickened and her palms sweated.

How had stopping for coffee and a pair of ugly socks landed her in Storyland, dressed in a ball gown standing next to a prince…a miserly, grumpy and greedy prince, but one she felt herself softening toward. Oh, she knew she couldn't have this prince forever and ever.

But maybe she could take a ride with him?

Or a ride on him?

The thought of making love with Brennan stuck in her mind, an ever-present unwanted pop-up ad for sex. Appearing at random moments. Luring her. Begging her to indulge.

"Here's your ticket…." Temptation beckoned.

MALCOLM SAT ON the flowery couch in the dressing lounge of the haute couture section of Henry's watching Judy and her fairy godmother eyeball each other. Gigi Malone had been with Henry Department Stores for over thirty years and was the equivalent of Coco Chanel in New Orleans. She might not design the clothes, but she paired the classic with the unique and wore designs with panache. No one doubted Gigi's eye. No one.

Not even stubborn Judy Poche, who had opened her mouth only once while Gigi tugged off the black sweater and glared at it as if it had been delivered from the back end of a dog before tossing it in the general direction of the gilded trash can in the corner of the lounge.

"Wait," Judy said, grasping the air where the sweater had once been held. "That's—"

"Darling," Gigi drawled, touching a finger to her black Buddy Holly glasses, "do you see the man sitting on that divan?"

Judy swiveled her head toward him, and he arched an eyebrow at Gigi. She was really over-the-top.

"He's Malcolm Henry, Jr., even if he's wearing a blinking nose."

"I know who he is," Judy said, frowning at Gigi as if the woman had sprouted horns or frothed at the mouth. He couldn't really tell if Judy thought Gigi was cracked or Satan himself.

"He does not squire about town with someone dressed in a habit unless it's Halloween."

Judy's mouth fell open. "I don't dress like a nun."

Gigi merely arched a well-groomed eyebrow.

His sweet date looked at him for help, and he didn't know whether to laugh or rush to her defense. So he did neither. He looked at Gigi and prayed she'd win over Judy.

"Not evident to these eyes, darling. Tonight you're to attend a benefit with the elite of New Orleans. Let's do you justice, darling," Gigi said, running a practiced eye over the black cotton tank she'd revealed and the skirt that hung to Judy's flats.

"Malcolm?" Based on her expression Judy appeared as though she might bolt...or punch Gigi.

"Judy, you're a beautiful woman, and Gigi will bring all you are to the surface. I trust her implicitly, otherwise, I wouldn't have torn her from her nightly cappuccino to dress you. Now, let her do her magic."

Gigi clapped. "Well, done, Malcolm, and don't think your sweet words will keep me from penciling in overtime on the time card."

"Wouldn't think of it. Now, time is money, and we have a date with the dance floor."

Gigi clapped her hands again and a young saleswoman appeared. "Fetch Mr. Henry a double scotch and then send for Beatrice at the Elizabeth Arden counter. Tell her to bring something suitable for a brunette. Also, tell Richard in Shoes to find strappy sandals in a size—" she looked at Judy's feet "—six and a half."

Malcolm nearly laughed as Judy's eyes widened. She mouthed "wow," and he didn't think he could feel happier at that moment watching his longtime employee ply her trade and his wares on the woman who likely had not worn anything designer in years, if ever.

Before long, Judy appeared wearing a beautiful champagne-colored sheath that hugged curves he'd never known she had. Her shoulders were exposed and, for a sixty-year-old woman, they were remarkably smooth and kissable. Her feet were bare and she wore no makeup. The dress was gorgeous, but the masterpiece wore the dress.

"Tsk, tsk," Gigi said, breezing into the room, her kitten heels clacking on the wood floor. "Metamorphosis not complete, darling."

Judy slid her gaze to the small woman wearing black Lycra, a Hermès scarf in jade and puce with matching harlequin-patterned shoes. "I don't want to look like a strumpet. Malcolm?"

"If I had strawberries, I'd dip them in you. You're like fine champagne, sleek but with bite."

Judy laughed. "Good gravy, I'm in trouble. Your words are like this dress—too good to be true…and a little naughty." She turned around and showed him a plunging back that stopped only just above the curve of her hips.

"Definitely that dress," he said, trying not to sound like a horny old sod.

Gigi clapped. "Back to the dressing area. Beatrice awaits and we must do something with this hair. I'll fetch pins."

The glance Judy threw him before disappearing around the corner was half desperate, half delighted.

Grinning, he went back to the drink that had already given him a cheerful glow. He had to be careful imbibing alcohol since the medications he took could be affected by the booze, but one more sip wouldn't hurt. Not when his hands trembled to touch that sweet woman wrapped in silk like an early Christmas present with his name on the tag.

When Judy reappeared, her hair had been pulled back

to show the face of a goddess. He didn't know what Beatrice got paid, but she'd be getting a handsome tip from him. Judy's face looked ethereal, glowing with excitement and a sort of radiance he'd never known cosmetics could create. Perhaps it wasn't cosmetics, though. Perhaps it was the glow of excitement making Judy look delicious and not quite angelic.

"Well?" she said, turning a circle, making his mouth water.

"Bewitching siren," he said, rising, giving Gigi a nod as she blew him a kiss and slipped from the room. He approached Judy, spun her into his arms and kissed those soft pink lips.

She melted against him, raising her elegant hands to frame his face.

Breaking the kiss, his gaze connected with hers. "What are you doing to me?"

"Exactly what you're doing to me," she breathed, smoothing the hair across his forehead before sliding her hand to his jaw. "This is like a fairy tale. The Malcolm Henrys of the world don't take the Judy Poches of the world to the ball. It scares me."

He rested his forehead against hers. "The world is wrong. I'm not worthy of you, sweet woman. I'm a hard-nosed cuss of a man who has waded through sin, vice and greed to reach a new shore to find an angel waiting for him. Please don't run away."

Her answer was to kiss him. Wonder flowed through him and he felt the way he had long, long ago with a girl he'd met, loved and left behind to marry the "right" woman. The emotion was as addictive as cocaine, this rush of exhilaration, this euphoria he wanted to tie himself to and ride until he was tossed into the grave.

"Let's go," Judy murmured against his lips. "We're late for the ball."

"It's a benefit gala," he said, nipping the delicate skin at Judy's neck.

"To me, it will be a ball and I'm not leaving one of these gorgeous shoes behind, neither." She kicked up an iridescent sandal with a gold heel.

"If you do, I know where to find you." He winked. "So, let's go to your ball, Judy."

She pulled a matching blinking nose from her bag and pulled it on. "Let's."

CHAPTER TWELVE

BRENNAN COULDN'T STOP laughing—his stomach felt sucked against the seat of the tilt-a-whirl car and the world whipped by in a blur of color and twinkling lights. The only thing clear at that moment was the giggling woman next to him and the thrill of remembering a time when life was worry-free.

"Oh, my goodness," Mary Paige shrieked, clinging to the metal handrail as the car took a sudden hard spin.

"This is awesome," he said, laughing at the way she squeezed those pretty brown eyes closed and braced herself for the next spin, which came quick and hard, twisting his gut and making him laugh.

Finally, after several minutes, the ride slowed and their car rocked from side to side before settling.

Mary Paige opened her eyes.

"You're not going to hurl, are you?"

She shook her head. "Though it would serve you right. Everyone thinks we're nuts climbing on this ride in these clothes."

Glancing around the new car with the purple, green and gold Mardi Gras colors, Brennan was reminded of an aged car with cracked red vinyl seats and black spots of ancient gum on the plate-metal floor—one he'd ridden with his father and Brielle. This time the memory didn't hurt, it merely gave him a warm glow as if his impish, silly sister would have approved of climbing aboard in dress-up clothes. "I like irony."

"Do you?" Mary Paige cocked her head. "Because this seems way outside your comfort zone. Never in a million years would I have expected a fuddy-dud like you to like carnival rides. Spur of the moment, too, I might add."

An older man wearing stained khakis and a T-shirt, with an unlit cigarette dangling between his lips, lifted the metal bar. "If I'd known there was a party, I'd a worn *my* tux," he drawled in a heavy New Orleans accent.

Mary Paige smiled. "Who needs a good reason to dress up, right?"

The guy didn't say anything. She shrugged as she hitched up her dress and tried to climb from the still swinging car.

"Here." Brennan extended a hand toward her, eyeing the greased axle beneath her shoes. Mary Paige wasn't the most graceful of women, and she needed that dress to stay intact and her bottom to remain grease-free.

"Thanks," she said, taking his hand as he tugged her a little too hard. Her heel caught on the edge and she stumbled into him. But he was ready—or maybe he'd subconsciously planned it—and caught her against his chest.

She raised those pretty eyes and there was nothing left to do but kiss her.

So he did.

"Don't mess up my hair," she said as his lips captured hers. Her demand made him smile, so the kiss that could have been passionate ended up tame by his standards.

A tap on his shoulder put a stop to anything more. Brennan released Mary Paige and turned to the carnival ride operator, who removed the cigarette from his lips, tucked it behind his ear and said, "My turn?"

The man laughed good-naturedly, which made Mary Paige laugh. Again, something he hadn't felt in a long time came over him. He almost didn't recognize the bubbling inside him.

Joy.

Good Lord, Brennan "Scrooge" Henry stood among tacky red velvet bows and Christmas lights in City Park smiling like a toddler high on sugar.

Was the world ending?

"Are you coming?" Mary Paige called over a very bare shoulder, trying in vain to tuck the hair flying at odd angles behind her ears.

He could have said something very dirty like "not yet, but if we go to my place in the Quarter, we can start working on it," but he didn't because this moment wasn't about sex, even though the skin she showed made him contemplate it. It was about what Mary Paige and his grandfather had said they'd embraced—being human.

"Yeah, lead on, lady."

So he followed her swaying dark blue backside, wondering what in the hell had happened to him. And wondering if he should run from Mary Paige rather than run toward her. Letting go of who he'd always been made his stomach ache…just like the tilt-a-whirl.

THE PARTY WAS in full swing when they walked into the Pavilion of Two Sisters…and it was crowded. Waiters in traditional uniforms swerved in and out of the revelers, who were dressed to the nines in mostly black, green and red.

"Is there room for us?" Mary Paige joked, waving off an attendant inquiring about a coat she didn't have. She eyed the rows of furs lined up at the coat check and wondered why anyone would need a fur in New Orleans. Then she remembered the abnormally cold temps the week before and acknowledged it would have been nice to snuggle into such warmth…as long as it was faux fur, of course. She wasn't into wearing dead animals.

"Take my arm," Brennan said as a slender brunette in a very short glittering dress advanced toward them. Creighton. Odd name, brash woman.

"I'm not your date," Mary Paige whispered, taking his arm anyway.

"Please."

That one word warmed her more than any fur ever could, but she didn't have time to think about it as Creighton halted before them, bright green liquor sloshing in the martini glass she wielded like a gun. "I waited for you to pick me up."

Brennan regarded her with hooded eyes. "Good evening, Creighton. Nice to see you."

Creighton blinked. "Oh, yeah. Good evening."

"You remember Mary Paige, don't you?"

Creighton's gaze moved to her. Nothing in her look was similar to the warmth she'd shown when Mary Paige had spoken to her in the elevator a week ago. "Of course."

Then Creighton focused on Brennan, dismissing Mary Paige. Something about Creighton's expression seemed as though she was contemplating a battle strategy…or disembowelment.

"I thought you were attending with Ian Massey. He said as much when I saw him at a meeting yesterday," Brennan said.

Creighton's shoulder lifted. "He asked, but I thought you and I had an understanding."

She said *understanding* like it was more than convenience. Like she had a claim. Mary Paige wondered if Creighton meant more to Brennan than he'd let on…or if she only thought she did. Mary Paige shifted in her somewhat uncomfortable shoes and looked away, as if that could give them needed privacy.

"This conversation is making me uncomfortable, Creighton, and here is neither the time nor the place to rehash our earlier discussion." Brennan glanced past Creighton at several people who seemed interested in their little trio. "Let's have a drink, shall we?"

"I already have a drink," Creighton said, swirling the cocktail in her hand.

"Of course, but I meant for me and Mary. Save me a dance, Creighton, won't you?"

She blinked and for a second Mary Paige felt sorry for her. Because Brennan had made it sound as if Mary Paige was his date, and she wasn't sure if it was because she was handy for fending off old girlfriends, or because he liked kissing her on tilt-a-whirls. Either way it felt a little uncomfortable—the exact kind of perilous situation she'd cautioned herself against.

Creighton, the daughter of a senator—okay, Mary Paige had done an internet search on her—was the sort of woman Brennan Henry would end up with. Not the hayseed farm girl turned accountant who shopped at the Army Surplus and made her own soap from a cool idea she'd found on Pinterest. She and he never would compute and Mary Paige trusted what computed.

"I don't dance." Creighton glided off, if one called her slight swagger a glide.

"Awkward," Mary Paige breathed, trying to free her arm from Brennan's grasp. He held tight.

"Sorry about that. She hasn't taken the fact she can't announce our engagement in the *Times-Picayune* well."

"Engagement? Are you two—"

"Only in her mind." Brennan steered her toward a table heaped with silver serving trays, extravagant flower arrangements and two ice sculptures shaped like Christmas trees. "We've never been more than friends—"

"With benefits? You do realize women regard sex as more than sex? No matter what they tell you in the beginning, making love *is* different for us."

"Who said I had sex with her?" he asked, stopping in front of a carving station and examining the offerings.

"Every glance she gives you."

"I've never misled her—or any woman for that matter—about my intentions, so I don't need a guilt trip, Merry Sunshine."

Merry Sunshine did not sound like a compliment. All lightness disappeared as the facade of control, of bored indifference, slammed into place. Suddenly the man on the tilt-a-whirl vanished.

Mary Paige pulled her arm from his and this time he allowed it. Guess she'd upset the apple cart when she called him out on Creighton, and she really didn't care about Creighton and what he did or didn't do with the haughty brunette. Okay, she cared a little. She didn't even want to think about anyone other than herself in his arms…which was…

Damn it. She was tired of thinking of Brennan and Creighton and about sex. If he was so blasé about dumping a senator's daughter, a small-town accountant would be even less of a bother.

"I see your grandfather. Think I'll go say hello." She left Tall, Dark and Surly and headed toward the sparkling Malcolm Henry and the lovely woman standing next to him.

She felt Brennan's eyes on her as she took each step. Something inside her wanted to turn around, apologize for rebuking him and try to recreate the wonder of moments ago. But another part of her wasn't a bit sorry she'd called him out on his behavior. Maybe he'd made no promises to Creighton, maybe she had misinterpreted his clear intentions. But Mary Paige believed he'd used Creighton's emotions to his advantage, keeping her around as long as it was convenient for him, then cutting her loose when she no longer suited his purposes. Maybe Mary Paige was being unfair, but she hated to see anyone treat a person with so little care, to see someone manipulate another's emotions for a desired outcome—in this case, a romp between the sheets.

"Mary Paige," Malcolm said, reaching out a hand, ending her contemplation of men and dysfunctional relationships. Malcolm's hands were as warm as his smile and she could hardly reconcile him with the homeless man who had flipped her off when she'd met him nearly a week ago. This man was in his element, comfortable among the elite of society and relaxed in his role as CEO of MBH Industries. "Come meet my Judy."

The woman standing next to Malcolm glowed even brighter at the man's words. Mary Paige dropped her hand from Malcolm's and extended it to the woman. "Hi, I'm—"

"Mary Paige." The woman's eyes were soft and her smile gentle. For some reason, Mary Paige wanted to move closer to her, to hear her sing, or braid her hair or some other ridiculous inclination. All she knew was something special lived within Judy.

"Malcolm's told me all about you, and I feel you're a sister of my heart. I do so love a woman who cares for others over herself."

Mary Paige glanced at Malcolm, stunned to see such adoration in his eyes. It was almost mesmerizing.

"That's quite a compliment," Mary Paige said. "But I don't think I did anything all that remarkable. Just being a decent human being."

"Oh, but you did. Sometimes all it takes is the right person at the right time to reconnect you to something you'd forgotten."

Mary Paige nodded, trying not to look confused. Then she realized Judy's words were not for her, but for Malcolm. The woman wasn't even looking at her as she said them.

Again, Mary Paige felt awkward.

"Ah, and here's my heir," Malcolm said, pulling his gaze from Judy to a spot beyond her shoulder.

"Grandfather," Brennan said, moving beside her, holding a plate of oysters and that god-awful smoked salmon. "Judy, you look stunning."

"Thank you." Judy kept her eyes on Malcolm.

For a moment, no one said anything more. If anything, it felt even more awkward.

"Ah," Malcolm said, swiveling his silver head toward the entrance to his right. "Right on time."

They turned to see the progression trickling in led by an older black man wearing a shiny suit and a feather in his fedora. If not for the subdued color and cut of his suit, he might have been a pimp.

"What the hell?" Brennan said under his breath.

"Alvin." Malcolm waved his hand at the man giving directives to the dozen or so young men following him in, hands in the pockets of their khaki trousers, heads moving back and forth as if they expected to be hunted for their hides. "Over here."

The large man acknowledged the welcome and delivered a tremendous smile at Malcolm before indicating the boys should remain where they were.

"Grandfather, what's going on?"

The room grew quiet as the crowd registered the presence of the unexpected guests. Quickly they parted as Alvin approached, stacking up on either side, creating a path for the behemoth with the wide crocodile smile.

"Good, good. You've brought your young men with you." Malcolm beamed and offered his hand to the man, shaking it vigorously. "This is my grandson, Brennan."

Alvin extended a hand toward Brennan, who shook it.

"Alvin Dryer, the director of Hope and Grace Home for Boys. Happy to meet you," he said as Brennan shifted his eyes to the boys still standing in the entrance.

"Pleasure to meet you, Mr. Dryer," Brennan said.

Further introductions were made before Malcolm said, "Let's bring the boys in. I'd love to introduce them as my special guests and talk a little bit about how Malcolm's Kids will partner with your agency to create better afterschool programs. Do you think the boys will mind saying a few words?"

Alvin nodded his head, looking more and more like an overgrown St. Bernard than the ferocious Doberman who'd split the room with his intense bearing and huge stride. "I've asked Samuel and Darian to speak about what Hope and Grace has meant to them and how added funding will help other kids on the streets."

"Perfect." Malcolm waved toward the boys, who appeared to be between fourteen and seventeen years old and not exactly happy to be there. Several of them jerked their chins in acknowledgment but their faces remained guarded.

Mary Paige snuck a glance at Brennan as the band struck up a KC and the Sunshine Band classic loud enough to distract several of the attendees, who still stared at the young men and their fearless leader. Brennan looked confused, and disappointingly, alarmed. He kept glancing about the room at the people whispering together and casting worried looks toward the new arrivals.

"Let me get the boys settled. Maybe get them some sodas or food. You said there was a special table reserved? Faster I get them out of everyone's line of vision, the more comfortable they will be," Alvin said.

It struck Mary Paige how rare it was that a man cared more about his charges' comfort than the rich, white people holding wineglasses and eyeing the young men as if, at any moment, they might lurch toward the diamond necklaces and Rolex watches. Here was a man who had his priorities right.

"Please, do." Malcolm gestured toward a table near one of the huge arching windows adjacent to the dance floor. "There is more than enough room. We'll start the silent auction in half an hour and I'll introduce you and your esteemed young men at that time. Until then, enjoy the food and music."

Alvin directed the young men toward the table. One boy who looked older and less intimidated inclined his head and muttered something to the others. They started forward, stoic soldiers among the coiffed, sparkling crowd.

"Nice to meet you folks," Alvin said before moving to join his group.

"Are you insane?" Brennan whispered to his grandfather.

"What do you mean?" Malcolm's silver eyebrows drew together.

"You invited street kids to the benefit? Doesn't that seem ill-timed for a gala intended to raise money for our projects? Everyone looks wary. People don't loosen their pockets when they feel uncomfortable, Grandfather. Though your heart might be in the right place, I think it's a poor decision."

"Do you?" Malcolm's expression became serious with shades of disappointment. "I don't agree. I think these jackasses need to be jolted out of their comfort zones. They need help seeing for themselves what the money we raise eating shrimp cocktail and drinking champagne does for the community in which we *share*."

"By bringing in young men who obviously don't want to be here and forcing them to mingle with Boopie Charles and Trinity Van Pelt? Oil and water don't mix for a reason and there's no need to force either of these groups to be together when they don't wish it."

Mary Paige stared hard at Brennan, wondering why this man intrigued her so. Could his own jackassery be redeemed? She wasn't sure. She had the urge to do something to prove him wrong. To do more than stand there like a cow munching clover, content to dwell within her own little world, accepting Brennan's version of the truth.

Oil and water? The same could be applied to him and her, too.

"Excuse me," she murmured, handing Brennan her clutch as she slipped away from Malcolm and his thick-headed grandson and walked toward the group of boys at the immaculate white-clothed table with the overdone bloodred roses clustered in the center.

"Miss Gentry," Alvin said, setting down a plate filled with meats and cheeses. "Meet my boys."

She smiled, taking in all the young men, some in ill-fitting navy sports coats, others in long-sleeve shirts anchored with striped ties proving they attended a school requiring a uniform. "I would love to meet your young men, but I'm really itching to dance. I'm kind of old-school and can't sit out when they're playing KC and the Sunshine Band."

Alvin smiled and pressed his tie down. "Well, I guess I can let this here food set and give you a spin."

"Oh, no. Sit and eat. I was hoping he would dance with me," she said, pointing to the toughest-looking kid, who wore big diamond earrings in both ears and whose pants hung low in the style favored by gang members and rappers. "Would you?"

The kid inclined his chin, his dark eyes flickering with something that could be interest…or could be plans for choking her for asking him to dance. "All right."

"Great." Mary Paige held out her hand, praying she wouldn't tremble. Inside her stomach rocked because she really didn't want to dance, but she damn sure wasn't going to stand by while everyone treated these kids like a circus act. If Malcolm wanted community, someone had to reach out. Might as well be the woman he'd talked into being his Spirit of Christmas. It was sorta in her contract that she "get down on it."

"I'm Mary Paige, and you are?"

The kid grabbed her hand. "I'm Darian."

He didn't say anything else. Merely moved to the dance floor, where a few of the younger crowd twisted and wove, dangling drinks from their hands as they did their best to do the song justice.

Darian dropped her hand and started moving, his body fluid and graceful. He looked cool as he slid on the floor, hips loose and pants miraculously staying up. Mary Paige channeled her inner Chaka Khan and let her body move. She wasn't a great dancer, but she had moves in her repertoire that said, "I ain't no slacker."

Darian smiled as she lifted her arms above her head, executing a perfect dip with just the right amount of wiggle.

"Yo, you good," he said, appreciation in his eyes for the white lady with surprising rhythm. Okay, she tripped often and sometimes ended up on her rump, but she could shake a leg, butt or shoulder when called upon.

"Try and keep up," she teased as she gave him her back and dipped her shoulders, allowing her backside to shimmy toward the floor before turning and gyrating up to near standing.

"D'yam, that's what I'm talkin' 'bout," Darian said, snapping his fingers, his head bobbing with the beat.

Mary Paige laughed at herself, and for the second time that night she felt good about what she was doing. It wasn't the tilt-a-whirl with Brennan, but it felt satisfying to toss the unspoken rules of social behavior out the window. Darian's velvety laughter washed over the crowd, most of whom allowed themselves to also shed their inhibitions. Seconds later the dance floor was more than half filled with shaking, shimmying and some out-and-out white-boy dancing.

Malcolm and Judy bobbed by, each doing the proverbial shoulder dip and shuffle that lacked in style but proved their enthusiasm. Malcolm gave her a knowing smile she took to mean thank-you.

By the time the song ended and the band had launched into a zydeco-sounding version of "Brick House" several of the other members of the Hope and Grace House were on the floor, partnering with young women in short dresses and older women wearing more matronly dresses replete with sequined jackets and silver hair. All were smiling and the party finally felt festive.

Mary Paige grabbed Darian's hands and pulled him toward Creighton, who had been standing on the fringes watching with affected boredom. "Do me a favor and dance with my friend Creighton."

Creighton looked like she might take off at a full sprint. "Huh?"

"No favor. This chick's fine."

Creighton's mouth snapped closed and a little smile twitched at her lips. She moved off with Darian, who, even though he was a good eight or nine years younger than Creighton, was good-looking and a skilled enough dancer to make a woman feel flattered.

Mary Paige fanned herself and headed toward the bar for a ginger ale. She'd downed the first itty-bitty cup and was working on a refill when Brennan appeared at her side.

"Well, you really are Miss Merry Sunshine, aren't you?"

"Figure your family is paying me to knit rainbows and crap sunshine. Have to earn my pay."

"I see you even made yourself feel better about Creighton, too."

She looked hard at him. "Maybe you should make Creighton feel better about Creighton."

"Maybe you should climb off your high horse and stop casting judgment on others. You don't know anything about me and Creighton." His words were angry and she wondered if she'd ever thought he had any inkling of kindness in his ice-water veins.

"No, I don't. And that's a good thing to remember."

For a moment they were both silent—Mary Paige reaffirming in her mind she needed to stay away from a man who treated people like tools and Brennan thinking… well, she didn't know what he was thinking. And wished she didn't care.

"Your shareholders and moneybag friends aren't looking too uncomfortable now." She jerked her head toward the dance floor, still angry, wanting to rub his nose in his mistaken truth.

His gaze found hers, and in his eyes she saw a flash of admiration before he shuttered his emotion. "Yes, a relief. Look, I hope you realize I have nothing against helping a bunch of kids from the streets, but this isn't the place to drag them in and make them trot around like a ring of ponies."

"You think that's what your grandfather intended? To parade them about and make them feel out of place so he could feel good about himself?" Disbelief shadowed the irritation in her voice. Brennan obviously couldn't see the forest for his big-ass ego and misplaced idea of his grandfather's objective.

"Of course not, but others might view it as such. The goal tonight is to raise money, not change the landscape of the city by forcing people to—"

"Do you hear yourself?" She glared at him. She hadn't felt so angry, so out of her league in understanding a person, in so long. How could he not see getting one's hands dirty was the best way to bring about change? "Writing a check is all well and good, but it's not enough. Changing the world, creating a better place for all God's creatures, only happens when people's hearts are changed."

"You do realize people will never be equal?" Brennan said, his eyes narrowing in thought. "And not just economically, but in beauty, talent and desire. Not everyone can have a Rolls-Royce, a perfect set of teeth or turn a perfect cartwheel."

"You don't get it," she said, jerking a glass of champagne off the tray as a waiter passed by. "I'm not trying to make everyone equal or the same. I'm trying to show compassion, to treat others as I want to be treated, to use my talents and abilities to create a world where everyone gets the chance to better him- or herself. It's not about writing a check or—"

"But even you took the check," he said, taking the empty glass from her hand.

She stared down at his hand, registering she'd downed the entire glass of bubbly midtirade against Brennan's asinine idea of social politics. "Yes, I took the check. I'm a hypocrite, so why don't you go find someone else to bother and leave me alone."

"Fine, but first you might want to take this." He shoved her clutch, which he'd been holding, toward her.

"Why? You afraid one of the kids from Hope and Grace might take off with it?"

"No, but your ex-boyfriend might show up and need a loan," he said with a smart-ass smile.

"Ugh." Mary Paige grabbed the clutch, turned on her heel, tilted a little sideways, but corrected herself before making her way toward the ladies' room. Her blood boiled, even though she knew Brennan's words were partially true. No, she couldn't fix greed and depravity, but she could do her part to respect all the people who inhabited her world—from strangers on the street to the idiot in the tuxedo who was too damn practical, too damn set in his ways, too damn…sexy. Okay, yes, she found Brennan sexy. But that attraction didn't mean she had to agree with him.

Was her attraction what had her so angry?

And she hadn't missed the smallness in his remark about Simon…or the overtone of jealousy.

She pushed through the gleaming oak door and headed to the sink, glad she'd retrieved her clutch. She pulled out her lipstick and stared at it. She didn't really need a touch-up, simply needed to get out of there and grab some space.

"Oh, Mary Paige," Judy said, stepping out from a stall, "glad you're here. I can't reach the closure for this dress."

Darn. Just what she needed. Small talk. "Sure, I'll be glad to help you."

Judy washed her hands and then spun around, presenting her back. "I'm having such a good time. How about you?"

Peachy.

"Yeah, it's nice," she said, hooking the tiny closures at the neck of the dress.

"Brennan likes you, huh?"

"Brennan is an ass."

Judy laughed, turning toward her. "He's quite abrasive at times, but I've often found those brittle soldiers hide the most gentle of hearts."

"Really? Because I'm pretty sure his heart has shriveled into a tiny, dried-up…thing."

"Well, then he needs you more than you know." She paused briefly before saying slowly, "And I think his grandfather feels the same way. I'm inferring he wanted Brennan to escort you to these events so you might teach his grandson something about love."

Mary Paige shrank against the sink. "Love?"

"Oh, I don't mean necessarily in a romantic fashion. More in learning what it means to love one another as Jesus suggested—love your neighbor."

"Oh," Mary Paige said, snapping her clutch closed and tucking an imaginary strand of hair behind her ear. Just hearing the word *love* in association with Brennan had given her shivers, filling her with hope and something that felt like indigestion.

"But you two do look rather nice together, and he watches you constantly."

Another shivery thing did somersaults in her belly. "Probably making sure I don't do something to make the investors and shareholders sew up their wallets."

"I'm positive it's not that."

"Well, I'm not the kind of woman for Brennan Henry," Mary Paige said, before she could think better of it. Why had she admitted she even had hope? Because that's what her decree had sounded like. *I'm not good enough, but I want to be.* And she knew that wasn't the case. It wasn't a good-enough thing, more like a not-suitable thing.

Tilting her head, Judy looked hard at her. "I feel the same way."

"I beg your pardon?"

"Well, I know I'm all trussed up in this dress, but I'm the director of a school for special-needs kids and, up until twenty-six years ago, I was a member of the Dominican Order and known as Sister Mary Hyacinth. I no more suit a dashing millionaire than a donkey suits a knight."

A nun?

Mary Paige studied Judy. "I think he's a billionaire."

Judy's smile faltered. "That much? Well, I know I look incredible in this getup, but Malcolm took me to see his friend Gigi, who pulled a *Makeover Story* on me. The woman even threw my good black sweater set in the trash can!"

Mary Paige laughed. "She threw it away?"

"Yes, and implied I still wore a habit."

Mary Paige pressed her lips together and tried not to laugh again because Judy looked really upset about the sweater, but a giggle slipped out. And that made Judy laugh. They stood in front of the gilded mirror in the bathroom of a pavilion designed to look like an orangery dressed in their finest, giggling like schoolgirls. It was a perfect moment.

"Now I actually feel better about having to deal with Oscar the Grouch out there," Mary Paige said when she finally composed herself.

"Well, I'm glad something good can come from that woman throwing a perfectly good sweater away. Now, let's go out. Malcolm will be starting the silent auction and introducing those boys. You know the one you danced with has a full scholarship to Tulane next year?"

"Darian?"

"See? Can't judge a book by its cover. So maybe it wouldn't hurt to thumb through Brennan's pages."

Mary Paige didn't respond because her mind contemplated those very words…and the words Brennan had tossed at her before she fled to the bathroom. Maybe she should dismount from the high horse and stop making assumptions about *him*.

She didn't have to agree with him to respect he thought differently than she did.

She didn't have to like everything about him to appreciate his good points.

And she didn't have to love him to…

That's where her thoughts betrayed her because she'd been about to finish with *sleep with him*.

Mary Paige had no business going there, did she? No matter how much she wanted to, no matter how tempted she was to throw caution to the wind, he was not for her. She only had to consider the seemingly callous way he'd treated Creighton to know that she didn't stand a chance against him. There would be no way Mary Paige could protect herself from either his charm or being cast aside. And she would be cast aside once his interest in her was done.

So even if she wanted to read those particular naughty pages in the book that was Brennan Henry, it needed to remain *on* the shelf.

CHAPTER THIRTEEN

BRENNAN STOOD IN the shadows as his grandfather spoke about Malcolm's Kids and the new partnership with the Hope and Grace Home for Boys. Usually he stood beside his grandfather when he made these sorts of announcements, as a united front from the Henry family. But tonight he'd ducked away when his grandfather looked for him.

And he didn't know why.

Maybe because Mary Paige had chastised him, made him feel bad about being a realist. Made him feel like an ass for saying what others were thinking. Made him not want to get onstage and smile at Alvin and those boys he'd misjudged. He was thoroughly shamed at his thoughts.

No, he was more like dog shit on the bottom of a shoe.

"Hey," Mary Paige said quietly, sneaking up on him.

He looked at the woman who poked him with sticks and made him see the world around him in a different shade. "Hey."

"I shouldn't have—"

"I'm sorry—"

They both whispered at once before closing their mouths and exchanging glances.

He shook his head. "My fault, Mary Paige. I was wrong."

Her eyes reflected a mixture of pleasure and hope,

and something felt weird in his chest—sort of warm and slightly painful, making him feel as though he couldn't take a good breath.

"But not altogether wrong," she whispered.

A few people turned toward the palm tree where they hid, so he motioned her toward a door that led out to a stone patio. Thankfully, she didn't argue and followed him.

The night air was cool and clear, stars glittering as if they were part of the festivities. A puff of vapor emerged with his sigh as he faced Mary Paige, who looked up at the night sky, her features luminous in the light of the moon.

Incredibly beautiful were the two words on his tongue, but he held them back because they seemed selfish, designed to get him what he wanted, which was this woman beside him.

Mary Paige wasn't like Creighton, or the countless other women who had paraded through his life like accessories, taken only to complement his life.

It was a callous thought.

A mind-bending thought.

That he would see others as mere conveniences rather than people who felt, hoped, loved and had value.

God, he was desolate—an empty shell walking among those he disdained. A perfect misanthrope. A modern-day Scrooge.

Mary Paige hadn't been far off the mark.

"It's beautiful out here," she said, smiling at the sky.

"Yeah," he said, not taking his gaze from her.

"I shouldn't have been so judgmental earlier. You were right to call me out on it. I often forget people have opinions that aren't the same as mine."

He followed her lead to contemplate the world above

them. "Sometimes I wonder if I argue with you on purpose. You're gorgeous when you have that fire in your eyes, all that passion I want to see, to taste in you." He looked at her, wanting to see her reaction to his bold statement.

Mary Paige's eyes widened but she didn't turn his way. "You're saying you do that intentionally? Yanking my pigtails like a little boy wanting my attention. I find that hard to believe of you."

"I don't know why. It's strange really. I guess your ire is better than receiving no part of you at all."

She moved to study him, searching for something he hid far beneath the layers he'd built. "I want to understand you, Brennan, but those words make it difficult. You know I feel more for you than anger."

"Pity?"

"Maybe. A little. I certainly wish for more for you. Honestly, I don't think you're as complicated as I once thought. Quite simply, you're scared."

"Of you?"

She stepped closer to him. It was what he wanted, but suddenly it felt too much. He felt naked and not in a good way. "Perhaps, but the more I know you, the more I see you're afraid of loving…and losing."

He fixed his gaze on a crack in the base of a huge planter holding some shrub—anything to avoid her seeing too deeply into him, seeing through his bluff. "I'm not afraid of anything."

Her touch on his jaw was the brush of angel wings. "Everyone is afraid of something."

"Yeah?" He met her gaze. "You've been analyzing me? Thinking about how I lost a sister and then my parents? About how I blame that on Christmas? On God?"

Her hand stilled. "Do you blame God?"

"You think I haven't been to therapy? Haven't thought about why I am the way I am?" He grabbed her hand and jerked her to him, enjoying the surprise in her eyes, liking the way her mouth opened, the way she didn't shrink back. Mary Paige wasn't afraid of him.

He watched her breathing grow erratic, felt her heart beat hard against his chest…and acknowledged the very essence of her soft body against the unyielding planes of his. This woman fit him, not like a glove, but like a well-cut dinner jacket, not too tight, not too forgiving, but perfect in every way. She balanced him, and for once in his life made him feel hopelessly inadequate.

For this woman, he wanted to be a better man.

Brennan lowered his head and kissed her. Maybe he wanted to silence her or climb back in the driver's seat. Maybe he didn't want her probing the parts of him that still throbbed like a bruised thumb, never easing. Or maybe he wanted to wrap her around him, make her part of him, let her become what he needed more than anything he could give voice to.

Her hands slid into his hair, and she met him, opening her mouth, giving him all she was. In true Mary Paige fashion, the kiss was generous, passionate and enthusiastic.

His blood sang.

Somehow his hands found her delicious ass and he pulled her closer, feeling her meld to him, knowing she could feel his heart, his erection and maybe even his damaged soul.

He broke the kiss, sliding his lips down her throat, catching the vibration of her groan. She tasted so good, salty and sweet, mixed with a heady spiciness, some crazy elixir created to drive men to the edge of lust. One hand slid up her satin dress, while the other held her to him, bending her back so he could graze the top of the beading with his teeth.

"You're making me crazy," she murmured, her hand anchoring his head against the silkiness of her chest.

He reached for her zipper as riotous applause sounded inside.

Mary Paige stiffened, her hand uncurling from his hair. "Oh, my…stop."

He released her and took a step back. "Shh, no one saw."

She pressed a hand to her lips. "But if they had— I mean, I suppose everyone thinks—"

"Come with me," he said, taking her hand.

"Where?"

"Away from here," he said, drawing her into his arms, moving them away from the doors and into the shadows.

"You're talking about something more than leaving here," she said, shivering as he brushed his lips against her collarbone. Mary Paige felt so different in his arms. This was no carefully constructed woman with sharp angles and practiced moves. Mary Paige was like a newly opened bloom.

New, wonderful and fresh.

He brushed his mouth across her jaw, moving to her ear. "Please, come with me. Let me love you, Mary."

Her hands stroked the hair at his neck, making the fire inside him crackle. Then her hand found his jaw and she pushed him away slightly so she could see his eyes.

"I want to go to your place," she said.

He grabbed her hand and started to move toward the entrance.

"But I can't."

Her words stopped him. "Why not?"

The chill of the night air filled the space around him

as Mary Paige stepped away, raising trembling hands to her face, pushing blond strands of hair behind her ears. "Because I'm not like Creighton, or any of the other girls you sleep with. I can't lie to you and say it won't mean something to me. I'm not wired that way…even if I really, really want to be."

He felt stupid, unable to comprehend her words while he stared at the creature who was exactly what he wanted, but who denied him on principle.

"You make it sound like you're some paragon of virtue…and I'm the very devil. Do I need to marry you? Is that what you're saying? You don't sleep around? You don't—" Anger flooded him, which was childish, churlish and any other "ish" he could think of.

Brennan tried to control his emotions, but Mary Paige's words hurt. Her actions stung. He knew she wanted him, but she treated him like something she might get on her hands and have to disinfect to get off. Was he really that horrible of a person? "You make me feel like a bad person all the time."

"I don't mean to."

"But you do." He regarded the same crack in the same planter, hating himself for caring what Mary Paige thought, for opening himself to pain.

"I don't think you're bad, Brennan, but I don't want to be treated as a plaything."

"Really? That's what you think? I'm some martini-swilling bachelor who sticks my Johnson in anything that moves with little regard for a woman's feelings? You have a damn bad opinion of me, don't you?"

"No," she said, her eyes dark in the shadows, but defensive. She didn't care for his words? Fine. He didn't care for being treated like some lothario who jumped from bed to bed with no consequence.

"Doesn't show," he said, turning from her.

"Wanna know the truth, Brennan?"

"Hmm, let's see… I'm a Scrooge. I have no soul. I—"

"I'm afraid of what I feel for you." Her words were soft and brutally honest, and they soothed the injury done to his pride, reined in the sarcasm before he let loose.

"Why? What do you think I'll do to you?"

She shook her head. "Don't you know? Can't you feel how attracted I am to you? Don't you think I know I'm not the kind of girl you date?"

"That's a lot of *don'ts* and *can'ts*." He took her hand. "Look, I'm just a guy trying to figure out what's going on between us, too. I'm not using you."

"But we're so different. Our views on life are so polar opposite I'm surprised I can even see you. And I can feel myself sliding toward you. It's like my house is shifting and I can't get any footing. Soon, I'll slam into love with you. I don't think either of us should flirt with disaster."

Love? The sound of that word on her lips clicked like handcuffs. Sobering. He'd never thought about love. It had always seemed like a word guys used to get what they wanted, and then regretted when they had to spend Saturday at Home Depot looking at pansies rather than watching the Masters. Love had always been a trap, so he couldn't account for that particular feeling.

"Say something," she said.

"I don't know what to say."

So for several seconds they simply looked at one another.

"I want to go home with you, but there will be consequences to making love. You have to understand because I don't want to show up at your office in several weeks only to be sidelined like a naughty puppy, pushed aside because I'm bothersome. If that's what's going to happen, it's better that I go inside and tack on my smiley face."

He didn't know what the hell to say. Is that how she thought he'd treated Creighton? Like a naughty puppy? Because on the surface it might look as such, but underneath there had been stalkerlike overtones to Creighton's pursuit of him. She called several times a day, showed up unannounced and told friends they'd be married by the following year. He'd dated her for only a month before he found the *Bride* magazines. If he'd been callous, it was only as defense against her relentless hounding even after he'd out-and-out told her he wasn't interested in a future with her.

"I can't make promises about anything other than I highly doubt you'd come to my office as anything less than the woman you are—passionate, proud and not likely to be pushed aside."

She tilted her head. "You think I refuse to be pushed aside?"

"Not in my experience."

Mary Paige's lips tipped up. "That's a first. In fact, this whole thing—" she swirled a hand between them "—is atypical for me. I'm usually a marshmallow, a total easy pushover. But somehow I'm not with you."

"And that's good?" He snorted, allowing lightness to emerge between them again. They needed to ease out from beneath the heaviness of the words spoken earlier. They needed a reprieve. "'Cause I really wanted to see what you're wearing beneath that blue satin. Why'd you have to get all staunch and guarded now?"

Her smile looked so much better than her frown. "Oh, you know me, I'm either falling down or denying you sex. I like to keep you off-kilter."

Yeah, Mary Paige had him spinning in circles, and he

didn't know whether he loved that…or might throw up. It was disconcerting.

But he wanted more.

Mary Paige tilted her head. "On the upside, you're bringing out something good in me—my backbone."

"I'd rather see your backbone and what lies below it… along with other choice parts of you." He offered her a flirty smile as the acid in his stomach quieted and a sense of rightness settled in his veins.

Slow down. Don't force. Deep breath.

He exhaled and acknowledged this woman had been sent to move him from the prison in which he'd been enclosed. When he'd climbed off that tilt-a-whirl hours ago, he'd essentially broken through the padlock he'd placed over his soul. Now he emerged blinking and uncertain. Better to go slow. Get his bearings. Where he stood with Mary Paige wasn't comfortable, but it was necessary. She was part of his journey to something more in life.

Didn't know how or if she'd stay with him.

But he needed more.

Mary Paige was his something more.

"So this thing between us. Maybe you're right. Sleeping together might be too much too fast, so let's not rush that," he said.

"Brennan Henry, New Orleans's notorious playboy, agreeing to forego the horizontal mambo?"

"Well, said like that…" he teased, glad to find steady ground again even though he knew the journey ahead would be more of a carnival ride, whipping left then right, looping hard, spinning almost out of control.

"How about dinner this weekend?" she asked.

"Like a date?"

"Like something we're not forced to do together as part of this Henry's Spirit of Christmas thing."

Perhaps seeing Mary Paige on those terms would bring him clarity. "Sunday afternoon?"

"Brunch?"

He nodded. "I'll pick you up."

Mary Paige's smile reminded him of a child on Christmas morning, and he felt something inside the shell of his heart ping. He figured he liked making Mary Paige smile as much as he liked making her angry.

"I haven't been out to brunch in New Orleans."

"Then it will have to be Commander's Palace Jazz Brunch."

She clasped her hands together with a delighted smile, and suddenly he was okay with not relieving her of her gown. He didn't quite understand why going slow with Mary Paige seemed so right, but he was glad they'd tapped the brakes.

He jerked his head toward the double glass doors. "I want to dance with you."

"How did I go from wanting to punch you to wanting to kiss you…almost in the same breath?" She moved toward him.

He picked up her hand, which was cold from the night air. In fact she looked a little chilled all over. He pulled her against him, enjoying the way she fit perfectly beneath his arm. "I wish I knew."

Before they entered the room where the band played "Moon River," Mary Paige stilled him with a hand on his arm. "Brennan?"

"Yeah?" He looked at her, finding her amber eyes soft with apology. "I don't think you're a bad person. I really don't. I think you have some hard corners and a few dings here and there, but none of us is perfect, are we?"

He shook his head.

"I think you have more potential than any man I've ever known."

Their gazes met and in that moment, something sincere bloomed between them. No words for it. A mere knowing between two people who didn't know what the future held, but did know they'd always hold each other in an honest regard.

"Dance with me, Mary Paige?"

She tightened her grip on his hand and nodded.

At that moment, dancing was enough.

MITZI PULLED OUT a glittery, bright orange shrug and waggled it. "Now, this came from a boutique where the chi-chi shop. What do you think?"

"That I'd look like a deranged tangerine," Mary Paige said, sitting on the edge of her bed as Mitzi, wearing a curly red wig reminiscent of *Annie,* pawed through the bundle of clothes she'd brought over to help Mary Paige find the "most awesome" of outfits to wear on her date with Brennan.

"Well, he's rich."

"And thanks to his grandfather, so am I."

Mitzi cocked her head. "Dude. You so are. So why are we going through all this crap when we could be buying you something that would make his jaw drop to the floor?"

Because I have no idea what to do with that kind of cash and just the thought of it terrifies me. "Because I don't like wasting money. Besides, I haven't even deposited the check."

"Are you nuts? You don't have an alarm system. Put it in the bank already." Mitzi flung the orange shrug on top of the stack and put her hands on her hips. "What's the deal?"

Mary Paige wished she knew. It was lame that an accountant, someone who had lifelong history of being so careful with money that it leaned toward frugality, would be so intimidated by the money. She should put it in the bank and trust that she'd figure out how to invest it and disperse it thoughtfully. But something held her back. "I will. Soon. Just have to figure out what I want to do with it."

"I've got an idea," Mitzi said, an unholy gleam entering her eyes. "Let's go shopping, darling."

Mary Paige looked over at her poorly stocked closet and sighed. "I guess we could go to the mall."

"The mall? Uh-uh. We're going to Saks or Henry's and buying something worthy of a millionaire." Mitzi sat beside her and picked up Mary Paige's hand, examining it closely. "You could stand a manicure, too. Oh, and maybe a Brazilian wax. Lots of guys love when you're all bare down there."

"Crap on a cracker, Mitzi." Mary Paige pulled her hand away and reared back against her extra fluffy pillows. "I'm not waxing down there."

"Well, at least give him a landing strip."

Mary Paige threw a cross-stitched throw pillow at her crazy friend.

Mitzi ducked. "Hey, don't get mad because I know what guys like."

"I know what guys like, too," Mary Paige groused, looking around for her tennis shoes.

"What?"

"Girls who know the difference between a holding penalty and an offside penalty. Girls who cook like their mamas. Girls who—"

"Go down on them."

"You are *so* bad." Mary Paige grabbed her favorite fuzzy hoodie and pulled it over her head.

"All part of my charm," her friend said. "Let me grab my boots and wallet, and I'll make sure you knock this man's socks off."

"I don't really want to knock his socks off."

"Of course. His pants, then?"

"I think you're the one who needs some action. Seriously, you're obsessed with sex."

"I know. It's been too damn long." Mitzi's cheerful expression shuttered for a moment, and Mary Paige could feel her friend's deep sorrow.

Since her diagnosis, Mitzi hadn't dated or hung out with her regular friends at the pub down the street. For some reason, though she remained positive about her prognosis, she wouldn't resume the unfettered, carefree life she'd once embraced, electing instead to hang out with Mary Paige and watch movies or help her mother with the catering business. Mary Paige suspected the loss of both her friend's breasts had affected her more than she'd let on, causing her to narrow her world as much as possible. Mary Paige couldn't seem to budge Mitzi from the street where they lived, so she was surprised to have an accomplice for her shopping spree.

"Meet you on the stoop in five," Mary Paige said.

Forty-five minutes later after spending ten whole minutes looking for a parking spot downtown, they browsed through Saks eyeing the sale racks.

"I feel guilty not shopping at Henry's."

"Why?" Mitzi asked, raking through the mismatching pants, sweaters and skirts on the fifty-percent-off rack. "You don't owe them anything."

Mary Paige shrugged as she pulled out a sweater in a

nice shade of cranberry and held it up. "Guess not. But I'm spending their money on a competitor's wares."

"Then spend your money. You have a job, don't you?" Mitzi grabbed the sweater from her hand. "Screw this sale crap. Let's go over there." She pointed to the couture section, where a mannequin wore a tight electric-yellow dress with strategically placed cutouts.

"That's a little much."

"Come on, M.P. Don't you wanna look like a total Betty?"

"You've been watching *Clueless* again, haven't you?"

Mitzi laughed. "Stop changing the subject. You need to look hot. Scorching. Babelicious."

"Why? I've never fit any of those descriptions. I'd rather look like me." Mary Paige sighed, returning the sweater to the rack.

"Okay, enough of the I'm-so-plain-and-simple-I-make-my-own-soap routine. Every girl likes to feel hot. So let's move in that direction," Mitzi said, pointing a finger toward the section that likely contained not a single garment for less than a hundred bucks. "Because this is your opportunity to wash the taste of that bum Simon out of your mouth with a guy who will treat you right."

Mary Paige stopped between a stand of bathing suits and one of business suits. "Who says he'll treat me nice? What's so great about being an afternoon amusement for Brennan Henry?"

"Negativity from Mary Paige Gentry?" Mitzi spread her hands out and looked around as if she didn't know where she was.

"What are you doing?"

"Trying to figure out the parallel universe I got sucked into," her friend joked. "Come on, stop being negative. What's wrong with a little afternoon entertainment?

You're a big girl. Maybe you need to use him and not let it be the other way around. Sex could lead to friendship, friendship could lead to love. Whatever."

Mary Paige ignored the idea of using anyone for anything but she couldn't ignore the last part. Her heart throbbed with the mere thought of a happily ever after with Brennan. It wouldn't happen. There was no alternate universe. Just reality.

"Here's the deal. He has a fascination with me because I'm a regular girl. I have a fascination with him because he's gorgeous and rich and all that our mothers told us to chase after with a leash. But he won't fall in love with me, ask me to have his babies or take me to live in his mansion on the hill."

"New Orleans doesn't really have hills, you know," Mitzi said, shaking her head and rolling her eyes. "Besides, why can't he take you off to have his babies? It's not like he's freakin' royalty and you're some tavern wench. You act like he's special."

"No, but gazillionaires don't fall in love with prostitutes and marry them like they do in movies."

"*Pretty Woman?* Really? That's why you're cutting off your nose to spite your face? Besides you're not a prostitute."

"Okay, maybe basing my reasons on a movie isn't so valid, but if you play with fire, you get burned."

"Or light a torch that will burn forever."

Mary Paige started moving across the polished aisle toward the section with the vibrant yellow dress. "Never knew you were such a romantic under all that acerbic wit and blustery bravado."

"I don't even know what those words mean. I went to public school." Mitzi unwrapped a piece of gum and popped it in her mouth. "And if you're going to play with fire, you might as well look *ah-mazing* doing it."

"But only if you let me buy you something, too."

Mitzi stopped in front of a mannequin wearing a full-length faux fur and looked down at her thin body clad in a bulky jean jacket and leggings. An expression of infinite sadness flitted across her face before she said, "In the children's section?"

"If you'd wear the prosthetics, no one would know." Mary Paige slid her arm through Mitzi's then tucked a red curl behind her friend's ear.

Mitzi swatted her hand away. "I know."

"Mitz, lots of women have breast cancer and have surgery like yours. Why don't you go to the support group and talk—"

"Stop trying to fix me. I'm trying to fix you," Mitzi growled, her eyes almost feral.

So it was too early for her friend to greet the reality of life without that part of herself. "Fine, but I'm buying you something. At least a manicure."

"Deal. We need to go to the spa anyway." Mitzi turned toward the section where Mary Paige would drop a lot of coin. No doubt about it.

Mary Paige could do a new dress, but she was absolutely not getting any unmentionable areas waxed. A gal had to draw a line somewhere…and it wouldn't be a landing strip.

CHAPTER FOURTEEN

MALCOLM ROLLED OVER and looked at Judy sleeping in the morning light that streamed through the sheer fabric hanging in the oversize windows of his room. She looked like an angel, and his heart swelled with love.

Last night had been the best night of his life. He'd laughed, loved and fallen hard for the small woman with the huge heart. It felt incredible.

Why had he waited so long to ask her out? Why had he waited so long to fall in love again?

He knew that answer.

He'd made MBH Industries his life, ignoring anyone with a heartbeat, including his only grandson.

"Morning," Judy whispered, her lovely gaze finding his, caressing him with the softest of looks.

"Morning, beautiful." He lifted a strand of brown hair from the pristine whiteness of the down pillow.

Judy rolled over and stretched, her shoulders bare, her face relaxed. "I can't believe I slept so late."

"It's not late. Only eight-thirty."

"Late for me." She glanced down at her body covered by the sheet. "I can't believe I slept naked."

Malcolm laughed and tugged the sheet down so that one of her small breasts was exposed. "Let me see."

"Malcolm Henry," she shrieked, jerking the sheet to her chin, but laughing. "Oh, no. It's morning."

Her gaze found his, and in it he saw the tiniest flicker of regret. Not something he wanted to see, not when the night before he'd found such beauty in her arms. There had been nothing tawdry about the way they'd loved each other. "And why?"

"Because," she said, staring up at the ceiling. "Because."

"Marry me," he said.

Judy jerked her head toward him, her eyes growing wide. "What?"

"Marry me, Judy," he said again, angling his body toward her. "I know this isn't moonlight, roses and a big engagement ring, but it's all I've thought about over the past few days. I want you beside me every day and every night."

"You don't have to marry me just because we slept together," she said, sitting up but still clutching at the sheet like it was a life preserver.

"I'm not. Why would I want to marry you because we had the most amazing sex last night?"

"Malcolm," she said, her cheeks blooming with color. "You say the most outrageous things."

"But true." He pulled her into his arms and kissed her cheek before nuzzling his nose into hair that smelled of lilacs, or what he thought were lilacs. He'd never been good with flowers. "Marry me."

"Are you serious?"

"I'd say as a heart attack, but that's flirting with danger." He smiled against her hair. "Thing is, I love you and I want you beside me for as long as I have left on this earth. You make me happy and make me want to be a better man. If that isn't a recipe for marriage I don't know what is…unless you don't feel the same?" He eased away and studied her.

Her eyes were soft, glistening with unshed tears. "I never thought I'd fall in love."

Leaning forward he caught her declaration with a kiss. "But…?"

"I left the order, not because I wanted to marry, but because I knew I'd made a huge commitment when I was too young. Mother Regina Agnes sensed this in me after many years and when she approached me about my faith and purpose, I lashed out because I was scared to be out in the world without my family of faith around me.

"But I did it. For the past few decades I've created a new family and, every evening, I ignored the loneliness that beset me. The first time I met you an excitement I'd never felt before filled me. I fell in love with you when you played basketball with the boys, letting Perry win when it became obvious he needed to win. I've never felt the way I feel when I'm with you."

He embraced her. "Oh, sweet woman, if you will stay with me forever, I'll be the happiest, most fulfilled man on the face of this earth. Say you will be my bride. Tell me this will last forever."

She looked him in the eyes, and kissed him before saying, "I love you, Malcolm Henry, and I will stay with you and love you as long as you will have me."

He smiled and felt his entire body flood with sheer joy.

Judy laughed and fell back onto the plush softness of his bed. "I can't believe this."

He shed the robe he'd tugged on earlier and slipped beneath the covers. "I can think of a good way to celebrate."

Judy giggled but held out her arms. "You've corrupted me, Malcolm."

"You've saved me, angel." He was so glad he'd taken

a leap of faith and pursued sweet Judy Poche, so appreciative that he'd been given a second chance to find happiness.

Finally, he'd found the love he'd lost so many years ago. His first love was no longer an option, but his last love lay in his arms, looking adoringly into his eyes, sliding her hands over shoulders once broad, loving him for the man he was.

Not the man he'd been.

Blessings so great for a man not deserving.

But at that moment, he didn't care. He only loved.

BRENNAN PARKED HIS Harley-Davidson at the curb to pick up Mary Paige. Rarely did he take the bike, but since they would spend the afternoon in the French Quarter, it seemed like good choice for weaving around carriages and taxis. Besides, he wanted Mary Paige straddling the hog with her arms around him.

It would be like prolonged foreplay.

Mary Paige emerged from her house wearing a tight pair of pants, some beautiful brown boots that stretched over her knees and a sweater the color of tobacco that fell below her hips. Her blond hair swung jauntily and, at that moment, Brennan felt a wave of longing so intense he had to adjust himself on the seat that was vibrating from the still-running engine.

"A bike?" she called over the noise.

He gave her a wolf's smile. "If you don't want to ride on it, we can take your car."

"No way. I love riding on a motorcycle." She took the helmet hc offered her, shoved it on her head and strapped the chin strap. Then she swung one of those long delicious legs over the back of the bike and slid into place, her thighs clasping his butt and her arms linking across his stomach.

He silently begged her to keep her arms high so she didn't feel his erection.

Because, damn, she'd made him rise to attention with her touch. Her smell. Her essence.

He hit the throttle and sped away, eating up the pavement, dragging his focus to the road before him and away from the incredible feeling of Mary Paige clinging to him. He wove through the narrow streets bordering midtown, heading toward the heart of the city. The day was moderately cool but sunny, and caused Mary Paige to cuddle tight to him, which was another nice result of taking the bike.

Minutes later, he pulled up at his town house off Conti in the center of the bustling French Quarter—aka Vieux Carré. Of course, it didn't really look like a town house because the whole first floor was occupied by a daiquiri shop.

"We're getting drinks already?" Mary Paige asked climbing off the bike, removing her helmet and shaking her hair.

"You want one?"

"No."

He pointed above the already-hopping business toward the gray stucco walls from which a small black wrought-iron balcony extended. "My place is up there."

Her eyes followed the lines up the several-storied town house. "I guess I never thought about people living above all these businesses. Doesn't the noise bother you?"

He tucked his helmet under his arm. "Nah, the contractor put in state-of-the-art soundproofing. Now, let me toss these helmets inside and then we'll get going."

She handed him the helmet and turned a full circle, looking at the world passing by on the street. "I'd love to see your place."

"Maybe later," he said, sliding a glance her way. Her cheeks looked pink and she didn't make eye contact. A good sign? Not a good sign?

But then she caught his eye as he unlocked the wrought-iron door not five feet from the entrance to the shop. "If you're lucky."

Suddenly, he wanted to be lucky. So very lucky.

After stashing the helmets in the narrow foyer, he re-locked the door and gestured down Conti.

"I thought we were going to Commander's Palace."

"If it's okay, I thought we'd do brunch at the Court of Two Sisters. I have a friend who's playing in the jazz quartet. Then maybe Commander's later for dinner?"

She nodded and they set off toward Royal Street, stopping so Mary Paige could admire the pricey antiques displayed in the storefronts. On Rue Royal all the antiques seemed overdone baroques, a bit like the city itself—lazy indifference to the rest of the world, lavish in its excess and not the least bit apologetic for it. Peppered throughout the antique joints were art galleries and the occasional specialty shop. It took longer than usual to walk the few blocks to Two Sisters, but Brennan didn't mind. He enjoyed seeing Mary Paige admire the art, enjoyed seeing his city through her eyes.

Ten minutes after she'd exclaimed, "We have to come back here," regarding a kitchen specialty shop, they were seated near the fountain in the lush courtyard of a restaurant that had been serving jazz brunch on Sundays for as long as Brennan could remember.

A waiter with a broad smile, a tidy white suit and a fondness for teasing brought them mimosas and invited them to help themselves at the buffet tables inside the restaurant.

As they entered the area teeming with diners heaping crawfish and other Louisiana specialties on their plates, he said, "Maybe we should have gone somewhere quieter."

"No way." Mary Paige grabbed a plate then headed toward the omelet station. "I love a good buffet," she said over her shoulder.

Brennan didn't so much, but he made do with the turtle and sherry soup and a cold salad plate. When he reached the table, Mary Paige sat with three dishes heaped with food.

She made a face. "It all looked so good."

"It is good. I haven't been here in years. My mother always loved brunch here. Said the lights above the awning, the sound of the fountain splashing and a rendition of 'Do You Know What it Means to Miss New Orleans' in the background made her happy she met my father and moved to New Orleans."

Mary Paige took a bite of her omelet and sighed. "Yum. So you're mother wasn't from New Orleans?"

"She was from Baton Rouge and met Dad at a game. He played ball for Louisiana State."

"Football?"

"Baseball. He even played some minor-league ball for a few years. Before my mom insisted he come home to help Grandfather with the company. But Dad never gave up on baseball. He was one of the guys who worked to bring a Triple A team to the city. He loved baseball as much as he loved my mother. Or that's what she said."

"This almost feels normal," she said, taking a bite of a cold pasta salad with olives.

"Why wouldn't it be normal?"

Her brown eyes narrowed. "Because…just because, I guess."

"Well, I *am* on my best behavior. Haven't rolled my eyes or kicked a homeless person all day. I even hummed along with a Christmas carol while I showered."

"Wow, that could be, like, a Christmas miracle."

"I wouldn't go that far," he said, taking another bite of soup and wondering if the bread pudding was as good as he remembered. Perhaps today was a day of total indulgence. Gym be damned.

"What I meant is you're intentionally being agreeable and it feels—"

"Scary?"

She frowned. "No, it feels nice."

"Well, I'm not the devil incarnate. I am capable of more than holing myself up to count all my gold and plot world domination."

"Oh, you mean you have a heart?" she teased, scooping a spoonful of soup from his bowl and popping it in her mouth.

"Who said you could have some of my soup?"

Her mouth fell open a little and she blinked twice. "Oh, I can't believe I did that. I'm so sorry."

Smiling, he shook his head. "I was teasing."

"But I didn't realize I'd even done it. That's so bizarre."

He wasn't sure anyone had ever casually taken a bite off his plate before, but it didn't bother him for some reason. It felt comfortable, as if it were something they'd done a dozen times. Seated at a table, teasing one another and scarfing samples off one another's plate.

He reached over and scooped some of the pasta with the olives and salami. "There. We're even."

Mary Paige laughed and turned as the jazz quartet entered the courtyard, playing a Dixieland rag that made diners spontaneously tap their feet. He caught Jonathan Posey's eye, a guy he'd gone to Newman with many moons ago, and gave him a wave. Jonathan hadn't been in his crowd per se, but Brennan had always liked the kid who played trombone and drew funny caricatures of all their teachers.

Brennan and Mary Paige leisurely finished their meal, interspersed with delicious mimosas, working up a nice buzz and enjoying the experience of dining with live music. He even managed to clap along once, which seemed to please the woman across from him. Her whole face was as readable as the eye-exam chart.… Well, for someone with twenty-twenty vision.

By the time he'd paid the bill—over her protests, of course—he'd fallen half in love with Mary Paige…and didn't really care that he headed in a direction he'd never wanted, needed or believed in.

Maybe it *was* a Christmas miracle.

"Don't talk to the guys who tell you they can guess where you bought your shoes. It's a scam," Brennan told Mary Paige as they walked past Jackson Brewery toward Woldenberg Park, which skirted the Mississippi River.

"How is it a scam?" She was stuffed to the point of being uncomfortable. The food had been so delicious she'd kept eating…and eating. Good thing they were walking. Maybe she'd be able to work some of those calories off and manage to stay out of the Spanx.

"Just trust me," Brennan said, taking her hand and directing her toward the winding walk that paralleled the muddy churning waters of the Mississippi yards away. Big ships lined the banks.

Mary Paige was fascinated with the cruise ships, craning her neck to look at them as she and Brennan passed. She'd always wanted to take a cruise, but growing up there'd never been money or time for a vacation.

Of course, there was that check in her jewelry box. If she cashed it, there would be nothing stopping her from sailing whenever and wherever she wanted. So why didn't she? She'd worked really hard through school and on her job—didn't that entitle her to a little self-indulgence?

Thoughts of the check and how that huge sum of money would change her life felt uncomfortable—worse than the Spanx—so she shied away from them.

A young guy headed their way, his intent obvious—to work a tourist out of a few bucks. But Brennan's stern frown had the youth swerving around them, searching behind them for some other sucker to hoodwink.

"Well, you didn't kick a homeless person, but you did shoot that kid with your eyes."

Brennan looked at her. "What?"

"He didn't try to guess our shoe size because you scared him."

"So you would have taken the bait? Parted with some money?"

She shrugged. "What would it hurt?"

"You really are the strangest woman I've ever met."

His words made her stiffen because she'd been called strange too many times to name, and that moniker had never sat well with her. "I'm not strange. Just different."

"Definitely different. But in a good way."

"My mother's words," she muttered.

"Tell me about your family, about the place you grew up," he said suddenly.

They paused to look out over the river, spanned by the Crescent City Connection Bridge. A boat's horn sounded and people passed them carrying shopping bags.

"Nothing spectacular. My mother never married because she never wanted to. Her parents spent their entire lives chained to one another, hating one another until, in a drunken rage, my grandfather drove off a bridge and killed both himself and my grandmother. My mother, luckily, was home with a babysitter. Gave her a bad impression of love and marriage. And that didn't get better being raised by a maiden aunt—we called her Granny Wyatt and she was lovely, but definitely not a fan of marriage.

"When Mom turned seventeen, she abandoned the family farm to run off to California with a guy who played bass in a crappy band. Later she came back pregnant with me, and single-handedly started an organic farm ten years before people cared anything about eating naturally or before it was financially feasible. Mom got pregnant with my brother, Caleb, when I was seven, and I really don't know how."

Brennan smirked.

"Well, I know *how.* What I meant is I don't know how she found the time and with whom. To this day she's never admitted to who his father is. She's extremely stubborn, proud and could care a flying fig whether anyone likes her. She's who she is, and very proud that she didn't need a man for all she accomplished. Except for the actual procreation, I guess."

"And you call that uninteresting?"

"I didn't say uninteresting. I said nothing spectacular."

"Right." The bright sun had him pulling a pair of Ray-Ban Aviators from his pocket. When he put them on, she was immediately reminded of Tom Cruise in all those '80s movies. In fact, there was something Tom Cruise-ish about Brennan—dark hair, sexy grin and together look... not to mention he was a control freak. He'd probably look good skidding across the floor in his underwear, too.

The sounds of traditional Christmas hymns grew louder as they approached a pavilion nestled in between the benches and sculptures of the park. As they rounded the corner, they saw a choir wearing robes and holding hymnals gathered beneath the shelter.

"Oh, wow," she said, moving in time to "The Little Drummer Boy."

"Oh, no," Brennan breathed, but allowed her to tug him behind her. "Christmas music."

"Don't even say it."

His mouth had started to form the *B* sound and he snapped it closed and smiled. "Okay. Best behavior today."

Mary Paige moved closer to the mixed crowd. Likely they were from a nearby church, bringing fellowship and fun to the December afternoon...an early Christmas present.

Brennan tugged her hand and jerked his head toward an empty bench to their left, beneath a small nearly bare tree.

She followed him to the bench, sitting then leaning back as he curled an arm around her shoulders. Something about the simplicity of the carol, the wind off the river blowing her bangs into her eyes and the warmth of a man holding her created such peace within her. It didn't seem to matter right now how different she and Brennan were in their philosophies or that their future was unknown. It merely felt good to spend the afternoon with no agenda, no constraints and no expectations.

Of course there was one niggle of an expectation inside her she didn't want to give credence to—the expectation of a kiss, of passion, of seeing what color sheets Brennan had on his bed.

"Why did you decide on accounting?" Brennan asked, rubbing her shoulder through the hand-knitted angora wool, unintentionally stirring moths around the flame of desire igniting in her belly. She tried to ignore the way the fluttering caused warmth to pool in her pelvis and instead concentrated on his question.

"Numbers make sense. They're concrete, finite and there's always a solution. My life with my mother and my younger brother felt like walking in a minefield. Nothing in my house went smoothly despite my mother's intentions. There were always broken dishwashers, burst pipes, new medications for Caleb and bills left unpaid. Drama, drama, drama. But with numbers, everything works, you know?"

"Why did your brother take medication? Is he sick?"

"Oh, no. Not really. He has cerebral palsy and is confined to a wheelchair, which sometimes lends itself to other problems. But mostly he's healthy."

Brennan studied her as the choir hit a stirring chorus, soft and plaintive in the bustle of the sunny afternoon, almost intentionally juxtaposed. She could tell he didn't know what to say to her declaration, so she beat him to it. "Caleb's normal in his mental capacity, and my mother has involved herself in creating a charter school for challenged students like Caleb. My brother has a nice future laid before him."

"And you?"

What about her? She leaned forward, propping her

elbows on her knees, stroking the supple leather of the boots she was embarrassed to have bought. "I'm taking my CPA exam in a few months and will hopefully have an offer from Ivan to become part of his firm, maybe even his partner one day."

"So you want to stay in the city?"

"I never liked living on a farm much. My mother took comfort in it, probably because she'd had an adventurous life in California, living on the road with various musicians."

He arched an eyebrow, and she shrugged. "Okay, she was a groupie, but life had harder corners than she expected. After a bad breakup with a boyfriend she refuses to talk about, she came back to Louisiana to lick her wounds and heal from the skinned knees she'd gained playing fast and loose with men who played faster and looser. She loves living in the middle of nowhere, milking cows and goats, making cheese and growing zucchinis, and I'm happy she's good with where she is. But I never wanted that life for myself."

"You wanted...?"

"To live in a city full of interesting people, to have a job that supported me and that I could take pride in, to have something more to contemplate than the grass and sky, as nice as they are at times. I wanted to do things, you know?"

He nodded. "Idealistic."

"Yeah, a little. Mushy and easily persuaded to rescue people, but rooted in enough reality to know not all dreams are realized or achieved. But there *is* something worthwhile in the trying."

For a moment, they were silent.

Brennan placed a hand on the back of her head then slid it down to her neck, gripping it in the manner of a coach to a player, but his touch was soft. When she turned his eyes were admiring. "I've never met someone like you before."

"I've never met anyone like you, either. Not many guys in Crosshatch who drive Maseratis and live in town houses above daiquiri shops. More like John Deere and small farmhouses. Even the guys I dated in college were more ramen noodle than filet mignon."

Brennan sighed, releasing her. "It's an Aston Martin, by the way, and I don't see myself the way you do. I guess I grew up accustomed to a certain way of life without thinking too much about it, though I suppose I like some luxuries well enough—especially the car." He smiled and the devil appeared in his eyes. She decided she liked that little devil. Liked seeing the pleasure he took in all things from the bread pudding he'd eaten at brunch to the machine he drove.

"I noticed you like that car."

"Anyone would like that car," he said, clapping politely as the choir finished the song. After the choir started a new song, he tugged her into the curve of his arm. "You know money isn't the most important thing to me, don't you?"

"Yeah. Control is."

He stiffened. "I was actually thinking more along the lines of personal achievement or security."

Mary Paige idly stroked his thigh, enjoying that she could take the intimacy without waiting for him to make a similar gesture, reveling in his body tightening, this time not in indignation. "Most people want control of their lives. Even me. A job, a title and a nest egg in the bank make me feel as if I'm in the driver's seat, as if I can handle the fall better when it happens. Opening up to others, trusting them though they might deceive, hurt or disappoint takes a good deal of courage."

"So you're braver than me?"

Was she? She trusted people easily. Maybe too easily. But she was also afraid of loving Brennan. Simon seemed a veritable pussycat compared to the heir to the Henry throne, and she'd eaten a lot of Ben & Jerry's after Simon and she had split. What would loving and losing Brennan do to her? She wasn't sure there was enough Zumba offered to cover that. "In some ways, but in others, I'm just as scared."

He stilled her hand. "I don't like being painted as scared."

"Who does?" she asked, not looking at him, not wanting to show him she was as fearful as he. She didn't want to love a man who, while he may not kick a homeless person, dismissed them all the same. She didn't want to love a man who hated Christmas because it reminded him of pain. She didn't want to love a man who thought so much about the bottom line, he forgot about the people who contributed to that bottom line. But she knew she was already halfway there.

She could stop now and go home, tucking her tail and hiding in the shadows because it was safe there, but that would make her less than who she needed to be.

Mary Paige Gentry hadn't been raised to duck her chin and feel unworthy of any man…and she hadn't spent the past few years of her life reinventing herself merely to run away at the thought of getting hurt.

"I'm not as strong as I'd like to be," she said, turning her hand over so that she clasped his. "But I don't want to shut the door on you."

The words of "Silent Night" washed over them. She

looked at him, at those gray eyes no longer immeasurable, but clear with intent.

"Good, because I'm really trying to be a man worthy of you."

"That's ridiculous. I am exactly what you said last night. Just a girl. Not a do-gooder or Merry Sunshine or the Spirit of Christmas any more than you're just a billionaire playboy who sneers at Santa Claus. We're both people."

A man with a box holding small white candles approached and offered them each one. At first she thought Brennan might wave him off, but he surprised her by taking the candle and saying, "Merry Christmas."

The man responded in kind and moved on to a clump of older women holding oversize shopping bags.

"Wow," Mary Paige breathed. "You *are* trying to be good."

His response was to stand and offer a hand, which she accepted. He hauled her to her feet, winding an arm around her as if he'd done it many times before.

And at that moment, they didn't need any more words.

Being in the moment and listening to the sacred strains offered by the choir was enough.

AFTER SPENDING THE AFTERNOON doing touristy stuff he'd absolutely never done before in all his time of living in New Orleans, Brennan could only desire two things—a good meal and Mary Paige in his arms.

"Are you sure you don't want to go to Commander's?" he asked as Mary Paige poked through the offerings on one of the tables in the French Market. She held up a bracelet and the woman across the table immediately barked, "Twenty dollars."

Mary Paige shook her head and set down the bracelet.

"Fifteen?" the woman asked, crossing her arms as if she were insulted to have to come down in price.

"I'll give you ten," Mary Paige said, looking the woman in the eye.

The vendor, who wore a full-length trench coat and had hair dyed the color of coal, sighed. "Deal."

Money exchanged hands and Mary Paige tucked the treasure in her bag. "This will be perfect for Lars's wife, Pris."

"Who's Lars?"

"The man who helps my mom with the farm. He's nearly seventy years old, but doesn't act it. He refuses to slow down, though Pris fusses constantly about old men acting like wet-eared pups."

Lars and Pris. Tractors and goat cheese. Wheelchair-bound brothers and former groupie mothers. The life Mary Paige had led certainly didn't sound as boring as she'd made it out.

"Reminds me of my grandfather chasing after Judy. Thinks he's in his twenties the way he's been acting."

Mary Paige passed a booth filled with leather bags and coin purses and stopped at one selling cashmere wool scarves. "She seems to make him truly happy. I don't know him well, but you can't miss that gleam in his eye."

Her hand stilled a moment as she lifted her gaze, focusing on something beyond the edge of the marketplace. For several seconds she was silent, and he wondered why the spark in Malcolm's eye demanded contemplation.

"What?" he asked.

She blinked and jerked her gaze back to him, her brown eyes soft like chocolate chips in the cookies his mother used to make. "Nothing."

"So about dinner?"

Mary Paige tilted her head. "You know what sounds good?"

"What?"

"Takeout and a tour of your town house."

And with that decree, Brennan knew the night would likely be better than the afternoon he'd spent with Mary Paige.

CHAPTER FIFTEEN

Mary Paige looked around the gorgeous subway-tiled modern kitchen and sighed. "This is truly beautiful."

"Thanks. I actually did some of it myself," Brennan said, pouring pinot noir into a wineglass and handing it to her.

She wasn't much for red wine, but her nerves were humming so she took a sip. "Really? What parts?"

He smoothed a hand across the wood of the center island. "This wood was reclaimed from an old ship that went down in the Mississippi River. I got it at a salvage yard and worked with a carpenter to get the right patina."

"It's beautiful." Cripes. She couldn't stand there like mud on a fence post saying everything was "beautiful," but her tongue felt stuck to the bottom of her mouth. She took another sip of wine, hoping it would help her relax.

After all, she didn't have to have sex with him.

"And when the tile guy came, he showed me how to set the tiles in here, so I did a little home improvement myself and installed the mosaic tiles in my bathroom before the stucco guy came and put in the plaster."

"I'm impressed. You like to get your hands dirty."

"Surprised?"

"What?"

"It's just you have this image of me you won't let go. Rich playboy waited on hand and foot."

"I don't think you're waited on hand and foot. I can

see how much your job means to you, how hard you work at your office." She stopped because she really hadn't seen him working—he'd only accompanied her to all the events lined up for the Spirit of Christmas promotion, so she was making a logical assumption based on the files he had stacked on the coffee table and the way he'd conducted himself thus far. Here was a man who put elbow grease into what he tackled.

He took a sip of wine. "I do work hard…and I always liked hands-on projects even as a small child."

She smiled. "I built boxes for the wood ducks on the river, and I volunteer every fall for a local church who build wheelchair ramps. We always need good carpenters."

"And I can weld. Took a welding class when I was in high school. I told grandfather I was out studying."

"Really?"

"I thought I wanted to be a sculpture artist for a while. It was a phase." He set the glass down and gestured toward the living area. "Want to see the rest of the place?"

She took another gulp. "Sure."

They walked slowly through the town house, Brennan pointing out the heart-of-pine floors original to the building and the clever way he'd hidden his state-of-the-art TV and components in a console. Everything was tastefully decorated and screamed expensive, sophisticated and put-me-in-a-magazine.

Brennan stopped in front of the open door of the master bedroom. "We don't have to have sex."

"What?" she squeaked, nearly sloshing wine onto the pale gray carpet.

"You're just making me feel creepy," he said, taking the glass from her hand, making sure the wine steadied, before handing it back to her.

"I don't— What I mean is, I didn't realize I was acting nervous."

"But you are." Brennan pointed toward the huge bed centered in the room. "I'm not going to pounce on you as soon as we get in there, you know. I respect the decision to take this slowly, to find our footing before jumping into bed."

"Well, what if I want to jump into bed?" Her heart felt like it was galloping in the Kentucky Derby and her palms were sweaty.

Brennan smiled. "I'm not unopposed."

She laughed. "Know what I'm tired of?"

"No."

She set her wineglass on a built-in shelf in the small hallway. "I'm tired of talking."

"Oh, yeah?"

"Yeah." She lifted herself slightly and placed her lips right on the cleft in his chin.

"You missed," he breathed.

She tilted her head back and shook her head. "Guess I need practice."

This time she kissed him—full-on, sexy, wet kissing. It didn't last long, but it got her point across. This wasn't about a tour of his house. This was about a tour of…other things.

"I'm willing to be your dummy. For, you know, practicing the whole kissing thing."

Mary Paige couldn't believe how bold she was being, but Brennan seemed to appreciate it. And something about the way he looked at her with those lips tilted up and pleasure pooling in his eyes emboldened her further.

"Well, should we get it on now or wait until after dinner?"

He opened his mouth to respond but the doorbell sounded. "Dinner."

"Okay, so dinner first?"

"No, I meant that's dinner at the door," he said, pulling away from her and walking toward the living room. "By the way, I like cold Chinese food."

She grabbed her liquid courage and followed him into the living room, standing on the jute rug as she admired the backside he presented on the way to the door. "I'm good with cold Chinese food, too."

When he opened the door, a frazzled-looking delivery girl stood there, balancing two white bags from someplace called Moon Wok. "Really?"

"No," she said, sinking onto the leather sofa and contemplating the huge cypress stump that had been converted into a coffee table. Clever idea…for the furniture and the name of the Chinese place.

She could hear the laughter in Brennan's voice as he paid the delivery person and something in his tone made her feel nearly content in the midst of anxiety over having sex.

Brennan dumped the take-out boxes on the coffee table, disappeared and came back holding the glass he'd left in the kitchen. "I'm guessing you want your hot food right now."

"Maybe."

He sank onto the couch and grabbed a control. After he pushed a gazillion buttons the sound of the clarinet filled the room. "Coltrane," he said.

"Oh."

"You like jazz?"

"Not really, but it sounds nice."

"Coltrane's my seduction music," he said with a grin,

before opening the first steaming tak-out carton. "Like on *Jerry Maguire*."

"It does sound sort of sexy," she said, eyeing the offerings. "So food first?"

Brennan turned to her. "You're acting like having sex is akin to a doctor's appointment. So why don't we enjoy the wine, the music and the lo mein then see what happens?"

"Because then I'll have major garlic breath," she said.

"But we both will, so who cares?"

He was right. She was treating this like some have-to thing and she didn't have to do anything. Brennan may have been the stereotypical alpha male with a reported Don Juan reputation, but he was also a gentleman. He knew she wanted him. And she was certain the feeling was mutual if that bike ride earlier had been any indicator. So why sweat it?

"Lo mein?" he said, holding out a container.

She looked at it. "My stomach feels too nervous."

Brennan sat the carton on the coffee table before turning to her. "Okay, let's do this already."

Her eyes widened. "Sex? Right here?"

He started unbuttoning his shirt. "You're not eating until we get it on, so no sense in waiting, right?"

Laughing, she grabbed his hands. "Stop. Wait."

He tugged her hands, hauling her neatly into his lap. "I like cold Chinese food, remember?"

His hands moved to her waist, slipping beneath her sweater to her naked back, stroking up and down as his mouth found the pulse in her neck. She sighed. "Okay, I guess."

"Mmm," he said, doing some spectacular kissing of the sensitive flesh of her throat as his hands traveled up farther, unhooking her bra with one flick.

"Wow, you're good," she said, angling her neck so he had better access.

Brennan jerked his head up and finished unbuttoning his shirt. "Okay, your turn."

She laughed. "Really?"

"I'm not seducing you. You're seducing me."

"No, I'm not," she said, wondering what his game was, but chuckling because she really didn't care. Brennan the Scrooge was fun in the sack...ahem, the couch.

"Standing outside my bedroom you took charge, and I've decided I like a bossy Mary Paige."

"I was?" She played along, touching the skin he revealed. His belly was flat, but not bodybuilder, six-pack flat, just nice-and-yummy flat. "Yeah, I was, but I don't have to be."

He pulled her on top of him and suddenly it was no longer light, flirty and fun. It was hot. Really hot.

"Oh, wow," she breathed as his hands caught her bottom, moving her against him as his erection found a home right where it belonged. Her mouth found his and she did her best to seduce him with her mouth, with the hands she slid into his hair, even as she enjoyed the warm, bare chest beneath her, sprinkled with dark hair, so masculine, so hard.

His hands traveled from her bottom and he tugged the sweater up. She felt air on her naked back and shivered, but she wasn't certain if it was from the exposure or the magic this man performed on her. Quickly, she tore her mouth from his and helped him remove her sweater and bra.

"Ah, sweet, sweet," he murmured, rolling her over so his hands cupped her breasts. She'd always wished she'd been bigger on top than on bottom, but at that moment, Brennan made her feel like the sexiest woman on the planet. His thumbs flicked over the nipples that had puckered and she sighed.

"Good?" he asked, lowering his head to suck one into his mouth.

"Ah," she said, lifting her hips, grinding them against his erection as she held his head in place. His mouth was so hot, felt so damn good on her. Liquid fire spilled into her belly, coating her with a need so intense, she lost herself in the sheer deluge. "Oh, oh, oh."

He smiled against her breast as he slid one hand to the waistband of her jean leggings. "My thoughts exactly."

Then he shifted his attention to her other breast as his hand slid beneath her leggings, past her new flirty panties to cup her sex.

His touch set her on fire. Like seriously over the edge of sanity. She pushed him back a little and he lifted his head and looked at her. "Too much?"

Shaking her head, she said, "Not enough."

One finger moved, parting her. "Oh, dear...ah. You're not playing around."

"Oh, I am, Mary Paige. I'm definitely playing," he murmured, continuing his assault, diving in to capture the nipple he'd abandoned.

Mary Paige stroked his head, reveling in the feel of him loving her. Her hips moved against his hand and she could feel an orgasm gathering. That was how hot she was for this man. But she didn't want to go so quickly. She wanted to savor the languidness of exploring each other for the first time, so she stilled his hand with her own.

"Thought I was in charge," she said when he lifted his head.

Those gray eyes were as she'd envisioned when making love with Brennan—dilated with passion, crackling with intensity.

His eyes alone made her shiver.

Or maybe it was his hand, which refused to leave its place between her legs.

"Yeah?"

"Can we go to your room? I want to see you naked. I've had fantasies."

"Oh, really?"

"Really," she said, recalling her naughty imaginings then forgetting momentarily as he did something marvelous with his hand. "Oh, dear Bessie, I've got to take these pants off so you have better access."

Brennan chuckled. "You are something else, Mary Paige Gentry. And, guess what?"

"What?"

"I've had my own fantasies," he said, dropping a kiss onto her shoulder. "Ever been tied up before?"

She shook her head.

The look he gave her she felt all the way to her freshly painted toenails and it made her laugh with anticipation.

Yeah, having sex with Scrooge was going to be lots of fun.

TEN MINUTES LATER, they sprawled naked on Brennan's bed. All the pillows had been tossed on the floor and there hadn't been time to tie anyone up or to leisurely explore the boundaries of desire. Once they'd hit the bed and managed to get her stubborn boots off, passion had ignited, inflamed and exploded. Kinda fast.

"Whoa," Mary Paige said, panting as she stared at his ceiling fan, which wasn't moving.

He picked up a strand of her hair and looped it around his finger. Her hair was so soft…just like her body. He loved the silky texture of both. "I hadn't intended to go so fast. Sorry. You drive me crazy, lady."

She turned her head and met his gaze. She smiled, slow, sweet and very Mary Paige-ish. "From the very beginning, right?"

"From the moment I saw your Spanx and you tried to leave the boardroom. Why do you have to wear those anyhow? Your ass is spectacular."

He couldn't really tell if she blushed or not because night had fallen. But enough light from the street spilled in to show him how beautiful she was splayed naked on his bed.

"It's a *smoother.*" She sniffed. "Almost all women wear them."

Brennan laughed softly, pulling her to him. "A smoother. Gah, you women do nutty things."

"All in the name of attracting a man. I almost waxed my hoo-ha yesterday in anticipation of tonight. Can you imagine? That has to be so painful."

He laughed, a full-on belly laugh—which probably wasn't the least bit attractive while naked—but he couldn't help himself. She was so funny and made his heart sing.

The last thought hit him between the eyes and he stilled. "Want to go eat our food? It's probably still warm."

Mary Paige lifted herself onto an elbow, which did wonderful things for her breasts. They were small and slightly sloped, ending in upturned pale nipples—breasts that made his palms itch to cup, his mouth water to taste. And her ass... Good heavens, it was a masterpiece— smooth, rounded and perfectly plump. Made for sex.

He felt himself stir and saw Mary Paige look down. "Oh," she said.

Moving quick as a cat, he rose above her and flipped her over.

"Hey," she said.

"I'm seeing what needs smoothing out," he said, running his hands over her quite marvelous bottom. "Nope, I see nothing that needs smoothing. It's perfect."

"You're insane." She giggled into the goose-down comforter. "Now I know why I like you."

She liked him? Hmm…something about those words wiggled inside him, multiplying in his heart. This woman who fought him, who saw him as an asshole extraordinaire, who looked down her goody-two-shoes nose at him liked him. When had things changed so much between them? When had it become so important to please her, to love her?

The thought was too much for him to contemplate at the moment. Not when this woman lay before him, wrought for his pleasure, perfect for his kiss, his touch, his soul.

He rained kisses down her spine, stopping at the small of her back. "Admit it. You want me for my sexual prowess."

"Meh," she said.

He smacked her bottom and she flipped over, reaching out to wrap him in her arms. Her mouth found his and again, the words fled as the desire took over. No need for words when there were sweet actions to perform, to savor, to revel in.

Her mouth opened to him and he took full advantage, delving into all that was Mary Paige as her thighs fell open, welcoming him. But this would be no quick lovemaking. No, her body was a playground, and Brennan had spent far too long being a man who never played, who never savored.

So tonight he would eat that cold Chinese food.

Gladly.

CHAPTER SIXTEEN

MALCOLM WATCHED HIS nephew, Joseph Asher Henry, sip his whiskey and eyeball the soup with a curled lip.

"Thought you loved seafood gumbo?"

Asher tossed him a jaded look. "Been so long, I suppose my tastes have changed. I'm much more accustomed to European cuisine."

"I can't imagine turning down Ernestine's gumbo," Brennan said, passing a basket of French bread from Leidenheimer, a bakery that was tops in turning out delicious, crusty loaves. "But to each his own. At least have the bread."

Asher took a piece and set it on the Limoges china, and for the second time that evening, Malcolm wondered if it was a good thing Asher had come home in time for the company party after all. The past few weeks had been so smooth and joyful—two things not normally associated with Brennan. Malcolm was loath to have anything upset this new delicate balance.

"So Brennan told me you're going to marry again," Asher said, favoring the liquor in his tumbler over the food. "Who's her family?"

Malcolm shrugged. "She's a Poche. From Chalmette."

"Chalmette?" Asher looked puzzled.

"Or thereabouts," Malcolm said, picking up the spoon and dipping it in the broth, allowing it to sail away and come back to his lips in proper soup-sipping fashion. "Her father's a retired plumber."

Asher shot a look at Brennan, who merely arched his eyebrows in a don't-ask-me manner.

"I suppose you thought her family was an old Creole one? Or perhaps her great-grandfather an oil tycoon?"

"No, merely surprised. I thought you'd never marry again after being tied down to the original ballbuster." Asher gave a look that was probably designed to encourage male bonding—a look more suited to the locker room than the dining room. "Aunt Cammie was the kind of woman who inspires a vow of bachelorhood."

His nephew had always been a bit of a jackass, even if he was correct about Malcolm's late wife, Camille. Before his illness, Asher's snot-nosed attitude hadn't bothered him much. The boy had sold his shares of MBH Industries, married a European supermodel and moved to Switzerland. Asher was extraordinarily good-looking with enough polo-playing haughtiness and charm to get him invitations to any exclusive event he wished.

Brennan had always admired his older cousin to the point of obsession. Sunshine always seemed to sit upon Asher's shoulders, and people often lingered near, as if his beauty and fortune might brush off on them. Few saw that beneath the perfection, he was a total charlatan. But the boy *was* family.

Still, Malcolm suspected something was rotten in Denmark, or rather, Switzerland. They had not seen hide nor hair of Asher in more than four years, and that trip had happened only because his wife, Elsa, had an American photo shoot.

"Judy's the director of a home for mentally and physically challenged children and young adults, and is the sweetest woman I've ever met. I'm honored she's accepted my proposal," Malcolm commented as Asher pulled out his phone and stared at the glowing screen before repocketing it.

"Then I'm pleased for you," his nephew said with a nod. "Is Ellen coming for dinner?"

"She texted me she'd be late," Brennan said, finishing the last of his soup. He had been particularly cheerful for the past few weeks. Even more peculiar, he left work early nearly every day, disappearing with little word of his planned activities. Of course, he still attended all the obligatory events for the Spirit of Christmas campaign alongside Mary Paige, except for the St. Thomas's Christmas Bingo Bash. Mary Paige had chosen to attend her company's small holiday dinner instead. Malcolm didn't know whether it was wishful thinking on his part, but Brennan had appeared a little lost calling out numbers without her beside him. Hope had burgeoned at the thought Brennan might find a similar joy, as he had. At the very least Brennan might learn how beneficial service to others could be by experiencing it with Mary Paige.

"Ellen has a habit of being late, but because it's often a result of her throwing herself into her work, I always let it slide." Malcolm chuckled, taking another piece of bread even though he knew he shouldn't. Never could resist the bread from Leidenheimer's. "How are things for you, Asher? All is well in Bern?"

"Of course. Elsa would have come but decided to stay in Atlanta with friends. She sends holiday greetings and kisses, of course." Asher tossed a glance toward Brennan, almost as though to rub it in that he was married to Elsa.

Irritation rose inside Malcolm at the reminder. Little shit.

Brennan had been the first one to meet the blonde model at a promotional shoot for a line of bathing suits.

After they'd been dating for a while, it was clear Brennan was quite smitten with Elsa. She'd seemed to return his affections…until Asher had encountered her while on a summer jaunt in Rome. He'd culled her, wooed her, then stolen her away, giving no apology to his cousin for blatantly doing so.

Even worse than that foul act had been Brennan's reaction. He hadn't been devastated; had merely accepted the situation, as if it were understandable Asher would win.

Malcolm felt the sharp pinch of guilt at the role he might have played in perpetuating Brennan's hero worship of Asher. Through his preoccupation with the business and making money, Malcolm had failed to provide guidance and a positive role model for Brennan. In that absence, he had fixated on Asher, who, on the surface, seemed almost perfect—gilded with money, success and good genes. What Brennan didn't seem to see was that Asher was a professional at twisting all things to his advantage. In short, he was a shyster. And Malcolm should know since he'd spent most of his life acting in a similar fashion.

"Is Elsa well?" Brennan asked, a subtle inquiry since Elsa had suffered a miscarriage nearly a year ago and it had devastated her.

"Of course," Asher said, rising and retrieving the decanter of whiskey from the sideboard. "She's at a spa getting a bit of needed rejuvenation. She's booked for the spring and summer."

"And Aare International? Still dazzling the world of high-end luggage?"

Asher glowered. "What is this? Twenty questions? Of course everything is well. I came to New Orleans because my older sister has henpecked me until—"

"You finally came," Ellen said from the doorway, a

huge smile on her face even though she'd caught her brother complaining about her.

Asher swiveled his head. "Ah, she squawks."

Ellen leaned over the chair, wrapping her arms around her brother, bussing him on the cheek with a kiss. "Yes, I'm squawking. Can't believe you finally came home. I've missed you so much."

Asher returned the hug, smiling at his sister. "In the flesh."

She pinched him.

"Ow!"

"Just making sure you're real," Ellen said before brushing an air kiss near Malcolm's cheek. He patted her hand, enjoying the pleasure she took in seeing the brother who was nearly twelve years her junior. The girl had virtually raised the boy until she'd gone off to college. The relationship was more maternal in nature and Ellen had never seen beyond the drooling toddler she'd taught to walk to the spoiled man he'd become.

Ellen sat, beaming as bright as the Victorian tree Ernestine and Gator had put up that week. "Evening, Brennan."

Brennan nodded at his cousin. "Saw the article in the *Times* about the success of the campaign, Ellen. Congratulations."

"You should congratulate yourself. You and Mary Paige have caused a sensation. Saw another picture of you two at Celebration in the Oaks a few days ago. I hadn't realized you'd decided to go the fake romance route."

Brennan's expression shuttered. "I've enjoyed spending time with Mary Paige. Once we got past our philosophical differences, of course."

"I've noticed you've been less grumpy," Ellen teased.

Much to Malcolm's surprise, Brennan didn't seem to mind the gibe in the least. Interesting.

"Didn't you love that one story about the pregnant lady on the bus and the man who helped her, only to figure out she was a friend he hadn't seen in over a decade?" Ellen asked Malcolm. "The writer did a great job of creating an *aw* moment. This Spirit stuff really is sweeping the city. And, as we'd predicted, Henry's bottom line isn't suffering a bit by the giveaways."

"Brilliant suggestion you had about letting our employees award the gifts rather than hire that out. Wish I had your marketing mind," Brennan said, his expression sincere.

"I'm surprised at this about-face from you, Brennan," Malcolm said as Ernestine brought in the pork roast, fingerling potatoes and Creole green beans.

Brennan stood and helped the woman with the dishes, something Malcolm was certain he'd never seen the boy do. Hmm…

"I can admit when I'm wrong. The entire Spirit of Christmas campaign has been successful on so many levels," his grandson said, setting the bowl of beans beside his plate. "This looks fabulous, Ernestine. Thank you."

The woman sent a disbelieving look at Malcolm then smiled. "You're welcome. Hope you enjoy it."

"What's this Spirit stuff?" Asher asked.

Ellen gave him a brief rundown of the campaign, adding in the way the media had spun a romance between Mary Paige and Brennan.

"*You're* faking this?" Asher asked.

"No," Brennan said, regarding his cousin over the rim of of his wineglass. "Just letting public perception to trump."

Asher made no further comment, instead contemplated the chandelier and sucked at the highball glass.

Malcolm regarded the dynamics of this small family gathering. Ellen seemed pleased to have her brother here, while Asher acted as though he'd done them a favor to sit down with them for a meal. Brennan ate and occasionally stared off with a half smile on his face. What would his Judy think of them and how would she handle what was left of the Henry family?

What was left.

My, how he wished for new life in the family.

Judy would do her part to add another perspective. But with Ellen's recent divorce making her wary about relationships, it was likely that by the time she remarried—if she did remarry—she would be past childbearing years. Asher and Elsa might yet have children and therefore carry on the name. But Brennan... Yes, Malcolm had high hopes his grandson would bring a new generation of Henrys into the beautiful, mysterious city he loved.

"The Henry Christmas party is this week, and I've decided to change the venue. This year I'm hosting it on the top floor of the Canal Street store."

Ellen frowned. "That's a storage area. How are you going to manage that?"

"You'll see," Malcolm said, his head spinning with the visions of the party he'd planned with Gigi and her flamboyant designer Max, who had conceived the concept one day when Gigi had shown him the old window stages housed in storage. "Christmas in the Attic" had emerged from that foray and Malcolm was excited about showcasing the flagship store's past as they contemplated the future of the company. "And I can't wait for Asher to meet Judy."

"I'm so thrilled for you, Uncle, and I know Asher

will like Judy," Ellen said, looking happier than she had in months.

Malcolm caught Brennan's gaze. "Sometimes we over-look what actually suits us in favor of what we *think* should. I'm truly blessed by that woman's love."

Brennan's eyes deepened slightly before he shuttered the emotions. "Shall we toast my grandfather and the woman who has captured him?"

"Hear! Hear!" Ellen said, lifting her goblet.

"Hear! Hear!" Ernestine popped her head into the din-ing room, holding a diet soda.

They laughed and toasted Judy, and all Malcolm could hope was that each Henry at the table would find what he'd found—peace, joy and love.

Sappy, sentimental and optimistic, sure, but he wished it all the same.

MARY PAIGE STRAIGHTENED the sheer black maxi dress, wondering for the third time in ten minutes if she were bold enough to pull off this outfit. Beneath the fitted see-through sheath she wore black satin hot pants and a matching bustier. It was the sexiest thing she'd ever put on her body, but the way she'd felt over the past few weeks had emboldened her. Something about spending time with Brennan made her forget she'd beaten Brit-tany Bolden in the corn-shucking contest at the parish fair when she was fifteen. She felt worldly, sophisticated and very much Spanx-free.

Mitzi clasped hands to her cheeks when she entered the bedroom. "Holy crap!"

"Oh, God. It's too much," Mary Paige said, cast-ing a desperate glance at the mirror. She'd thought the Victorian-style dress covered enough, but Mitzi's reac-tion said it all. "I'm taking it off."

"Don't you dare," Mitzi shrieked, tossing the dark tresses of the wig she wore over her shoulder. "You're smoking hot and sweet at the same time. Don't know how, but you are. If you take that off, I will hold my breath, fall on the floor and pitch a fit."

"Okay. Fine. I'll go in this even though it's probably not appropriate. The invite said party attire, and it's supposed to be a Christmas in the Attic theme. I didn't really think things out when I bought this dress."

"Where did you get it?" Mitzi asked, walking around her, plucking at the material.

"I found the maxi at that new vintage shop on Magazine. It's obviously not true vintage, but it's not brand-new, either. And then I went to Frederick's of Hollywood for the bustier and hot pants. I'm no fashion genius, but I knew it would look awesome." Mary Paige looked at her reflection critically and had to admit her instincts were right. The outfit was fabulous…but was it her? Could she wear this in public?

Mitzi met her gaze in the mirror. "I'm almost speechless."

"Now I *know* I need to take it off."

At her friend's narrowed eyes, Mary Paige laughed. "Guess there's no time to change?"

Mitzi grabbed her and pulled her into a hug. Mary Paige caught the sheen of tears in her friend's eyes and pulled away fast. "Is everything okay? I know you went to see your doctor today."

Mitzi shook her head. "No, nothing like that. In fact, the PET scan was good and I don't have to do any more treatments this spring."

"Whee!" Mary Paige embraced her friend. "That's the best news I've had in forever."

"You won two million dollars less than a month ago. Surely this isn't better than that."

Mary Paige released Mitzi and gave her an affectionate shove. "Yes, it is."

"Well, I'm happy for you," Mitzi said, an embarrassed flush on her cheeks. "You've been glowing for weeks. Being with Brennan has unleashed you. You're bold and wonderful. You, but like ten times better. It's really cool to see the power of love right in front of me. Makes me believe it can happen for me one day."

Love? Mary Paige wasn't sure she wanted to be that obvious in her feelings for Brennan. It made her feel more naked than this dress. Could everyone see the way she felt? Could Brennan?

"I'm not sure it's love, Mitzi. I'm just enjoying being with him. It's been easier between us at all these charity things we've gone to. But, there has been no talk of anything more once this whole campaign ends."

"So why not ask him about the future?"

"Says the woman who won't even return the calls of her old friends. Honesty's hard."

Mitzi's warm glow disappeared. "Maybe I don't want to hang at biker bars anymore. Maybe I don't want to drink beer and smoke cigarettes and sleep around with guys who don't care about me."

"I'm sorry. That was out of line." Mary Paige had been friends with Mitzi long enough to know that she never faced anything until she was ready to. And it didn't take a genius to add up all those Saturday nights with her mother as company and come to the conclusion that Mitzi wasn't ready to return to the social life she'd had before the diagnosis. "Guess I hate seeing you sitting home alone when you have so much to offer."

Mitzi crossed her arms. "I never bothered you about

not getting out after Simon left you. I brought the ice cream, remember?"

"Yeah."

"And for your information, I'm trying. I actually accepted a date with Robbie Theriot for this weekend."

"The guy who fixed the transmission on your mom's car? The one with the Sylvester the Cat tattoo?"

Mitzi's nod seemed hesitant, as though she were braced for Mary Paige's reaction. Well, no judgment here. She couldn't be happier for her friend.

"That's awesome. I'm proud of you for putting yourself out there." Mary Paige embraced Mitzi again, letting the action convey how she felt about this brave woman who was her friend.

"I know." After a long moment, Mitzi pulled away and blinked suspiciously fast. "Now, you better get going. Is the B-man picking you up?"

"I'm taking my own car since it's at the flagship store, which is, like, three blocks away from his place."

"He's changed, you know?"

Mary Paige's hand stilled. "Brennan?"

"No, the Easter Bunny. Of course, Brennan."

"How would you know? You've never met him—only seen him when he's come to pick me up."

"He has to be better just for knowing you, Mary." Mitzi smiled sweetly. "I'm so glad you came across the street to borrow an egg from Mama after you moved in. I don't think I've had a friend like you."

Tears pricked Mary Paige's eyes, which would never do. She needed to be flirty and fierce, not misty and maudlin. "Don't you dare make me cry."

"I can't help you're an angel," Mitzi said, directing her toward the door.

"You so know I'm no angel. I'm just a person who

does what a person should do, Mitzi. I'm kind of tired of being painted as some paragon of perfection. I'm not. I have a wart right here on my left thigh." She pointed at her leg. "And I once poured milk on a kid's head because he called my mother Farmer Freda and made a milking motion at pretend boobies. And one year I paid my taxes late. And I barfed in my mom's begonias after drinking vodka then lied about it."

"The horror!" Mitzi called behind her as she grabbed the sparkly red clutch Mama Cascio had found in her trousseau trunk and loaned to Mary Paige. "Go have fun. Tell Brennan you love him. Be bad, Mary Paige!"

Mary Paige rolled her eyes and trotted down the steps, heading toward her faithful compact car and a night of possibility.

She'd never been happier. Never. Brennan had been attentive, humorous and fun these past few weeks. They hadn't fought once over any issues, and he'd rolled his eyes only twice. Once when a volunteer at the Mr. Bingles Jingle Run wanted him to invest in some exercise program she'd created. And the other when his grandfather had introduced her as the mild-mannered sweet servant who'd raised him from the depths of wet cardboard and destruction. She wasn't sure if that eye roll was the result of Mr. Henry's dramatic embellishment or the fact he'd called her mild-mannered. She was fairly certain it was the latter.

Marshmallow? Check. Naive? Check. Mild-mannered? Not really.

Just the thought of their shared enthusiasm when they were in bed, coupled with the fun they had working together, made her smile as she reversed out of the drive and headed toward the glittering city and the party that waited.

And the man who waited.

As she drove, she contemplated Mitzi's challenge.

Tell him you love him.

Before she did anything so drastic, she had to define her own feelings. Did she love him?

Smitten was the word that came to mind. On some level, it probably went deeper than that. The potential for something great hovered beneath her heart, bumping against it, nudging her to open and risk so it might come to fruition.

She was afraid.

Plain and simple.

But wasn't everyone afraid of getting hurt? Anyone who took a risk stood to get trampled, shoved and broken by failure.

She and Brennan had stumbled into something that, at the moment, felt right. But what would happen when reality set in? When they weren't dressed in fancy clothes, tasting lobster dip and living in some campaign that, for all intents and purposes, was some fairyland for her?

No matter how well she'd handled it thus far, Brennan's world was not hers.

And that was the one thing squashing the hope brushing against her heart.

BRENNAN WATCHED THE people who worked at MBH Industries mix, mingle and engage in forced conversation—or so it seemed to him. Same old company party scene even if the setting was fantastical. The entire top floor of the store had been turned from a wasteland of old racks and mannequins into a unique winter wonderland, utilizing the holiday accessories and window settings from years past. Huge stage lamps tilted toward the vignettes and walking through the room was like walking through time.

Large old-fashioned Christmas lights traversed the un-finished ceiling, brightening a party that still felt same old, same old....

At least until Mary Paige arrived.

Two and a half weeks of wonder, of feeling like a different man, had resulted from their one unscheduled date. They'd broken away from "have to" and explored "want to." He couldn't remember being as content as he'd been since they'd made love. It was an odd feeling.

Since then, he hadn't wanted to stay at the office and read reports until his eyes crossed. Not when there were little Italian restaurants where they could share a delicious meal, Christmas lights strung in parks to stroll through hand in hand and beds that beckoned to be wrinkled from vigorous, mutually pleasurable, hot, dirty, sweet, wonderful—

"Who are you looking for?" Asher said, arriving at his elbow as the word *sex* reverberated in his brain.

"Mary Paige."

"That Spirit of Christmas person Uncle Mal told me about?" Asher drawled, one hand in pocket, the other cupping likely his third or fourth drink. "Shouldn't she arrive on a cloud with a heavenly chorus strumming harps?"

Brennan smiled at the image. He'd have to tell her about it. Then they'd laugh about her lounging on a cloud in a white satin bra and thigh-high hose and garters. "Yeah, something like that."

Asher eyed him with a steely look. "You like this girl."

Brennan met the gaze with his own forthright one. "I do."

"She must be gorgeous, then. Don't think I've ever seen you slumming. You slept with her yet?" Asher's questions were inappropriate and the words were slurred slightly. He hadn't been the same since he arrived a few days ago. He'd seemed sad, at odds with the man who would usually work the room with a charming smile and biting wit.

"Haven't you had enough to drink?"

"I'm on my second scotch, and I'm fairly certain I can handle my liquor. But you, if I remember correctly, should be drinking ginger ale." Asher smiled and in the blink of an eye, he was once again the man Brennan knew.

The kind of man Brennan had always aspired to be— bold, fearless in the business world, respected by all and married to such gorgeousness it was almost a crime. Asher had always been Brennan's ideal in manhood.

"I was seventeen, Asher. No one holds his liquor at seventeen. Besides, I think that was actually a stomach virus that swept through Newman that week."

Asher grinned. "Yeah. Right."

Brennan ditched his whiskey and accepted a flute of champagne from a passing waiter. Lifting his glass, he murmured, "To our misspent youth."

"Whose misspent youth?" Mary Paige asked, swiping a glass before the waiter disappeared into the crowd.

Brennan turned and his mouth gaped. Jesus, she looked… He wasn't sure there were words.

She wore a black sheer dress that covered her from wrist to neck to towering stilettos. Yet he could see right through the gown to the satin bustier and short panty-looking things she wore beneath it. Little black satin bows trailed ribbons down her thighs and mimicked the ones along the front of the dress. It was both stunningly original and fascinatingly sexy. He was certain his tongue had stuck to the roof of his mouth.

"Well, now, you must be the intriguing Mary Paige." Asher's gaze flicked over her with lazy interest.

Brennan felt his radar rise and beep…and if he hadn't been among his coworkers, standing next to his cousin, something else might have risen and, well, not beeped. But risen. Definitely risen.

Mary Paige gave a smile worthy of any silent-screen film goddess. "And you must be the charming Asher Henry." She held out a hand and he wouldn't have been surprised if she'd murmured, *"Enchanté."*

In fact Brennan almost muttered it for her.

In true continental fashion—or maybe it was Asher simply being Asher—he brought her hand to his lips.

"Charming is such an overstatement." Asher smiled, holding her hand a little longer than necessary in Brennan's opinion.

Something flared in him, something he hadn't felt in so long he almost didn't recognize it. Jealousy.

"Somehow I doubt that," Mary Paige said, her eyes sparkling with humor. "Brennan has warned me about your lethal charisma."

"But he did not warn me of your absolute deliciousness. Bold choice, Miss Mary Paige." Then his shark of a cousin swept his gaze down her body as bold as an eagle or another such predatory bird with no shame.

And with that, his sweet, gentle Merry Sunshine turned on the ball of her foot and executed a nonclumsy pirouette. Where had that awkward blonde in the ill-fitting skirt and Lycra gone? This woman taking her place flirted with his cousin with a skill he'd never seen her use outside of the bedroom.

"You have been holding out on me, cousin," Asher said, not bothering to even toss a glance Brennan's way as he muttered the accusation.

"No, I haven't and why would I? You're married, re-member?" Brennan didn't feel so happy anymore. He felt grumpy. Why did he have to be here gabbing endlessly with the same people he saw every day about where ev-eryone would spend Christmas? Watching Asher eyeball what belonged to him? He wanted to grab Mary Paige, take her home where they'd snuggle on the couch, eat extra-butter popcorn and watch *CSI* reruns.

But duty called.

As it often did for him.

So he'd endure the party, the cousin who wasn't quite himself and everyone taking in the sexiness Mary Paige had on display. Then later he could have Mary Paige to himself.

That thought both excited him and alarmed him. When had she started meaning so much to him? When had he started putting her above his company on his personal priorities list?

Maybe they were moving too fast. Maybe he needed some distance from her instead of spending every mo-ment he could with her.

The woman ever in his thoughts flashed dimples and said, "And your wife didn't get to come to New Orleans for Christmas. You must be so disappointed to be with-out her."

Asher nodded. "Of course, but I've found once a woman makes up her mind, it's hard to steer her in a new direction. I'll miss her."

Perhaps Brennan imagined it, but there was a lack of sincerity in Asher's words.

"Can I get you a drink, Mary Paige," Brennan said, touching her elbow. He could feel the warmth of her body, and all he could think about was stripping that dress off of her and indulging in the naughtiness of what was evident beneath. Only a few more hours of chatting, dancing and popping cocktail shrimp into his mouth and they could leave and go back to his place.

Or maybe he should start inserting that distance between them?

Mary Paige looked at him with smiling eyes and he decided he'd think about getting space from her next week. Tonight he needed her beside him. "I'm drinking what you're drinking."

He looked at the glass in her hand and felt stupid.

"But we were toasting something, weren't we?" she asked, linking her arm through his.

Pleasure flooded him. It was the first time she'd staked her claim on him publicly. Until now, they'd squirreled themselves away, keeping their personal relationship private while maintaining a friendly, yet polite distance in public.

Asher seemed to notice the gesture and something about his expression altered. An acknowledgment of what her touch meant. An understanding of the intimacy, the claim.

"We're toasting my cousin—" Asher lifted his tumbler "—and his excellent ability to choose so wisely."

"Choose what?" Mary Paige asked.

"Everything," Asher said.

Brennan dutifully sipped, but an unpleasant feeling sat with him. For some reason, Asher's words seemed like a warning. But a warning of what, Brennan had no idea.

CHAPTER SEVENTEEN

MARY PAIGE SURVEYED the buffet, snagging some delicious crawfish-stuffed meat pies and some sort of soft-shelled crab with a coconut coating, while she watched the employees of MBH laugh and freely partake of the free wine and champagne circulating the room. She'd seen a line of cabs waiting outside and knew many of the people surrounding her would need them when the party ended.

She caught Judy's eye as she conversed with a woman wearing Elvis Costello–style glasses and a dress made of ivory lace with a neckline that plunged almost to the navel. A black patent and rhinestone belt cut the simplicity of dress and added the appropriate holiday sparkle. Obviously the woman had been waiting for an introduction because she dragged Judy over to Mary Paige.

"Darling, who are you wearing?" she said, not even bothering to introduce herself.

"Beg your pardon?" Mary Paige said, darting a glance toward Judy, who looked as if she might laugh.

"Mary Paige, this is Gigi Malone, the manager of— What are you the manager of?" Judy asked, a small flush spreading across her cheeks.

"Haute couture," the woman said, pinching the fabric at Mary Paige's hip and studying it. "Carolina Herrera?"

"Oh, is that a designer?" Mary Paige asked, feeling completely out of her depth. "I'm not sure. I actually got this at a secondhand store."

The woman literally stepped back. "Well, it's stunning and quite brilliant to pair it with substantial lingerie. A little last season, but you wear it so well, and that's half the battle. I applaud you, my dear."

Substantial lingerie? Jeez, what was the woman's idea of non-substantial? "Thank you—I think." Mary Paige was almost positive Gigi had paid her a compliment. "And may I say you look equally stunning? You, too, Judy."

Judy wore her hair in soft swooping waves à la Rita Hayworth in *Gilda,* and it matched the '40s-style taffeta dress that had to have a petticoat beneath it if the skirt's volume was any indication. She looked pretty adorable and her smile matched the flash of the small diamond on her left hand.

"Thank you, Mary Paige."

"Well, I'm off to find Ellen and Mark. They've promised to give me a ride home. Cheers, ladies, and very nice to meet you, Mary Paige."

"Likewise," Mary Paige said, turning to Judy as Gigi strode away, chin up, back straight, parting the crowd with her very aura. "I heard about the engagement. Congratulations, Judy. I'm so pleased for you and Mr. Henry. I don't think I've seen a man preen before, but he's a regular peacock."

Judy held out the ring. "Isn't it perfect? Not big but Malcolm says there isn't a single flaw. Crazy man thinks it represents me, which is silly. You and I know, no girl is perfect."

Mary Paige looked at the ring—so simple and suitable for Judy—then lifted her gaze to the woman who had been a steadying force each time Mary Paige felt a stormy sea rocked beneath her. She marveled at that special something Judy had, that knack for making everyone feel comfortable.

"Nope, none of us is, but to Malcolm you're perfect for him, and you can't argue with that."

"I can." Judy looked at the ring before shaking her head in wonder. "But I won't. Both he and I are too old to argue about such things. If that man says he loves me and wants me next to him every morning when he wakes, I'm not standing in his way because I feel exactly the same way."

"It's what every person wants," Mary Paige said.

"But many never have, so I feel incredibly blessed." Judy studied Mary Paige—not the dress as everyone else had—but her face, her eyes. It was as if the woman had taken out a trowel and dug around until she found the roots beneath the surface. "And you?"

"Me?"

"I haven't known Brennan for very long, but he's definitely spinning in circles over you. And, while I don't know you well, either, you're different than that night several weeks ago. Something more peaceful—" she gestured toward Mary Paige's dress "—or secure."

Secure? Not in the least. Mary Paige mostly felt as if she were walking on a ledge trying not to look down. Her relationship with Brennan was strange—like meeting a guy at summer camp. Everything was good while living in that bubble, but real life tended to be a long pin that popped the bubble, leaving a girl exposed, blinking at the sun, wondering what happened.

"I'm not secure, just inspired when I saw this dress. Guess I felt like being bold for once in my life, but that proves nothing."

"Okay," Judy said with a little smile that made Mary Paige want to argue with her, to convince her otherwise.

But what did it matter what Judy believed? All that mattered was what Mary Paige believed, and when it came to her and Brennan, she didn't have a clue what that was.

So she simply wouldn't think about it.

Spying Brennan across the room, she started toward him. His dark head was angled toward the woman she remembered was his secretary. He looked so different than when Mary Paige had first met him. Maybe it merely seemed that way because she knew him better. Had seen the gooey center in the hard man he showed the world, had seen beneath to the man he could be.

"Dance with me?"

She spun at the touch on her shoulder and the sound of the voice in her ear. "Oh, Asher. You startled me."

His smile could melt the ice sculpture. "You were deep in thought. Sorry." He held out an expectant hand.

She cast a final look at Brennan, who was still talking, and took the proffered hand. "Sure."

"Perfect." Asher let her pass in front of him as they moved toward the dance floor centered in front of the band the Funky Meters, which included members of the Neville family. The New Orleans originals played their own music mixed with funky versions of traditional Christmas music.

Asher spun her into his arms as the band launched into a soulful number with jazzy snare drums and rich guitar, inspiring a wicked dance groove. He was a good dancer, light on his feet with natural grace. No awkward jerking or silly-looking footwork.

"You're an amazing dancer," Asher said, his blue eyes traveling yet again down the length of her body. It made her a little uncomfortable, but she supposed she'd asked to be looked at when she took the plunge and wore the overtly sexy outfit.

"Not so bad yourself," she said, her breath growing labored as she twisted and turned with the sexy beat of the song.

After several minutes, the song wound down and Asher jerked his head toward the nearby bar. "Let's grab a drink. I'm not used to getting down New Orleans–style anymore."

She nodded because she really needed water. It wasn't warm but her skin was coated with a light sheen of perspiration anyway. She'd let her exercise routine lapse with the busyness of the Spirit of Christmas campaign and her whirlwind romance with Brennan, and it was evident.

Asher ordered a whiskey while she sucked down a glass of water. Wiping her brow, she smiled. "Whew, I need to get my butt back in the gym. I'm out of shape."

"Not from where I'm standing," Asher said, his voice like silk.

What the hell? He was starting to set her teeth on edge with the flirting. Hadn't she made it clear she was "with" Brennan when she'd jabbed her arm through the crook of his and beamed at him like some starstruck teenager? Despite what seemed a very obvious staking of claim, Asher acted like he was seducing her. Maybe it was the way he treated all women…after all, he *was* married.

She never cared for men who hid their intentions behind honeyed words. Probably why she liked Brennan so well. He said what was on his mind whether she liked what that was or not. "Actually, I am. That wore me out."

"Then you should sit down. Come with me." He took her elbow and steered her toward a door behind a vignette of funky '70s dresses and a tinsel tree with peace signs attached. She tried to pull back but he tightened his hold, and since she didn't want an all-out struggle she went with him. He *was* Malcolm's nephew, Brennan's cousin and surely there was no harm in getting to know him better, even if something in her brain shot out a warning.

"Let's go to one of the tables over there." She pointed, and made another attempt to wrench her elbow from his grasp.

"But it's so loud in here, and I need to talk to you about Brennan," he said, his smile suddenly harmless.

"Brennan?"

"Just some insight about him and his past relationships you might want to hear."

Something inside her gut twisted. What could he tell her about Brennan she didn't already know? That he'd never get serious about her? That he had some stunted heart that wouldn't allow for love? That he used his charm to get what he wanted then left a gal to pick up the pieces, smelling the gasoline vapors on the side of the road as he took off for greener pastures.

Asher didn't wait for a response. He opened the door and pressed her inside, hitting the light to reveal a small office with a desk covered with papers and several coffee mugs. A calendar with scantily clad women hung on the wall beneath a huge clock.

"You should sit," Asher said, gesturing toward the chair.

"Wait, what's going on?" She should leave. Her gut told her so, but Asher had dangled a carrot she found hard to resist.

He shoved a hand through his light brown hair, the highlights catching in the fluorescent light, making her wonder if he highlighted his hair or if it was natural.

"Look, I can see Brennan has you under his spell. He's

very good at that, Mary Paige. I know firsthand because he did the same to my wife."

"Your wife? Brennan dated your wife?" Her heart sped up as she sank onto the proffered chair.

Asher stared out the window at the glittering night sky, his face a study of contemplation and concern. "Yes, and he toyed with Elsa the same way. Poor girl thought he was serious about her, but he wasn't. Brennan never is."

"Why are you telling me this? This is—"

"Because you're like Elsa. A nice girl who doesn't deserve to pin her hopes on a man who doesn't have the word *commit* in his vocabulary. Every woman thinks she can heal Brennan, and he plays on that, strings her along but it never works. Elsa's heart was broken, and it was a long time before she could trust again. I feel so fortunate I was there to help her pick up the pieces. I merely thought you should know."

Mary Paige shook her head, wondering why she was listening to Asher. It wasn't his place to tell her of Brennan's past, but still she sat glued to the chair. "No, I can't believe that. Brennan wouldn't treat a woman so callously."

"Wouldn't he?"

Creighton's face bloomed into view in Mary Paige's mind and something twisted hard in her stomach. From what she could tell, Brennan had toyed with Creighton then dropped her the moment she started expecting something from him.

"Look, I love my cousin. He and I were so close… before he broke Elsa's heart, before he threw himself so fully into the family business. I wish Brennan and I could be close again, but he guards himself. Holds himself apart from everyone. I know you've seen this in him."

She stared at the little flecks in the tile at her feet.

"Brennan has endured loss in his life, so it's only natural he protects himself. And, besides, I think your concerns are premature. We've only been hanging out."

"But you should ask yourself who stands to gain. I heard my sister commend him for allowing the entire city to think you're falling in love. To him this is a game played to help the only thing he really cares about—the company." Asher approached, taking one of the hands that hung at her side. He cradled it between both of his and she felt nothing. It was as if she were having an out-of-body experience. "And it's very obvious you've fallen for him in spite of it all."

He said it in a how-very-sad voice that felt like a razor slicing across her heart, making her overlook the fact this man hadn't been around Brennan in years, permitting her fears regarding the man she'd tumbled into love with so quickly to surface.

"I haven't," she said, but even she could hear the lie in her voice.

"Sweet Mary Paige." Asher pulled her from the chair, and gently wrapped his arms around her. "I see such beauty in your soul. You're like a tender flower, grace and love in each petal. But like that flower you trust people not to step on you, not to pluck your petals and leave you abandoned."

She stood woodenly in his arms, every cell in her body screaming out against the truth in his poetic words. Had she wanted to love Brennan so badly she was easy plucking? Had she been the softhearted idiot yet again, allowing Brennan to do on a larger scale what Simon had done—use her?

She felt shell-shocked.

Stupid.

Asher's lips brushed her cheek.

What the hell? She stepped back, but his arms held her firmly.

"I appreciate your concern, Asher, especially when you've just met me. I can assure you I'm okay. My heart isn't broken and your words are unnecessary. I'm a big girl."

He looked at her, his blue eyes so sincere. "Yes, you are. Still, there is something delicate in you, something a man needs to protect."

Mary Paige read more than goodwill flickering in Asher's eyes. He looked strange, and acted even more strangely.

She pressed lightly against his chest, attempting to break his hold. "Let me go. I'm stronger than I look."

His eyes dipped to her lips and the last thought she had before he kissed her was, *Oh, crap.*

Mary Paige struggled to move away, but Asher's hand caught her head as his other arm locked her in place. His lips were demanding and he tasted like whiskey.

She tried to turn her head. "Stop."

Vaguely she heard the door open and her mind tripped into the land of disbelief. She didn't have to look to know it was Brennan standing looking at them.

Suddenly, she was in a soap opera, her lover catching her with another man.

She stomped on Asher's foot and he released her finally, then turned toward Brennan with a sheepish smile. Mary Paige dragged the back of her hand over her mouth, trying in vain to erase Asher's touch.

"What the hell?" Brennan said, his eyes flickering from her to his cousin.

"It's not what it—"

"Sorry, man," Asher said, shaking his head, spreading his hands out as he shrugged. "We danced and we couldn't help ourselves."

"No," Mary Paige said. "That's not what happened. He said he had to tell me something about you, and then all of a sudden he kissed me."

Brennan's eyes had narrowed and anger pulsed in the room like a live animal, devouring all in its path. She'd never seen fury so quiet before and knew how the poor gazelle felt right before the lion pounced.

"Come on," Asher said, shaking his head. "I'm a married man. Do you think I would endanger my marriage over some girl I just met? She flirted with me, and when I offered her a sympathetic shoulder, things happened."

Mary Paige's mouth dropped open and she punched his arm. "You're a liar. I did no such thing."

"I watched you go with him. You came to this room with him." Brennan's words were calm...and cold as ice water.

"Well, yes, but only because he said he wanted to give me some insight about you." She couldn't believe what was going down. The whole situation felt preposterous, and Asher was a damn snake in the grass...or party. Either one.

Asher sighed and delivered a bemused smile. "Come on, Mary Paige, you don't have to pretend with Brennan. He knows the score."

She gasped. "You're making this look like something it wasn't, and Brennan's not stupid. He knows me and knows I wouldn't act like that."

"Act like what? Flirt with me? Dance with me? Kiss me? Isn't that what you've been doing with my cousin all along? How am I different from him? Besides, Brennan doesn't really know you, does he?"

Mary Paige couldn't believe the spin. It felt so designed. In fact, how had she not seen his intent? But why would Asher want to sabotage her and Brennan? What did he care who his cousin dated? Especially when he'd implied their dating was all an act contrived by Brennan.

She looked at Brennan, who stood motionless at the door, expression grim as if trying to pierce through to the truth. "Brennan, say something."

BRENNAN HELD ON to the doorknob of the storage office as if it were a life raft, glad the office was hidden behind one of the displays so no one could see what a fool he was to have trusted either Asher or Mary Paige.

His heart pounded in his ears and his stomach flipped over and over, churning the small amount of alcohol he'd consumed.

"I don't know what to say." And he didn't. His eyes didn't lie. He'd seen Mary Paige in Asher's arms, her hands splayed across his chest, and it was déjà vu. Years slipped away and it was Elsa, naked in Asher's bed, sorrow in her pretty eyes.

Mary Paige stomped her foot. "This is ridiculous. You know I would never entice a man to an office I don't even know about and make out with him while my boyfriend was in the next room. Who does that?"

"Who said I was your boyfriend?" Brennan said.

She looked as if he slapped her. In fact, he felt as though he *had* slapped her. His mind reeled and all he wanted to do was punch the hell out of Asher, leave the party and forget he'd ever met Mary Paige. Because his damn heart thumped louder and louder, a roar in his ears, fracturing with each pulse.

He *knew* he should have left her alone. From the very beginning he knew she would be trouble for him. But like a dumb-ass he stumbled right into this bizarre relationship with her, living in a fantasy, never bothering to think about how it would end.

He wasn't sure what happened between her and Asher. And while he couldn't really say he trusted his cousin anymore, he'd seen her flirting with Asher earlier. She'd done so right in front of Brennan's own eyes. And she'd dressed so differently tonight—so not Mary Paige—and he'd noted how confident she seemed.

This was no clumsy, gauche accountant with her head in the clouds. Nope, not this woman.

Did he really know her? What if everything she'd claimed to be had been an act simply to get more money than what the Henry family had already given her? She could be the most skilled of con artists ever encountered. After all, she had yet to confess what she'd done with all that money his grandfather had given her.

His thoughts turned toward accusations a logical part of his brain knew were unfounded, but he couldn't seem to stop his mind from venturing down those paths. What if she'd tricked him all along? What if it were all a big lie?

Who was Mary Paige Gentry?

He examined her standing beneath the ugly fluorescent lights, virtually in her underwear, as Asher leaned casually against an old filing cabinet.

Brennan didn't know the truth, but he knew he couldn't deal with this right now.

"I thought we had something," Mary Paige said, stepping even farther away from Asher, reaching a steadying hand for the chair that rolled backward when she grabbed it. She teetered, but pulled herself upright, her brown eyes pools of despair.

Her expression tugged at him and he didn't want to look at her. Didn't want to feel the hurt that flooded him.

Goddamn them both.

He was better off feeling nothing than this.

Asher shrugged. "I should leave you two to talk this out."

Mary Paige crossed her arms. "Sure. Leave us in the rubble, you bastard."

"Don't bother," Brennan said, stepping toward the party. "I'll go."

"The hell you will," Mary Paige yelled, stomping her foot, not looking quite so shaken. "It's not going to happen like this. This isn't some damn soap opera."

"No, it's not. It's my company's Christmas party, and it's neither the time nor the place to discuss what will happen between me and you after this debacle."

"Well, I'm not letting you leave it like this. It's not fair." Her words trembled with tears. Real or crocodile? Was it all part of her plan? Two million dollars was a lot of cash. But hooking him through the nose and getting him to the altar would be worth much more. Hadn't every other woman he dated wanted the same? Jumbo ring equaled jumbo bank account.

"Don't you know life isn't fair, Mary Paige? It pretty much sucks most of the time…something I forgot for a while."

"Brennan…" Her plea floated out to him, but he didn't wait any longer. He shut the door on her and Asher.

Gone was the anticipation of another night in her arms.

Gone was the joy that shimmered inside him, vibrating like a string plucked over and over.

Gone was the man he thought he could be.

How could he have so easily forgotten who he was, who he'd always been? He'd been blinded by the image of being with someone good and kind, someone who could guide him out of the walled fortress where he lived. He'd been confused by her contrived benevolence. He'd been suckered by the whole festive promise of the season, allowing him to forget what he knew for a fact—Christmas was a sour, grim and a cruel reminder that love didn't exist for Brennan Henry.

He cut through the crowd, ignoring the shouts of "Merry Christmas" and "Happy New Year." Emotion clogged his throat and he was afraid he might actually break down and cry like a damn baby in front of everyone who mattered to him—his grandfather and the company.

Pressing the elevator button, he spotted a small tinsel tree blinking beside the entrance.

Like a hurt and angry child, he walked over and kicked it. As it hit the floor, he felt a little better. He walked toward the opening elevator doors.

As the doors slid shut, he glanced once again at the revelers. No one even noticed he left…or that he'd kicked over a Christmas tree.

"Bah, freaking, humbug."

MALCOLM PERUSED THE crowd for Brennan, but didn't see him. It felt marvelous to have all his employees, along with the board of directors, in attendance. He'd asked the board to the party after they had all voted to approve Brennan as the new CEO of MBH Industries mere days ago. Brennan wasn't aware of the secret meeting called to select the next executive in charge, and Malcolm had been waiting until this event to announce the decision.

It was a Christmas gift for his grandson.

Maybe not as important as the gift of love, but a nice one even so.

Malcolm had submitted his letter of resignation a week ago and would not be returning to MBH Industries after he and Judy returned from Charleston and Savannah on their honeymoon in a few weeks. It was long past time he started enjoying his last few years on earth, and he wouldn't spend any more time worrying about profits, the market and whether or not they should purchase another piece of land for a new store. Time to sleep late, make love to his pretty new wife while he still could and walk Izzy every afternoon. Time to really live.

But he couldn't make the announcement if he couldn't find his grandson.

He spotted Mary Paige across the room, standing near one of the vignettes, and moved toward her.

"Evening, my dear," he said, pulling her into a hug before she could protest. "Where has my grandson gotten off to?"

"Good evening, Mr. Henry," she said, her voice oddly choked. Her pretty brown eyes were filled with tears and her smile was tremulous.

"Are you well?"

She pressed her lips together and shook her head.

He narrowed his eyes. "Where's Brennan?"

"I don't know. He left, I think." She swallowed hard, as if she could swallow the emotion away.

"What's happened?"

She seemed reluctant to say anything so Malcolm waited her out. Finally, she spoke. "A misunderstanding, but it doesn't matter because nothing was real. It was just a bubble…it was a…mistake."

What had his grandson done? Everything had seemed so good for Brennan over the past few weeks, and Malcolm had hoped it might lead to something more lasting, something close to what he'd found with Judy. He wanted his grandson to find love before it was too late.

Before he was old, gray and past his prime.

Mary Paige's gaze flickered over the crowd, stopping for a moment.

Malcolm turned his head to see what gave her pause and spotted Asher dancing with a clerk from accounting.

"Did Asher have something to do with this?" he asked, a warning flag shimmying up the pole of realization.

Her gaze jerked to his and she wiped a single tear from the corner of her eye. "Why would you think that?"

"Because in my experience, he always has something to do with things going south for Brennan."

She sighed. "It isn't Asher's fault. It's an issue with the nature of who Brennan and I are. Trust me, this is all for the best."

"Not really."

Her touch on his arm was gentle. "No, truly. Brennan and I are not meant to be. We're too different, and we forgot that for a few weeks."

"It's not true. Look at me and Judy. Look at—" Excruciating pain struck hard and fast. Malcolm clutched his bow tie as a hammer struck him again and again in the center of his chest, the last one pressing him down. He sank to a knee, his mouth open but unable to make a cognizant sound.

"Juuu—"

"Oh, my God!" Mary Paige reached for him, grabbing his elbow as he fell.

Lights swirled above him.

Judy.

He needed Judy.

"Help!" Mary Paige screamed, dropping beside him.

He felt others move his way, the band playing on and he knew he was dying.

Dying without ever making Judy his bride.

Dying without teaching Brennan about love.

Dying with so much left unfinished.

It wasn't fair.

But when had life been fair?

He closed his eyes and then there was nothing more.

CHAPTER EIGHTEEN

BRENNAN SAT IN the waiting room of ICU staring at the clock, willing the minute hand to hit the six for no other reason than he was tired of it being on five. The cardiologist on call had tersely told him earlier in the emergency room it was touch and go for Malcolm and they'd know more when they got him on the cath table. That news had made Brennan's gut cramp and his head pound with dread.

His heart was already bleeding from the episode with Mary Paige and Asher, so he wasn't in good shape.

Judy sat across from him, her skirt bunched up and her face pale and worried. Her fingers knit together, twisting and turning over and over until he thought he might scream.

"He'll be okay," Judy said for the third or fourth time in ten minutes. It was the new mantra that had replaced the "Oh, God, please save him" that she'd repeated for over an hour.

"He will," Brennan replied, not feeling the words. Knowing this could be it, and in the snap of his fingers, he'd be utterly alone. Well, he'd have Asher and Ellen, but that thought wasn't comforting even though he cared for his cousins. Well, at least he cared for Ellen.

Finally, after forty minutes of finger-twisting by Judy, the cardiologist, Dr. Jim Grantham, pushed through the doors and headed their way. Brennan stood.

"Mr. Henry, sorry for my shortness earlier. I wanted to get your grandfather on the table as soon as possible to see what we were dealing with. Time is always of essence during an MI event."

"No problem. How is he?"

Judy stood and touched the doctor on the arm. "I'm Judy Poche, Malcolm's fiancée."

"Oh," the doctor said, turning to her as he pulled off the brightly colored surgeon's cap and tucked it into the waistband of his scrubs. "I'm Dr. Grantham, and your fiancé is stabilized and recovering."

"Oh, thank God," Judy said, closing her eyes and drawing in a deep breath.

"For some reason he threw a clot in that stent and there was an immediate cardiac event. We fixed the blockage and placed a new stent. The heart muscle was further damaged, but it looks as if he's going to pull through."

Brennan nodded his head, relief spiraling through him at the doctor's prognosis. "We can't thank you enough, Dr. Grantham."

"I'm glad you got him here quickly and it wasn't something more serious. We're running some tests to see why his body formed the clot in the first place—usually it's not taking the prescribed blood thinner. We'll know more soon and I'll consult with his personal physician."

Dr. Grantham patted Judy on the back and gave her a gentle smile before he left. The older woman wilted like a daisy in a drought and sank onto the vinyl armchair, tears rolling down her cheeks as she clutched her stomach.

"I thought I'd lost him. I'd just found him, found love, and I thought it could be gone before we'd even got started." Her slim shoulders shook, and Brennan didn't know how to comfort her, so he sat beside her and rubbed her back.

"But it's okay, now. Grandfather will get stronger and we'll make sure he takes his medicine. He's got you to watch over him now, and I'm banking on the fact you'll make him eat right and exercise. He'll be up and around in no time."

She nodded, but didn't stop crying.

Judy had been scared silly. Not because she thought she stood to lose a fortune. But because she thought she might lose the love of her life.

This wasn't about money or social position. This was about love, pure and not so simple.

Love.

He'd always fought against that particular emotion, but he didn't always win the match. He loved his grandfather and could hardly stand the thought of being without him. When Malcolm had first had the heart attack in late spring, Brennan had felt frozen—scared stiff—to such a degree that he avoided the hospital, pretending it hadn't happened. But now, he knew he couldn't run from his grandfather's delicate health, couldn't pretend Malcolm Henry, Jr., the strong, powerful tycoon, was made of steel and would never change.

Because he wasn't. And he had.

Life didn't seem to care what Brennan wanted. It kept chugging forward, throwing surprise curves and blinding tunnels his way.

Mary Paige.

Her image popped into his mind—blond hair swishing, brown eyes snapping as she belly-laughed while watching *America's Funniest Home Videos* on his couch. Her giggles had made him laugh and then they'd looked into each other's eyes and he'd felt that zing, that little zap that said, "You belong with her."

And he'd believed she was his destination.

Until he'd caught her in Asher's arms, and doubt had poured over him coating him like hot wax.

Was it wrong to think so poorly of her? His past experiences colored him, made him doubt her intent from the very beginning. This he knew, but he didn't want to hurt again, especially not from her falling into his cousin's arms. He'd already danced that dance, and knew how it left him—alone and embarrassed. And, deep down in the recesses of his heart, hurting.

"You okay?" Judy patted his thigh. "You look pale. Should I get you a soda?"

He shook his head, impressed that Judy, whose face was blotchy and swollen, was concerned about him. "No, I'm fine. Relieved."

The doors Dr. Grantham had disappeared through parted and a large nurse with a wide grin came through. "Well, I'm guessing you're here for Mr. Henry. He's in recovery, awake, asking for his Judy. And someone he called a knothead."

An almost hysterical bark of laughter burst through Judy's lips.

The nurse looked at him. "I'm assuming you're the knothead? Unless you're name is Judy?"

He raised his hand. "Knothead."

Judy raised hers. "Not the knothead."

The nurse nodded and they followed her into recovery, where his grandfather lay, hooked to beeping machines and an IV. Brennan's heart stopped when he saw how sick his grandfather looked. Near death.

"Judy," Malcolm breathed, lifting his hand slightly.

"No, no," she said, pressing his hand down with hers as she cupped his jaw. "I'm here, darling. You're okay."

His grandfather's eyes searched over her shoulder and landed on him. "Bren."

Brennan felt the tears in the back of his throat choke him. His knees shook and he thought he might pass out. Instead the tears escaped along with a sob.

"Oh," Judy said, reaching for his hand, drawing him near to her and his grandfather.

Brennan allowed himself to be pulled next to the bed, trying like hell not to cry like a damn idiot, but failing. He clutched his own chest because it felt as if it might break apart.

"Bren," his grandfather said again, reaching for his and Judy's hands twined together. "Don't, son. Don't."

But Brennan couldn't stop the flood. It overwhelmed him, sucked him into fear so intense and relief so sweet. Judy's arms wound around him and this woman who loved his grandfather held him as he cried the tears he'd stored for years upon years.

Finally, Brennan reined things in and wiped his face with the sleeve of his tuxedo, feeling exactly what his grandfather claimed he should embrace—vulnerability.

"Sorry," was all he could manage to say.

"Why?" his grandfather whispered, his voice hoarse and gravelly. "For caring? For loving? Don't be. It's a gift."

Brennan shook his head. He didn't know what he apologized for. Maybe for being weak.

"Come here."

Judy gently pushed him toward Malcolm. Brennan went because this was his grandfather…and he'd nearly died. Again.

Brennan bent toward his grandfather to catch the faint words.

"You're a complete idiot."

Brennan drew back. "Why? Because I—"

"No, not because you cried, but because you made that woman cry. That woman who loves you."

"Mary Paige?"

"No, the friggin' Virgin Mary."

Judy gasped. "Malcolm, that's—"

"Sorry." Malcolm cleared his throat. "Shouldn't have said that. But Brennan is obtuse as a da— Uh, darned, moron."

"Asher—"

"Is an ass. He looks to undermine you at every turn, something you refuse to see because you think he's better than you. But he's not. You're ten times the man he is, and Mary Paige doesn't deserve to fall victim to his selfishness. And neither do you. Wake up, boy."

Brennan couldn't say a thing. His mind jumbled around those words, at the thought of his cousin intentionally ruining his relationships. Why? Jealousy? He couldn't grasp the concept.

"Bren," his grandfather croaked, his eyes sharp as stone. "Remember the spirits in the book."

"What book?"

"In *A Christmas Carol?*" Judy asked, smoothing the sheet beneath Malcolm's chin.

"Yes." Malcolm coughed, his neck muscles straining. Judy patted him, her eyes worried. Finally, his grandfather quieted. "Remember the children beneath the robes?"

"Ignorance and Want," Brennan said to himself, his mind clicking as he grasped the implications.

"Don't let them win."

MARY PAIGE FOLDED her favorite Christmas sweater and put it in the suitcase.

"When will you be back?" Mitzi asked from her perch on the bed.

"I took the whole week off. Ivan the Terrible wasn't happy, but then again, when is he ever happy?" Mary Paige placed a stack of underwear into the suitcase and secured them with the strap. Never knew how many undies a girl might need.

"What about Brennan?"

"What about him?"

Mitzi frowned. "Well, you never talked to him about his cousin, and then when Mr. Henry got sick…"

"There's nothing to say. We were never going to work. And I shouldn't have to explain myself to him any further. I told him what happened—he should have known I would never kiss Asher—and he refused to believe me. Instead he believed the worst of me. So it's over. Period. End of story."

Mary Paige believed the words she said. Most of them anyway.

She'd spent the past few nights lying awake, staring at the water stain next to the antique chandelier she'd scored for a song at the Goodwill Unique Shoppe, thinking about all that had occurred over the past few weeks… and thinking she needed to go by Ace Hardware and get some white paint to cover the stain.

At one point she'd gotten really philosophical and imagined Brennan as that water stain on her heart.

Would she ever be able to cover it up?

Then she'd gotten pissed because she was lying awake, thinking about him again, and making analogies out of old water stains.

So she'd but on her big-girl panties and stopped thinking about him.

Mostly.

"So that's it?" Mitzi asked, flopping against the pillows, messing up the bed Mary Paige had made that morning.

"That's it," Mary Paige responded, sitting beside her friend. "I went to the Rotary Club's Yuletide coffee and doughnuts yesterday morning, and as of today, I'm officially finished with the Spirit of Christmas campaign. Hallelujah."

"I let Robbie Theriot get to second base last night," Mitzi said.

She eyed her friend. "But you don't have a second base."

Mitzi giggled. "I know, so I let him get to third."

She looked so pleased with herself, the sparkle of the pre-cancer Mitzi evident in her face, that Mary Paige joined in.

"You always know how to make me laugh. So are you going out with him again?"

"Maybe."

"Why is it so hard to be out there?" Mary Paige muttered. "Dating sucks."

"Yeah. It does suck."

At that, they both lay there silent, contemplating life, love and…the water stain.

"You need to get something and cover that up." Mitzi pointed to the yellowed amoeba-shaped mark.

"Yeah."

"And you need to find Brennan and make this all right."

"No."

Mitzi rose to her elbow. "Why won't you go after him?"

"Why won't he come after me? He was the one who chose to believe that moron's lies. He's the one who has to overcome the hurt of the past to see I wasn't repeating it. Brennan has the problem. Not me. I was ready to talk about our future…and he shut the door. No, he *slammed* the door right in my face."

"But the situation looked bad. You said so yourself."

Mary Paige sat up and crossed her arms. "I'm not being stubborn. I'm no longer sitting on my high horse looking down my nose at him and his narrow-minded tendencies. All I'm doing is saying I'm not chasing after that man when he's jumped to hurtful conclusions about me, when he may have been using me all along. I never gave him any reason to doubt the way I feel about him or to suspect I'd jump into the sack with another man— especially not after leaving his sack the night before. I refuse to chase after a man who has that low opinion of me."

Mitzi sighed. "But he's damaged."

"And he'll have to fix himself. I wasn't put on this earth to save Brennan Henry from a joyless, petty life."

Mitzi looped an arm around her shoulders. "You're right. No woman should have to convince a man to love her. Good reminder."

Mary Paige tapped her friend's thigh. "I know you already got the tremendous gift of remission but I have a little something else for you."

Mitzi clapped her hands. "Oh, goody! A present!"

"Come on." Mary Paige tugged Mitzi toward the small living room, where the tree blinked in tune to the carols spilling out of the stereo. Okay, so Mary Paige hadn't synchronized the music to the blink, but it still looked as if they were in perfect harmony.

She reached under the tree and pulled out a small box and handed it to Mitzi. "For you."

"I have something for you at my house. I can go get it."

"I'll get it when I bring the cat over and give your mother her gift."

"Okay." Mitzi tore through the gold wrapping paper with little care for saving the bow. Pulling off the lid of the box, she gasped. "Ooh, Mary, it's so...sweet."

Lying on a square of cotton was a silver bangle bracelet with a pink cancer-survivor ribbon charm.

"You like it? I got it in October because I knew you were going to beat this."

Tears shimmered in Mitzi's eyes as she unhooked the bracelet and slid it onto her wrist. "What if I hadn't?"

Mary Paige smiled. "Eh, it would have kept until you did."

"Thank you."

"Oh, and I also got this for you." Mary Paige had finally put the money in the bank, realizing that ignoring it wasn't making it go away. And it was high time she figured out what to do with it. One of the things she planned to do was spoil the people she loved. "Here." Mary Paige passed an envelope toward Mitzi.

"What's this?"

"Open it."

Mitzi lifted the flap and pulled out a brochure. Her eyes skimmed the first page before opening to the middle. "This is a brochure for breast reconstruction...oh, Mary Paige."

Tears spilled down Mitzi's face right before her expression crumpled.

"Don't cry, Mitzi. You'll make me cry, too."

"How did you— I can't let you do this. It's too much."

"No, it's not. It will make me so happy to see you happy again. To see you confident, wearing those skimpy halter tops you always wore before your diagnosis."

Mitzi laughed through the tears. "I can't believe you bought me a boob job. Do know how bizarre that is?"

"Well, it's a little—"

Her words were cut off by Mitzi's full-out sobs. And that made Mary Paige cry, too. Mostly because it felt so good to do something for her friend, something she knew Mitzi could never afford. She also cried because her heart had been broken into a billion itty-bitty pieces when Brennan closed that office door, ending their relationship as if it had meant nothing to him. Happy mixed with sad.

Hope mixed with despair.

Love mixed with loss.

"You're the best person I know."

"Sure." Mary Paige sniffed. "Don't you know I'm the Spirit of Christmas?"

Then it was Mary Paige's turn to sob into the arms of her friend. The love of a friend was a joy, but no substitute for the love of the man she wanted.

No doubt about it—Brennan Henry, the big, fat Scrooge, had broken her heart.

BRENNAN HENRY STARED out at the cold December night, feeling nothing but emptiness at spending Christmas Eve with Asher, who was drunk and intent on getting drunker if the bottle of scotch he'd pulled from the hotel minibar was any indicator.

"Appreciate you driving me," Asher slurred with an ironic smile. "Had a bit too much at dinner."

"Yeah, I know," Brennan said, looking out at the city he loved. The moon hung over the Hibernia Bank building, where columns glowed with red and green lights. The city was festive and bright, as it should be on the night before Christmas Day. Even the horns honking in the streets below sounded cheerful.

Asher knocked something over on his way toward the bed. "Have a drink. It's Christmas."

Brennan turned, hands in pockets, and contemplated his cousin in the weak light of the hotel suite. Asher had slipped his loafers off, loosened his tie and was now propped against the headboard, full glass of amber liquor in hand. Part of Brennan wanted to ask Asher about Mary Paige and the kiss, the other part of him wanted to ignore what had occurred, as if ignoring it could mean it had never happened. "I should be going. I'm taking care of grandfather's dog and I don't want a puddle on my pine floors."

"Come on, it's Christmas. Not like you have anything better to do."

Wasn't that the truth?

"Maybe one drink before I go. Not looking forward to walking her for blocks to find grass anyhow." He walked to the bar, grabbed a small bottle of merlot and poured the wine.

Brennan sank into one of the club chairs across from the bed and crossed one leg over his knee. "When will you leave?"

Asher blinked. "Leave where?"

"New Orleans. I assumed you and Elsa will head to Bern before the New Year."

"Oh, that. Well, I'm not going back to Bern," Asher said with a twist of his lips.

"Oh?"

"Elsa is, but not me. She and I are over, and she's moved on to another man. Ironic, huh? I stole her from you and he stole her from me. She's such a whore."

Brennan leaned against the back of the chair as his

cousin's admission sunk in, stunning him, angering him. *I stole her from you.* "So it *was* intentional? You always said you two fell in love."

"Fall in love with a whore? No way. They're all whores. Soon as you lose your money and your looks, they wrap their legs around the nearest Italian million-aire. Whores."

"And Mary Paige?"

"Who? That Spirit chick?"

"Never mind," Brennan said as the depth of Asher's bitterness washed over him, waking him up to what this man he'd admired truly was—not worthy. Brennan's anger turned to pity, the disbelief to bitter acceptance of how wrong he'd been about Asher. "You're drunk and need to sleep it off. Things will look better in the morning."

"Will they?" Asher's laugh sounded like a choke. "I doubt it. What you're looking at is a man returning home with his tail between his legs. I don't have anything left, Brennan. Nothing. The business, the houses, the Lear, everything is gone. *G-O-N-E.*"

"What do you mean?"

"Do I have to spell it out? You have to make me re-peat it, you bastard?" Asher's voice rose angrily in the room. "You win, Brennan. My house of cards has tum-bled down. I'm broke. As in, I'm not even sure I can af-ford this hotel bill. Got it now? The great Asher Henry, continent-hopping businessman, husband to the hottest swimsuit model in the world is finished. Done. Over."

Brennan didn't have words. He stared at the man who had once been the person he most wanted to pattern his life after. What had happened to change the man before him? Or maybe life hadn't changed Asher? Maybe it had changed Brennan.

Asher took a gulp of the scotch, spilling some down his shirt. "How you like me now?"

"Guess I don't."

"No? Well, get in line."

For a moment the room was as quiet as the pall before daybreak. Nothing but the clink of ice in Asher's glass and the sounds of the street below.

What does a person say to his cousin when he admits losing everything that made him who he was? To the man who admitted to stealing his girlfriend? To the man who had likely used Mary Paige to prove a point to Brennan? Asher was a playground bully and a selfish bastard.

Asher set the empty glass on the bedside table and pointed at Brennan. "I always thought you had it easy. Fancy boarding school, living in your grandfather's house, learning at his knee. And what did I have? I lived with my father, who was a drunk and hit my mother when he got angry. Did you know that? Did you know he hit her?"

"No. I was young. I barely remember your father's funeral."

"Too bad," Asher said, his face crumpling briefly before he caught hold of his emotions. "Because you won't remember how I didn't cry. I was happy. Glad he wouldn't live with us anymore. But then my mother married that dick from Philly and, well, let's just say Mom's attracted to a certain kind of cruelty."

"I'm sorry, Asher. I never realized, but that's no reason—"

"Why would you? And who cares. It made me who I was. Ambitious, hard and sometimes cruel. You know what I'm talking about because you're the same way. It's why you never squealed like a little bitch when Elsa ended up in my bed. All part of the game. All part of being a pawn to life. I'm just checkmated right now, huh?" Asher closed his eyes and shook his head. The action caused him to fall to the side. "Whoa, I'm a little drunk."

Brennan rose and walked to the window. Was he like Asher? He didn't want to think so, but here he stood on Christmas Eve—a cold, hard man shutting the world out, refusing to hold on to the one soft thing that made him want to be more. The one woman who made him a better man. "I'm not like you."

"Huh?"

"Me. I'm not like you."

"Of course you are. Look at you. Look at me. We're alone. *Alone.*"

Those awful words smacked Brennan harder than if Asher had punched him in the chest. He'd always been alone on Christmas—it was what he preferred.

Is it really?

Brennan shook his head, willing that little voice to go away.

You push everyone away.

You used the excuse of Mary Paige cheating to sideline your romance. So you wouldn't get hurt. So you wouldn't have to feel anything.

"Come raise a glass with me, cousin." Asher slurred even more, sounded sleepy in fact.

"I've had enough," Brennan murmured, wondering whether he meant the alcohol or the life he clung to… which was no life at all. Not without love.

"I'm still thirsty," Asher protested, his eyes closing as his head sagged against the upholstered headboard. "Wanna make it go away…"

Brennan stood there, a solitary sober figure in the lonely hotel room, and felt nothing but regret.

Regret for the man his cousin had become. Regret for the youth he had been and the admiration he'd once had for Asher. And regret that he, Brennan Henry, would ignore love in favor of…

He didn't even have an answer to why he held his heart so tightfisted. A person couldn't use his past as a reason to grow into a robot with nothing more than switches, gears and whatever else made robots function. At some point, if a man wanted to live, he had to know love.

He had to show love.

A random Bible verse filtered into his mind—and the greatest of these is charity.

Charity.

Love for his fellow man.

Brennan had experienced it these past few weeks, and now his soul craved a better purpose.

And his heart craved Mary Paige.

Asher started snoring, forcing Brennan's attention to the man who had unintentionally proven what a future was when one lived for oneself, not bothering to open the door for anything other than self-serving opportunities.

Brennan didn't want to be like Asher.

Didn't want to end up drunk and alone on Christmas Eve with no one to love but himself. He wouldn't let the ignorance and want in his soul win.

He walked to his cousin, who had virtually passed out, pulled the folded coverlet at the foot of the bed over him and turned off the bedside lamp. Brennan felt nothing but sorrow…and a smidgen of rage at the man who had hoodwinked him, who had seen Elsa as a game to be won, who had no doubt played the same game with Mary Paige. And Brennan was the bigger fool because he'd fallen for it, believing the degenerate over the woman he loved.

"Merry Christmas, Asher. You miserable bastard."

CHAPTER NINETEEN

MARY PAIGE FAKED a happy smile as Caleb sped into the living room of their old farmhouse like a NASCAR driver. She really wanted to be happy. Really wanted to enjoy Christmas, but her heart ached too badly.

"Caleb! You almost knocked down the Christmas tree," her mother shrieked, grabbing hold of the wheelchair arm and punching something.

The chair ground to a halt and Caleb grunted his displeasure.

"Well, I don't care. I don't want broken ornaments on the floor. I picked glass out of my foot last Christmas."

Caleb gave Mary Paige a look that said, *You see what I deal with?* and signed something to her.

Mary Paige laughed. "Caleb said to take a leap."

"Stop siding with him," her mother said, blowing her bangs out of her eyes but tempering her fussing with a smile. It *was* Christmas morning, which meant even a broken ornament wouldn't earn her anger.

"Can't help it," Mary Paige said, pulling her legs up onto the old velour sofa and looping her arms around her knees. She wore her traditional Christmas nightgown, sewn by Granny Wyatt right before the woman passed when Mary Paige was twelve. It was red flannel with white snowflakes and covered her from throat to ankle. Her wool socks with the fuzzy reindeer stuck out from the hem. "It's what brothers and sisters do."

Caleb grinned and slapped his hands together with jerky imprecision common in most kids with cerebral palsy. He'd just turned fourteen and was going to flip for the modified PlayStation 3 she'd bought him. The dude loved art, video games and playing practical jokes… which was hard for someone as challenged as Caleb. But he made out fine.

"Mary Paige, will you grab my coffee and then we'll open presents before Caleb destroys the house," Freda said, plunking down on the braided rug and sorting through the presents stacked beside the tree. This year she and Caleb had strung popcorn and cranberries as decorations. Tango, the small mixed terrier that was her mother's constant companion, gnawed some of the popcorn off one end of the tree. "Stop it, Tango."

Smiling, Mary Paige shuffled toward the kitchen, temporarily comforted by the sounds of a typical morning on an atypical day. The coffeepot was full and smelled like a toffee-flavored brew. Yum, her favorite. She grabbed a mug that said Welcome to Kansas from the faded cabinet beside the porcelain sink and filled a cup to the brim. She added a splash of creamer then searched for the mug her mother had already used. Before she located it, the doorbell rang.

"Coming!" she heard her mother shout.

Mary Paige found the mug beside the bread box right as the sound of a two dogs fighting reached her ears.

"What in the devil?" she said, grabbing both mugs as her mother started shouting.

She heard a man hollering "Sit!" at the top of his lungs, and nearly spilled the coffee all over herself when she rounded the corner and saw who was chasing two dogs around the Christmas tree, tangling the lead in Caleb's wheelchair.

"Brennan!"

He didn't stop, just kept grasping at the leash, which had obviously jerked from his hand when Izzy launched herself at Tango.

"Tango! Stop!" Her mother tried to catch the scrappy terrier, who ran like mad from the barking dachshund.

Caleb flailed his arms and legs, and Mary Paige couldn't tell if he was excited or upset.

Mary Paige set the cups on top of the bookcase and lunged forward as Tango headed her way. She scooped up the terrier and snapped, "Sit, Izzy!"

Izzy barked at her…or more likely at Tango, who panted and shook in her arms.

"I said, sit!" Mary Paige pointed at Izzy, who gave one yip and sat, looking up at her with her tongue lolled out to the side. Mary Paige lifted her gaze as Brennan brushed against the tree, causing several ornaments to fall and shatter on the hard floor.

"Well, hell," her mother said, looking up at Brennan, who made the strangest face Mary Paige had ever seen him make. It looked like he was half constipated and half embarrassed. Not to mention he wore that ridiculous elf hat they'd been given on the streetcar. In fact, Izzy wore hers, too, but it was riding low on the dog's neck.

Caleb quieted and Tango stopped shaking. Mary Paige looked at Brennan, who lowered his arms and swallowed hard. Her heart started thumping almost as hard as Tango's. "What are you doing here?"

He shrugged, spreading his hands apart. "Uh, I came to wish you a Merry Christmas."

"Who are you?" Freda said, rising from the rug where she'd landed in an effort to catch one of the dogs.

"I'm Brennan Henry." He scooped up brightly wrapped gifts he'd obviously dropped when chaos reigned. He wore a long-sleeved button-down shirt, jeans, running shoes…and were those Christmas socks? "Sorry about Izzy. I'm dogsitting her and couldn't leave her at my apartment. I'll pay for the ornaments."

Her mother took his hand, casting a look at Mary Paige before saying, "I'm Freda Gentry, and I don't really give a rat's ass about those ornaments. Got 'em at the dollar store."

"Oh, good to know they weren't heirlooms."

Mary Paige spied the smashed ornaments. One was an heirloom. She glanced at her mother, who had that expression that said "let it go."

"What are you doing here?" Mary Paige asked again, shifting Tango to her hip as Izzy sniffed about her feet.

"I needed to talk to you." He seemed as comfortable as a prisoner faced with the hangman's noose. "Maybe we could talk outside?"

Freda walked to the door and pushed it closed. "It's too cold to talk outside. Plus, Mary's in her nightgown. Better take this into the kitchen."

Caleb grunted and flailed his arms before thumping one on the tray affixed to his table. He'd removed the computer and voice synthesizer he used when at school because both Freda and Mary Paige understood him through modified sign language, which he used now.

"Let's go ahead and open, Mom." Mary Paige bent to grab Izzy's lead then handed it to Brennan. "Caleb wants to open gifts, and we've already made him wait while we fixed coffee and let Tango out. Talking will have to wait."

Her voice was firm because she was still mad at him. Still hurt by his actions…and inactions.

He nodded. "Sure. I brought some gifts, though I wasn't exactly sure what your brother or mother might like."

"Put them under the tree," Mary Paige said, setting Tango down near Izzy. "Make friends, Tango, and stop being such a wuss."

While Tango and Izzy eyed one another, Freda swept the shattered glass. Brennan perched on the couch, still looking like he faced execution. Caleb grew still and watched Brennan, fighting against his twitching muscles to achieve some sort of coolness.

"Brennan, this is my brother, Caleb."

"Nice to meet you, Caleb," Brennan said, stepping over to Caleb, who extended his hand. Brennan shook it, overlooking the way Caleb's arm jerked spasmodically.

Her brother made a few guttural sounds and then signed to Mary Paige. "He said 'back at you' and he likes your hat."

Brennan smiled, touching the elf hat as if he'd forgotten he wore it, and resumed his position on the couch, keeping one eye on Izzy and darting measuring glances in Mary Paige's direction. She tried to ignore him, but failed, of course. How could a girl clad in a homespun gown and reindeer socks ignore the man she loved sitting in her mother's living room wearing a ridiculous-looking hat?

"Okay, so let's do this," her mother said, returning from the kitchen and scooping up both the coffee mugs, handing one to Mary Paige. "Brennan, if you'd like some coffee, there's some in the kitchen along with cinnamon rolls. Help yourself."

"No, thank you," he said, looking at Mary Paige again.

She jerked her chin toward her brother. "Start with Caleb first. Give him mine."

Freda lifted the large box onto the tray and helped Caleb tear open the paper. When he saw the gaming system, he got excited, jerking and signing his happiness.

"You're welcome," Mary Paige said, pointing at the separate box taped to the side. "That's an EPOC specially modified for gamers with disabilities. It should sync with your computers and your chair, or at least that's what the sales guy said."

Freda looked up. "Spendy gift, Mary."

"You haven't seen yours yet, Ma."

Her mother wagged a finger. "You know the rules yet you're breaking them." The Gentry family never spent more than fifty dollars on Christmas gifts to each other, electing instead to make donations to local charities.

"I like to break rules. Open yours."

Freda picked up the small box wrapped in Christmas puppy paper. She jerked the bow off, removed the wrap then tugged the lid off.

Mary Paige leaned forward in anticipation, her stomach fluttering nervously as she watched her mother's face. It, perhaps, was the best present Mary Paige had ever received from her mother—a look of befuddlement and then utter disbelief.

"Oh, my goodness," Freda said, looking at Mary Paige. "This is a check."

Mary Paige grinned, clapped her hands and leaped toward her mother. "Isn't it fantastic?"

Freda rose on trembling legs and grabbed her daughter's hands and jumped up and down like a small child. "Oh, my God! Oh, my God! It's for one-point-five million dollars made out to the Crosshatch Charter School!"

Mary Paige jumped with her, laughing like a loon. Both the dogs started barking and Freda spun toward Caleb. "Look, Caleb, it's the money for the school, baby! It's for your school!"

Caleb hit a button on his electric scooter chair, sending it spinning in circles, and they all laughed, jumped, spun and cried.

Finally, Freda pulled Mary Paige into a tight hug. "Oh, my sweet girl, you don't know what this means to me. To the school. I gotta call Marjorie and tell her. She's going to flip. This means we can start in the spring. Oh, my Lord!"

Freda gave her a final squeeze and ran into the kitchen.

Mary Paige winked at her brother and then turned toward the couch. What she saw nearly brought her to her knees.

Brennan was crying.

Actually crying.

His gray eyes had filled with huge tears that splashed onto those beautifully hewn cheeks.

"Brennan," she said, walking to him. "Are you okay? Is it your grandfather?"

He shook his head and swiped a hand across his face. "No, he's better. In fact, he'll be home tomorrow. It's just I—I— Shit."

She sat next to him, feeling her brother's eyes watching their every move. "Brennan?"

He turned a gaze so raw, so powerful, on her. "I'm a total asshole."

Caleb laughed.

"Okay, let's go into my bedroom. I'm not having this conversation in front of my brother—" she glared at Caleb, who pushed a button on his chair to make a honking sound "—who's being a total butthead considering I just gave his charter school a lot of money."

Caleb honked again.

"Watch the dogs, Caleb," she said, tugging on the arm of a too-emotional Brennan. "Come on, Bren."

Brennan leaned forward and gave his head a shake as

if he might clear it before rising, not even bothering to wipe his face. Mary Paige led him to her room, which was a total disaster since she'd been living out of the suitcase for a few days, had left wrapping paper and scissors on the floor and her bed was unmade.

She closed the door and turned to him. "Now what's going on? Why are you here?"

Brennan looked as if he wanted to pull her into his arms but instead, curled his hands and jabbed them into his pockets. "I'm an asshole."

"So you've said."

He frowned slightly but nodded. "I shouldn't have doubted you."

"Nope, you shouldn't have. Did you think that…that… miserable man would interest me?"

"Why not? I'm a sad man, but you were interested in me."

Mary Paige sank onto her unmade bed and ran her hands over the bedspread that had seen better days. This was the room she'd grown up in, still holding the remnants of her childhood along with a couple of sewing projects her mother had started and left in various stages of progress. It was as jumbled as her heart. "You're different, Brennan. Unfortunately, you can't see that."

He looked as if he might cry again. He really was a sad, sad man. Mary Paige sighed. "I can't fix you, you know."

"I know," he said, lowering himself beside her. "But maybe I'm ready to fix myself."

"I could be a lot more serious about this conversation if you'd take that elf hat off."

He touched the hat again and smiled slightly. "I don't want to take it off because I want to be changed."

"Changed?"

"Like Ebenezer Scrooge," he said, lifting one of his pant legs. "I even wore your socks. Stole them from Grandfather's drawer."

"Those are hideous socks." What did he mean by being like Ebenezer Scrooge? He couldn't merely wake up on Christmas morning and think putting on an elf hat and holiday socks made everything right.

"I had this epiphany—"

"Did three ghosts come for a visit?"

"In a way, yeah. These past few weeks I've seen my past and my present, and neither was very...pleasing. But last night, as I stood in my cousin's hotel room, I saw my future...and I didn't like the way it looked. It was cold, loveless and most importantly, Mary Paige–less. I don't want to live that life. I really, really don't."

She studied him, her heart kick-starting a little, even as her mind reminded her he'd so easily set her aside. "You hurt me."

"I know I did, and I wish I hadn't. I do, Mary Paige. I wish I had been as strong as you, as outraged as you, but past hurts clogged my vision. And you've been right all along—I'm scared and my fear has made me a hard man."

"But not irredeemable," she said. "You are the only person who can change yourself."

"But don't you understand? I have changed. These past few weeks have opened my eyes to who I was. I wasn't the worst person on the planet, but I wasn't even close to being the best. I lived blind and you smacked me out of it. The thing is, Mary Paige, you sort of saved me from myself."

"I'm not a miracle worker," she said, crossing her arms and feeling a strong urge to make him see who she actually was. It was as though everyone held a misguided perception about her and she *needed* Brennan especially to know the real her. "Everyone acts like I'm some angel, like this whole Spirit thing was all I am. But I'm no angel. I'm a woman, flesh and blood, and I make mistakes, screw things up, fall down and show an entire office my underwear. I once put Tabasco sauce on my dog's tongue just to see what he'd do. I have an evil side, a mean side, a petty side. So don't put me up on a pedestal and don't treat me like some—"

She couldn't talk anymore because he was kissing her, and in spite of the fact he'd broken her heart, it felt pretty dang amazing.

His hands slid over her face, cupping her jaw, bringing her to him as if he could drink from her…and she really dug the whole desperate-kiss thing. She was a sucker for romance, for sweet kisses on Christmas morning… for Brennan Henry.

He broke the kiss, pushing back her hair and looking deep into her eyes. "Thing is, Mary Paige, I know that already and it makes me love you all the more. You get it?"

She shook her head.

"Let me show you again."

He kissed her again, and this time it wasn't desperate. It was beautiful. As though all Brennan's hopes, desires and dreams were poured into that one kiss. She didn't feel it down to her toes this time. She felt it in her heart.

He pulled back. "You see now?"

"Huh?"

"I love you, Mary Paige. I do. Every time I think of you, my heart squeezes. Sometimes it's with love or desire. Other times it's with frustration or pain. But no matter, I feel something every second I'm with you."

"Brennan," she breathed, brushing his face with her hand, caressing him with her gaze. No one had ever said such things to her before. And not only said them, but also showed them. Emotion poured from this man who'd once been encased in ice.

"Say you'll forgive me for being an asshole. Say you'll come back to New Orleans and eat popcorn on my couch with me."

"I do like popcorn," she said, feeling something akin to awe flooding her, filling up all the corners of her heart. Brennan loved her.

Brennan loved her.

"Say you'll marry me, complete me, stay with me… even if I can sometimes be an ass."

"Marry you? Seriously?"

He dropped down onto his knee and yelped.

She looked over the side of the bed as he pulled the scissors from beneath his knee, grimacing as he tossed them aside.

"This is so not going as I planned," he said, reaching into his pocket and pulling out a ring.

"Oh, Jiminy," she said, staring at the prefect, not-so-small diamond winking in the morning light. "This is kind of sudden."

"No, it's not. When you meet the person who makes you want to be better, stronger and kinder to not only others, but to yourself, you don't want to waste a single second of time without her. I screwed up when I walked out of the room several nights ago, but I won't ever walk away from you again. If I do, you have permission to pick up the nearest heavy object and brain me."

Mary Paige pressed her lips together and tried not to laugh at this man wearing the elf hat, holding out the huge diamond and giving her permission to hit him when he got out of line.

"Now, I want to put this ring on your finger, but you've got to tell me if you want it. If you want me."

Smiling, Mary Paige slid off the bed so quickly she accidentally tumbled gracelessly to the floor. She overshot a little and hit her elbow on the sewing machine that sat beside the bedside table. "Ow."

He grabbed her arm and tugged her so she didn't hit the table and the ring flew under the bed. They both dived for it and ended up bumping heads.

"Ow," they said at the same time, before Brennan started laughing. "This is ridiculous."

She wrapped her arms around him, giggling as she kicked aside the wrapping paper. He pulled the ring out, blew dust off it and held it up.

"So?"

"So I love you and put it on already," she said, holding up her left hand.

His eyes turned to soft gray cashmere. "Yeah?"

She nodded. "Yeah."

He put the ring on her finger and lowered his head to kiss her. She met him halfway, which shifted him off balance, and he tumbled onto the hooked rug taking her with him, one of his hands sliding around her back while the other trailed toward her bottom.

Mary Paige felt the whoosh of the door opening, but didn't stop kissing Brennan.

"My lord," her mother said as the door banged against the wall. "What are y'all—"

Mary Paige's left hand shot straight up, and she didn't stop kissing Brennan, who tasted like coffee, salty tears and a man who'd love her forever.

"Oh, my God!" her mother shouted, obviously catching sight of the ring.

Then the two dogs ran in barking as Freda kept saying, "Oh, my God" over and over again.

Brennan broke the kiss and looked up at Mary Paige with a smile. "Merry Christmas."

She smiled back right before Izzy's tongue caught Brennan right in the mouth.

"Ew," he said, making a horrible face and pushing the dog away as he sat up with her still in his lap. "Gross. Dog spit."

Mary Paige laughed. "Bah, humbug."

He wrapped his arms around her and squeezed her tight. "I thought it ended with 'God bless us, everyone'?"

"Yeah, that, too." And then she kissed him in spite of the dog spit because he was a man who'd learned to keep Christmas in his heart…and she loved him.

* * * * *

COMING NEXT MONTH FROM
HARLEQUIN® SUPERROMANCE™

Available January 2, 2013

#1824 THE OTHER SIDE OF US
by Sarah Mayberry

After a few less-than-impressive meetings, Mackenzie Williams and Oliver Garrett have concluded that good fences make good neighbors. The less they see of each other, the better. Too bad their wayward dogs have other ideas, however, and won't stay apart. The canine antics bring Mackenzie and Oliver into contact so much that those poor first impressions turn into a spark of attraction...and that could lead to some *very* friendly relations!

#1825 A HOMETOWN BOY
by Janice Kay Johnson

Acadia Henderson once had a secret crush on David Owen. Then they went their separate ways. Now they're both back in their hometown trying to make sense of a tragic turn of events. Given what's happened, they shouldn't have anything to say to each other. Yet despite the odds, something powerful—something mutual—is pulling them together. Maybe it's the situation. Or maybe they're finally getting their chance at happiness.

#1826 SOMETHING TO BELIEVE IN
Family in Paradise • by Kimberly Van Meter

Lilah has always been the quiet, meek Bell sister, the one to follow what everyone expects from her. Then she meets Justin Cales. The playboy turns her head and she allows herself to indulge in a very uncharacteristic and passionate affair. But when that leads to an unexpected pregnancy, Lilah discovers she has an inner strength she has never recognized!

HSRCNM1212ENHRA

#1827 THAT WEEKEND...
by Jennifer McKenzie

A weekend covering a film festival is what TV host
Ava Christensen has been waiting for—her dream assignment.
But not if it means being alone with her boss! Jake Durham
recently denied her a big promotion, so Ava wants as little
to do with him as possible. That's virtually impossible at
the festival. Somehow, though, with all that time together,
everything starts to look different. Must be the influence
of the stars...

#1828 BACK TO THE GOOD FORTUNE DINER
by Vicki Essex

Tiffany Cheung has tasted big-city success—and she's hungry
for more. So when she ends up at home, working in her
parents' restaurant, all she wants is to leave again. Nothing will
change her mind. Not even the distraction of Chris Jamieson,
her old crush. Yes, the adult version of him is even more
tempting—especially because he seems equally attracted.
But her dreams are taking her somewhere else, and Chris's
life is deeply rooted here. There's no future...unless they can
compromise.

#1829 THE TRUTH ABOUT COMFORT COVE
It Happened in Comfort Cove • by Tara Taylor Quinn

The twenty-five-year-old abduction that cold-case detectives
Lucy Hayes and Ramsey Miller are working together is taking
its toll—especially with their attempt to ignore the intense
attraction between them. The effort has been worth it,
because they're close to solving this one. And once they do,
then maybe they can explore their feelings. But as they get
closer to the truth, they aren't prepared for what they discover!

Turn the page for a preview of
THE OTHER SIDE OF US
by
Sarah Mayberry,
coming January 2013
from Harlequin® Superromance®.

PLUS, exciting changes are in the works!
Enjoy the same great stories in a longer format
and new look—beginning January 2013!

THE OTHER SIDE OF US
A brand-new novel
from Harlequin® Superromance® author
Sarah Mayberry

After a not-so-friendly introduction to Mackenzie Williams,
Oliver Garrett is looking to make a better second
impression…and he may have found it, thanks to
their dogs! Read on for an exciting excerpt
from THE OTHER SIDE OF US by Sarah Mayberry.

OLIVER searched the yard for his dog, Greta. Finally he spotted her doing a very enthusiastic doggy meet and greet with Mackenzie's dachshund.

How did he get over here? Obviously there must be a hole in the fence between their properties.

Suddenly Oliver saw his best chance at a second meeting with his neighbor. Mackenzie would be grateful if he returned her wayward pet, wouldn't she?

He scooped up the dachshund, who wriggled desperately, but Oliver kept a tight grip the entire walk to Mackenzie's.

"Why do you have Mr. Smith?" she asked, frowning as she answered his knock.

"Your dog was in my yard. Seems our fence has a few holes."

"Thanks for bringing him back." Her tone was warm, even a little encouraging, he thought.

As he was about to respond, the phone rang inside her house.

"I need to get that." She was already closing the door.

"Fine. But we should talk about the fence or the dogs will keep visiting."

"I'm sorry, but I really need to take this call." There was a distracted urgency beneath her words.

He opened his mouth to respond, then stared in disbelief as the door swung shut in his face for the second time that day.

"You cannot be serious."

Okay, so he got the message. She was too busy for a friendship. Fine. He and Greta could live here happily *without* knowing their neighbors.

Oliver may have given up on a relationship with Mackenzie, but it seems Greta and Mr. Smith may have other plans! Find out in THE OTHER SIDE OF US by Sarah Mayberry, available January 2013 from Harlequin® Superromance®.

REQUEST YOUR FREE BOOKS!
2 FREE NOVELS PLUS 2 FREE GIFTS!

Harlequin

Super Romance

Exciting, emotional, unexpected!

YES! Please send me 2 FREE Harlequin® Superromance® novels and my 2 FREE gifts (gifts are worth about $10). After receiving them, if I don't wish to receive any more books, I can return the shipping statement marked "cancel." If I don't cancel, I will receive 6 brand-new novels every month and be billed just $4.69 per book in the U.S. or $5.24 per book in Canada. That's a saving of at least 15% off the cover price! It's quite a bargain! Shipping and handling is just 50¢ per book in the U.S. and 75¢ per book in Canada.* I understand that accepting the 2 free books and gifts places me under no obligation to buy anything. I can always return a shipment and cancel at any time. Even if I never buy another book, the two free books and gifts are mine to keep forever.

135/336 HDN FC6T

Name	(PLEASE PRINT)	

Address		Apt. #

City	State/Prov.	Zip/Postal Code

Signature (if under 18, a parent or guardian must sign)

Mail to the **Reader Service:**
IN U.S.A.: P.O. Box 1867, Buffalo, NY 14240-1867
IN CANADA: P.O. Box 609, Fort Erie, Ontario L2A 5X3

Not valid for current subscribers to Harlequin Superromance books.

Are you a current subscriber to Harlequin Superromance books and want to receive the larger-print edition?
Call 1-800-873-8635 or visit www.ReaderService.com.

* Terms and prices subject to change without notice. Prices do not include applicable taxes. Sales tax applicable in N.Y. Canadian residents will be charged applicable taxes. Offer not valid in Quebec. This offer is limited to one order per household. All orders subject to credit approval. Credit or debit balances in a customer's account(s) may be offset by any other outstanding balance owed by or to the customer. Please allow 4 to 6 weeks for delivery. Offer available while quantities last.

Your Privacy—The Reader Service is committed to protecting your privacy. Our Privacy Policy is available online at www.ReaderService.com or upon request from the Reader Service.

We make a portion of our mailing list available to reputable third parties that offer products we believe may interest you. If you prefer that we not exchange your name with third parties, or if you wish to clarify or modify your communication preferences, please visit us at www.ReaderService.com/consumerchoice or write to us at Reader Service Preference Service, P.O. Box 9062, Buffalo, NY 14269. Include your complete name and address.

HSR11